FIGHT DIRTY

A DAWSON FAMILY NOVEL

EMILY GOODWIN

Fight Dirty
A Dawson Family Novel
Copyright 2019
Emily Goodwin
Cover photography by Braadyn Penrod

UNCORRECTED ARC EDITION

❀ Created with Vellum

To those who still believe in magic

CHAPTER 1

CHARLIE

Maybe there is a rational explanation for all of this.

I twist my ring around my finger and pull it off my knuckle. Tears blur my eyes as I stare out at the water. Happy people walk the path behind me, and the air is full of typical New York City sounds.

Cars honking.

People laughing.

People arguing.

Music playing.

Hearts breaking.

I squeeze my eyes shut and a fat tear rolls down my cheek. Of course today of all days I chose not to wear waterproof mascara. I look up, blinking back the tears. The only thing worse than crying in public is going back to work and having people ask me about it.

Though there's a good chance I can't go back. That I won't be able to bring myself to walk through that set of double doors, pass across the busy lobby, and press the elevator button to take me up to the office.

Because he's there.

And I know there's not a rational explanation for all of this.

Part of me wishes I hadn't seen what I did. I wouldn't be standing here in the middle of Central Park debating if throwing myself off this bridge is a better option than facing the truth. I wouldn't be desperately trying to patch my heart back together before it falls into a million pieces too little to gather up and glue into place.

And I wouldn't feel so stupid, because I should have seen this coming.

He'd postponed the wedding twice. Went out for drinks "with the guys" when I knew the guys hadn't made plans to go out. Yet...I wanted to trust him. I wanted to get married and have the fairytale life.

I'm living a fairytale, all right. Just not the kind with a happy ending.

"I wouldn't do that if I were you."

I whirl around, bumping my knee on the side of the bridge, and see a homeless woman making her way over. There are a tragic number of homeless people in the city, but I'm a bit familiar with this woman. I've seen her on my morning runs through the park, and I gave her a coat, boots, gloves, and a hat last winter.

There's something about her that made her stand out to me, and it's not just because she slightly reminds me of the Bird Lady from the second *Home Alone* movie. One of the most the things that shocked me the most when I first moved from Eastwood to NYC was how easily people walk by and ignore the less fortunate.

And this woman...for some reason I noticed her. And then noticed her again. She's not that much older than me and I can't help but wonder what happened in her life that led her to be in this situation.

"Do what?" I sniffle.

"Throw expensive jewelry into the water like that old bitch from the *Titanic*."

I don't have a response to that. I push the ring back on my finger and try to blot up a tear with my finger. It doesn't work.

"If you're just going to throw it away, you can give it to me." She shuffles a bit closer. "I'll pawn it and use the money for booze," she admits with a shrug and then laughs. "Well, not all of the money. But a lot of it."

I blink a few times and try to get my head back on straight. "Are you hungry?" I ask her and she nods. "Want to get something to eat? I could really use some company right now."

～

THE HOMELESS WOMAN—WHOSE NAME IS JOLENE—RIPS INTO THE bread that's in a basket on the center of the table. "So, did he cheat on you?" She dips the bread into her pasta sauce and takes a bite. I haven't said much since we sat down at my favorite Italian restaurant. Out of habit, I ordered my usual pasta dish with the world's best side-salad.

Once the food came, the smell of the creamy pasta sauce soured my stomach. *He* was with me the first time we came here, discovering this little gem of a restaurant tucked behind a cell phone store. I ordered tea instead, but haven't been able to bring myself to even take a drink yet.

"Yes," I admit and my throat closes up. Memories flash before me, just like they do when your life is ending. I squeeze my eyes closed and take a deep breath as guilt starts to creep down my neck. I'm sitting here feeling like my life is over. Like there's no way I can recover from this. Like everything is too much of a mess to even try.

But I'm alive. I'm healthy. I have a job and a place to sleep tonight. Still, I can't help the pain that's radiating through me.

And the anger.

3

"You walk in on it or something?" Jolene asks and I shake my head.

"I wasn't snooping," I start, turning the white teacup around on the saucer. Steam billows up out of the cup. "I ran home to feed Tulip and then couldn't remember where I left my phone." I pick up the lemon wedge and slowly squeeze it over my tea. "So I grabbed his iPad to text me, you know, so I'd hear my phone dinging. And then I saw the texts from his assistant. I know you can't always interpret things in print the way they might be implied in real life, but there's only one way *I miss your cock* and *I want you inside me again* can be taken."

"That lying, cheating bastard doesn't deserve you." She breaks off another chunk of bread. "You're pretty, for starters." Slowly running her eyes over me, she mops up more sauce with the bread. "And you're kind. I don't see that a lot...especially from lawyers."

"How do you know I'm a lawyer?"

"Lucky guess." She smiles, showing off crooked and yellowed teeth. "And I've seen you carrying files with that fancy agency name on it."

"Oh." I smile back. "I was beginning to think you were psychic or something."

"Or something is right. Are you a public defender or something noble like that?"

I shake my head. "I mostly do real estate law. Nothing too noble; well, I did win a case a few months ago against a slum lord whose building wasn't up to code and was overcharging the tenants."

I wrap my fingers around the teacup and pick it up. My mouth is dry and my stomach clenched the moment I saw the texts and hasn't relaxed. I'm afraid if I put anything in there it'll just chuck it right back up.

"That's cool." She spends a few minutes eating in silence.

Once her plate is almost clear, she eyes my pasta. I slide it to her and she digs in. "What are you going to do?"

I shake my head. "I don't know."

"You're breaking up with the asshole, right?"

My head bobs up and down. I can't go back to the way things were. Some people can forgive a spouse for cheating, but I'm not that kind of person. Maybe if we had kids to consider, but we haven't even walked down the aisle yet.

"We work together," I whisper, feeling like I'm going to barf. Or cry. Or stand up, flip the table, and scream bloody murder. "And the...the other woman is his assistant."

"Oh shit, that's some reality TV drama."

"Yeah." My mind goes to Gemma, and I just don't understand what she has that I don't. What would draw him to cheat. She's only a few years younger than me, is rather plain-looking, and couldn't get into law school. She's always been nice enough to me, but she knows—she fucking knows—she's taking part in an affair.

"I just feel so stupid," I say in a small voice. Tears blur my eyes and my throat tightens. I pick up the tea and take a small sip, hoping swallowing something other than bile will keep me from puking. I squeeze my eyes closed and repress everything I'm feeling.

"I'm sorry," I tell Jolene.

"Don't be." She twirls noodles around on her fork. "It's easier to talk to someone who doesn't know you, who won't judge you or whose judgement doesn't matter than it is to talk to someone close sometimes."

"That's really accurate right now. But still, I'm sorry."

She shrugs. "If listening to you talk means I get some fancy food then by all means, keep talking."

I take another drink of tea and lean back, looking around the restaurant. People are carrying on like they didn't just find out everything they've built their lives around was a sham.

5

"How long you think the asshole's been cheating on you?"

I shake my head, wiping away a tear before it has a chance to run down my cheek. "I'm not sure." Todd's been working on a case for a big client for the last month. He's stayed late a lot over that time, but since I knew the case was legit, I didn't think much of it. His uncle is a partner at our firm, and is how Todd got the job…and how he was able to get in on such a big case so soon.

"So," Jolene says again. "What are you going to do?"

~

I STICK THE SPOON BACK INTO THE TUB OF ICE CREAM, DIGGING around for a piece of cookie dough. Jolene's question stuck with me as I started to walk back to work. Back to where *he* was. And my pain started to turn into anger.

What are you going to do?

I wasn't going to go back to work and stare at little miss redhead's face acting like everything was okay. And I couldn't promise I wouldn't go ape-shit once I got back to the office. So I called in sick, saying I got food poisoning. Todd texted me not long after that, asking if I was okay and telling me he'd be late.

Because he'll screwing his secretary on top of his desk.

Okay, he didn't say that, but it's what's going on, I'm sure.

It's nine-thirty at night, and the door to our apartment opens. Tulip, my black-and-white cat, growls when Todd walks inside. She's never liked him, and now I'm wishing I listened to her. Though that cat doesn't like anyone but me.

"Hey, babe." Todd tosses his keys in the bowl on the entryway table. Our apartment is small, way overpriced, and perfectly New York chic. It's what young lawyers new to the city are supposed to live in…well, if you're going off what you see on TV. "Feeling better?"

I trade my spoon for the bottle of wine I have wedged between the couch cushions. "I'm getting there." I close my eyes and welcome the dry red wine down my throat. "How was work?"

"Ugh," he starts and takes off his shoes. It's one of my few rules I put in place about living together. Take off your shoes when you walk in. Those things have been all over the city and it's gross. I'm not a germaphobe by any means, but you can't argue with the nastiness tracked in on the soles of your shoes when you've been on the subway.

Todd always hated it and often forgot to take his shoes off.

"This case is a tough one. Both sides have solid arguments."

"Those are the best cases." I take another drink of wine. "As long as your side is stronger."

"Oh, it will be." He hangs his jacket on the back of a chair before coming into the living room. His eyes go to the ice cream and wine on the couch. "I though your stomach was upset."

"It was. This helps."

"Really? Dairy is one of the worst things you can eat when you're sick."

"I'll take my chances." I shove the wine between the cushions again and go back for the ice cream. My heart radiates with pain, and the speech I had planned fizzles in my mind. I can call him out, tell him that I know he's been unfaithful, and then what? He'll give me a million excuses, all of them bullshit, and try to convince me it was somehow my fault.

He sits on the couch next to me, eyes filled with concern. I clench my jaw, not sure how he's able to do this. How can you act like you care when you're cheating?

There's no way I can deny this. He's cheating on me.

And sitting here like nothing is wrong.

My chest tightens and all the ice cream and wine slosh around in my stomach. I squeeze my eyes closed, words burning on my tongue. Tears leak out of my eyes, running down my cheeks.

It's funny, how you think you'd react if you were in this situation. I never thought I'd go mute, sitting here unable to make myself say the words. Yet here I am.

"I'm going to shower," he tells me. "Feel better, babe." He gets up, going through our little living room to the only bedroom.

What are you going to do?

"Wait," I say and move the ice cream to the coffee table. Tulip raises her head, sniffing the air as she stares at the tub of ice cream. Something sparks inside of me, lighting a strength I didn't know I had.

"Yeah?"

I swallow hard, clenching my fingers into my palms. I look right into Todd's eyes. "I know."

CHAPTER 2

OWEN

And then there was one.

I pop the top to my beer and sit at the kitchen table, looking around at my siblings, who've each been happily paired off. All I can think is *suckers*. Being stuck with the same person for the rest of your life? No fucking way. I'm a love 'em and leave 'em kind of guy, though I always make sure to lay out my no-strings attached ground rules from the start. I'm a player, not an asshole, and I love playing the game of getting new pussy almost every single day of the week. I don't have to listen to anyone, get to do what I want to do, and have a damn good life.

Logan, my twin, puts his arm around his wife, smiling down at her before she takes a seat across from me. Maybe it would be nice to have someone like—nope.

It's the single life for me.

I'm happy with how things are. I have three nieces and one pretty cool nephew, and I love being an uncle. I get the best of both worlds: spend time with my family and then give the kids back to their parents so I can go out for the night. Or stay in and play video games, watch TV, or do whatever the hell else I want.

"Can you hold Arya for me for a minute?" Quinn, my sister asks. "I have to pee."

"Sure," I tell her and take the sleeping baby from her arms. Arya's only a few months old but looks like a Dawson already, with dark hair and eyes a deep shade of blue that will no doubt fade to a soft green just like her mother's.

"You look good with a baby in your arms."

I look up to see Danielle smirking at me. Shaking my head, I roll my eyes. "Stop imagining me as Logan. It's creepy."

She holds up her hands. "Busted," she laughs. "Though really. You do."

"I look good no matter what."

"Just not as good as me," Logan quips. We're identical twins, and are able to fool just about everyone but our close family when we try to switch identities. It got us into—and out of—trouble more times than I can count when we were younger.

Macie, my mom's newest rescue dog, barks and wakes up Arya. Her little eyes fly open and she looks up at me, realizes her mom isn't holding her anymore, and scrunches up her face, getting ready to let out a cry. I stand up and gently rock her as I tell her it's going to be okay.

Her eyes flutter closed and she goes back to sleep. *Crisis averted*.

"You're a natural," Mom says, coming over to the table with a bottle of wine. Danielle reaches for it, filling up her glass and passing it to Kara, my other sister-in-law.

"Chicks dig me," I retort with a cheeky grin.

Mom rolls her eyes and calls Dad to come out of his office. Always working, Dad grumbles something about going over a client file for the morning but joins us. Quinn comes back, taking a seat next to me and telling me I can keep holding Arya since she's sound asleep in my arms.

"Archer is stuck in surgery," Quinn tells us, making a face as her older daughter, Emma, squirms out of her chair and into her mom's lap. So much for eating a meal in peace, right? "So let's eat."

We make it only a few minutes into our meal before the newest Dawson member, Violet, starts crying. My oldest brother, Weston, gives his wife a loving look and gets up to get their baby from the crib where she'd been napping.

See? Being single has its perks.

"One of my friends from Chicago is coming in this weekend," Quinn says, not looking at me as she digs into her food. She doesn't have to say it for me to know she's trying to low-key hook me up with one of her friends. It's not the first time and it certainly won't be the last. Quinn is a bit of a schemer, always has been, always will be. Now that Logan is married, Quinn shifted all her attention to me. Weston's wife Scarlet only encourages her. Throw in Danielle and my mother...

I reach for my beer.

"Let me guess. She's single."

Quinn moves her gaze to me, trying hard to keep her face neutral. "She is. Just got out of a relationship."

"Ohhh, bad move, sis," Logan says with a laugh.

"Why is that a bad move?"

Logan looks at Dean, who's smirking, and shakes his head. "Rebound se—" He's cut off, elbowed hard in the ribs by Danielle.

"Little ears," she hisses, but tries not to laugh herself. "And it's true."

"Hey now," I shoot back, trying to sound offended, but by now the whole table is joining in on it, much to Quinn's chagrin.

"Well," she presses. "You could at least meet her for drinks or something."

Logan lets out a snort of laughter. "You know what *drinks* is code for, right, sis? Or have you been out of the game that long you've already forgotten?"

Quinn narrows her eyes. "It hasn't been that long, but we all know I never played the same game you two dummies did."

11

"When is she getting into town?" I ask just to humor Quinn.

"Tomorrow. She's coming to Arya's baptism and then is staying with us until Tuesday."

"Send her to the bar."

Quinn raises an eyebrow. "Just like that?"

I shrug. "It's not like you're going to go out drinking, right?"

Shaking her head, Quinn lets out a sigh and turns to Scarlet, whispering something that I don't even care to hear. They've been trying to set me up with people for the last year and it's never amounted to anything.

Because the truth is, there is only one woman in this whole damn world who could get me to change my ways and want to settle down. She's amazing. Smart. Insanely gorgeous. She was mine once, and I fucked it all up.

So yeah...there is one woman out there for me. But she's the one who got away, and I'm still trying to learn to live with that.

CHAPTER 3

CHARLIE

I pick up the remote and flip through channels, needing to find something funny to watch. Or maybe something depressing. Or dark.

Yes. Dark is what I need.

Bonus points if there is cold-blooded murder committed by a scorned woman.

"Charlie?"

Blinking, I look away from the bright TV and see my sister's silhouette appear in the doorway.

"Hey."

"You look like shit."

I glare at her but don't have the energy to argue. Mostly because it's true. "You know people say we look alike, right?"

"We do. And trust me, I've been there and looked worse. Which is why I'm here. I'm taking you out."

"I don't want to go out." I flop back against the pillows of my childhood bed.

"You've been holed up here for days. I'm getting worried, sis." Carly comes into the room, going to the window. She draws the blinds, and I'm half tempted to hiss at the sunlight. "I get it. You need to grieve what you lost. But this isn't you."

Blinking as my eyes try to adjust to the sudden change in light, I look at my sister and try to find truth in her words. I've never felt more lost than I have this last week and a half. After confronting Todd, I packed my shit, got in the moving truck, and just drove, not stopping until I pulled into the driveway of my parents' house here in rural Indiana.

"And your friend Marcus has texted a few times." Carly sits on the edge of the bed. "You haven't texted him back, have you?"

I shake my head. "What am I supposed to say? Todd is the biggest dick I know, which is ironic considering his dick wasn't actually all that big in real life, and now I'm here, back home with Mommy and Daddy, not sure what to do with my life. Though sitting here, eating my weight in junk food and watching trashy reality TV seems like a good way to go out."

Carly snatches the remote from my hands and turns off the TV. She stands up and puts one hand on her hip. "You knock this off right now," she demands with a quiet sternness only a mother is capable of. "Yes, Todd was a grade-A asshole but you are not going to let that asshole turn you into...whatever it is you're doing right now."

"Wallowing in the failures of my life?" I supply, knowing I'm being overdramatic. It's allowed, right?

"Stop it right now. You get your ass up and into the shower because I'm questioning the last time you washed your hair. And then we are going out. I spent the last two days ridding my house of everything that doesn't spark joy, and Lord help me, we both need a night out."

"What were you left with?"

"My vibrator and my electric wine opener."

"Way to minimalize."

"I might have kept my old Buffy the Vampire Slayer DVDs

too. And a few of the kids' favorite toys. I'm going to snap before we get this house ready to go up for sale."

"Go out without me. I'm…I'm just tired."

"No excuses. Remember when Tommy broke up with me right before prom my senior year?"

I nod. "You were devastated."

"And you were boycotting dances for being sexist or something." She holds up her hand, keeping me from arguing my point on the subject. "But you put on a dress and went with me so I wouldn't have to walk through those doors alone."

"We had fun that night." I look up at my sister and smile. She's only a year and half older than me and was one grade ahead in school. We fought—of course—but for the most got along while we grew up.

"Now it's my turn to take you to prom. Well, kind of. So get up, get your stinky ass in the shower, and then get dressed."

Feeling a little emotional, I nod and get up, thankful for my sister. I didn't intend on getting here and hiding out like this, but as soon as I stepped foot inside my childhood home, all I wanted to do was lie down on the floor, hiding from sight. I have friends here, friends I haven't talked to much since I took the job in New York.

I never thought I'd be back here. Well, not in this sense at least. Yet here I am, and I don't want to have to explain to anyone how the man I thought loved me more than anything cheated on me with his assistant.

Closing the bathroom door behind me, I turn on the shower and turn around, staring at myself in the mirror. My blue eyes are bloodshot with dark circles underneath and my blonde hair is in a bun so messy I'm not sure I'll be able to untangle it without losing several strands of hair. I pull the band out and then strip out of my PJs.

I'm not one to feel sorry for myself, and I pride myself on being an upbeat and positive person. Funny considering I'm a

lawyer, I know. I worked hard to get to where I am—er, was—
and I'm not going to let some asshole pull it all out from underneath me. Eastwood is a small town, but my father's established
his own firm here and represents people from all over the
county, not just this town.

I always assumed I'd work with him and then eventually take
over the family firm after he retired. But then I met Todd, who
got me to visit New York City with him, which led to a job inter-
view at the high-powered firm his uncle was a partner at, which
then led to us both getting hired. I couldn't pass it down.

As a new lawyer, I couldn't ask for better experience. I got to
work with some of the best—and ruthless—lawyers in the city. I
had access to huge clients and got to sit in on some even bigger
cases. It was fast-paced, exciting, well-paying considering how
new we were...but it always felt temporary.

I tried to explain that to Todd once and he didn't get it. In
fact, it made him angry, and I thought then his anger was based
on the fact that I was talking about something he didn't understand. Todd always got weird when he didn't fully get something
because he didn't like to feel stupid.

I overlooked it then.

Called him ambitious.

Admired his drive.

But really, the guy was an asshole.

I'm better off without him, even though this hurts. Though
the more I think about it, the more I realize that it's my ego that's
hurting...and not so much my heart. Maybe deep down I always
knew exactly the type of person Todd was.

And that feeling of things being temporary was a warning for
me to run far, far away.

$\sim$

"They've really added to the downtown." I close the car

FIGHT DIRTY

door and look around The Square, which is the main block of Eastwood's downtown. "Is that a splash pad?"

"Yeah," Carly says, locking her car and putting the keys in her purse. "It went in about a year ago. After that new hospital went up, they started doing a lot of improvements to the downtown area. It's really nice now, and my kids freaking love that splash pad. I love it because there's a bar next door that serves half-priced margaritas during the day."

"You lush," I tease, smiling at my sister.

"You'd day drink too if you had three kids."

"I day drink and I don't have kids at all. Or a job right now." We slowly start walking down the sidewalk. It's nearing sunset, and the early June air is just warm enough to let me enjoy the night in a sundress, but not so hot that I have to put my hair up before my neck gets all sweaty.

"Have you talked to Dad?" Carly asks softly.

"Yeah. Mr. Fenton is retiring at the end of the year so it would actually work out perfectly for me to start coming in and taking over his client list."

"Ahh, that's awesome!" Carly grabs my hand and gives it a squeeze. "Call me selfish, but I always wanted you to come back here."

"Todd would have hated it."

"Fuck Todd," she says and then brings her hand over her mouth. "Sorry. Too soon? Are you still missing him? Wait, don't answer. Let's just grab drinks, walk around a bit and then go to dinner with no mention of him."

"We can talk about Todd," I say matter-of-factly. It's a professional habit to keep a neutral face when talking about something upsetting. Usually the issues aren't as personal, but I'm able to compartmentalize nonetheless. "And no, it's not too soon. Because fuck him. In the ass. With an extra-large dildo and no lube."

"I knew living in the Big Apple would harden you, sis," Carly

17

laughs. "But now I don't feel bad telling you we never liked Todd."

"We?"

"Justin and I." She makes a face. "And Matt. And Libby. Jack is too young to form an opinion, but I don't think he'd like *Uncle Todd* either."

"I'm glad you guys told me before I married the guy. Don't tell me Mom and Dad didn't like him either."

Carly wrinkles her nose and shrugs. "They never said anything even though I asked."

I playfully nudge her with my arm. "You asked!"

"Yes! I wanted to make sure I wasn't crazy."

"We all know you're crazy," I retort. "I'm the sane one."

"And that's saying something," Carly laughs and slips her arm through mine. "Until I knew that the little prick was sticking it in someone else's hole—"

"Way to be crude."

"Thanks. But anyway, before I knew that, I always thought he treated you well, but he's just arrogant."

"He is," I agree, feeling sick to my stomach about it. His hot, alpha-male personality made him perfect for romance novels. Strong-willed lawyer who doesn't take any shit? Sounds good on paper.

But in real life…he was just an asshole who put himself first regardless how it made other feel.

"I should have seen it earlier," I start.

"No, no!" Carly says. "Let's not do this. I just said he treated you well, and he did. Up until the end. And I'm sure he's already realized that he fucked up big time and lost out even more."

"He's tried calling me," I tell her. "I don't want to hear what he has to say. Not yet at least. It hasn't been long enough."

Right as we pass by a bakery, the door opens and a little girl goes toddling out. Carly stops short, her mom instincts kicking in fast, and she dodges in front of the girl, keeping her from running into the street.

"Emma," someone calls after the girl, just a step behind her. "You can't run away like that. You have to hold my hand." A man I presume to be her father picks her up. "Thank you," the man tells Carly. I tip my head, studying him. There's something familiar about his face but I can't place it.

Not until Dean Dawson steps out of the bakery behind him, carrying a newborn in his arms.

"Dean and Archer," I say, looking from one to the other. I should have known I would run into a Dawson sooner or later. Part of my hesitation over going out was in fear of seeing a particular Dawson brother...one who broke my heart into a million pieces years ago. My stomach gets all fluttery, and my throat tightens.

What if Owen is with them and he walks through those doors next?

"Charlie," Dean exclaims, shifting the sleeping baby against his chest. "Is that you?"

"In the flesh." I smile down at the little girl. Dean is several years older than Owen, and Archer became an honorary Dawson family member during their time in college. I'm not surprised to see them still together. "How are you?"

"Good," Dean answers and gently rocks the baby, who's starting to stir. "We're good. Arch, you remember Charlie Williams?"

"Yeah, I do." Archer holds the toddler against his hip with one arm. "It's been a while."

I nod. "It has. You guys look good, though, and have a cute family."

Dean turns to Archer, brows furrowing. "We're not...wait, what?" Dean mumbles.

"These aren't your children?"

Archer's eyes go wide and then he laughs. "We do make a

19

handsome couple."

"Oh my God." My hand flies to my mouth, trying to remove the metaphorical foot. Though, really, it wouldn't have surprised me. Logan and Owen used to tease the hell out of Dean and Archer about being best buds with benefits all the time.

Dean shakes his head, narrowing his eyes. "This jackass married Quinn. These are their kids."

Now it's time for my eyes to go wide. "Really?" Quinn was still in college when I left. The last Dawson news I saw over social media was a picture of her graduation from MIT. All four of her brothers were in that picture with her, and after that I did everything I could to avoid seeing that annoyingly perfect family again.

I couldn't risk seeing Owen, not knowing what that would do to me. My heart was so fragile I didn't think I could handle it.

But then I met Todd...and we all know how that turned out.

"Yeah," Archer says with a smile. "Our anniversary is coming up next week, actually."

"Congrats. Oh, this is my sister, Carly. I think you met her many years ago. Carly, this is Dean and Archer."

"I know who they are, sis."

"Right. Small town. I almost forgot."

"That and Dean's our contractor for our new house." Carly brings her arms in close to her body, getting exciting just thinking about building. "We're putting our house on the market tomorrow," she tells him. "I can't wait!" She turns to me. "I'm going to go in and grab some cookies for the kids." Without another word, she goes inside, leaving me to catch up with Dean and Archer.

"So you're back for a visit?" Dean asks.

"Kind of." Fuck. This is the part I was dreading. "You're working with your dad now?" I ask, hoping to deflect all conversation about myself.

Dean nods. "Yep. Things have really expanded over the years.

Are you still doing the lawyer thing?"

That's another *kind of* answer I don't want to give, dammit. "Yep. How's Quinn? What's she been up to other than having the cutest kids?"

"She does something with computers I don't understand," Archer laughs. "She started her own company with some friends a few years ago."

I look into the store, wanting Carly to get her ass back out here now. This conversation is going to go from small talk to awkward in three seconds flat.

"Oh wow, that's awesome. You were in med school the last time I saw you."

Archer nods. "It took a lifetime, but I'm finally done. I'm a surgeon now."

Dean rolls his eyes. "He loves telling people that."

"Don't be jealous," Archer shoots back. "But I do like it when you call me Dr. Jones."

"You two could really pass for a couple," I laugh and look into the store again. "Well, I don't want to keep you guys. Looks like you have a cupcake to eat," I say to Emma. Her eyes light up and she nods.

"I eat cupcake!" she jabbers.

"That does look good. Maybe I should get one."

"You should," Dean urges. "Everything in there is good. Logan's wife runs it."

Part of being a good lawyer is keeping my own expression neutral, not wanting to upset, give away info, or lead anyone on. But there's no stopping my eyebrows from hiking up and the slight rush of blood to my head.

If Logan settled down and got married, does that mean... Nope. I shouldn't care.

I don't care.

Because Owen broke my heart years ago, and I swore back then that I'd never make that mistake again.

CHAPTER 4

CHARLIE

I swallow hard, pushing my heart back down into my chest. I'm still getting over a betrayal so deep it cut right down to my heart. Owen needs to be the farthest thing from mind.

Though I know I never really got over him.

"Logan's married?" My voice comes out steadier than I expected. "That's a shock."

Dean laughs. "Yeah, we weren't sure if he'd ever settle down." He looks at Archer for a millisecond before looking back at me. "Wes got remarried too. They just had a baby girl."

"Oh wow. You all are doing so well." I shuffle forward. There's only one Dawson left to update me on, and thinking about him is making my heart start to hammer. I'm in an emotional head-space, that's why thinking about Owen is making me dizzy.

It's not because the feelings I swore were gone are slowly coming back like the walking dead. Haunting. Reaching for me. Surrounding me. Ready to pull me back down. The fall will feel amazing all over again.

But the crash...the crash will destroy me for good this time.

"Owen is single," Dean deadpans, trying to sound causal, but he's studying me as he speaks.

"I'm not surprised." My throat tightens. "I hope he's wised up some at least."

Dean makes a face and laughs. "Just some." His eyes go to my left hand, no doubt noticing the lack of engagement ring. Though, really, that doesn't mean much. There are lots of reasons to have an engagement ring and not wear it...oh who am I kidding?

Dean is leading the construction on Carly's house. It's going to get out sooner or later. And I'm banking on later.

"I heard you're getting married," Dean goes on.

Dammit.

Carly steps out of the bakery right before I have to answer. Thank fucking goodness.

"I got us cupcakes," she says with a smile. "Now let's go find a bottle of rosé to go with it."

"Sounds good to me."

"Daddy, I hungry," Emma says, looking at the box of cupcakes in Archer's hand.

"It was really nice seeing you again," I say and loop my arm through Carly's. "Tell everyone I said hello." I give a small wave and practically drag Carly away, not taking a breath until we're a good block away.

"You didn't tell me you hired the Dawsons to build your house."

Carly cocks an eyebrow. "I didn't think you'd care. And they're pretty much the only reputable builders in the county."

"True."

"Why do you care?" she slowly asks, turning to look at me as we walk.

"I don't. I just haven't seen them in a while and it caught me off guard."

"And it has nothing to do with the fact you and Owen Dawson dated for what, seven or eight years? And how you thought you two were going to get married and start popping out babies the day you graduated?"

I glare at my sister. "That was years ago. Why would I care about any of those things anymore?"

Carly shrugs. "Oh, you wouldn't. Not at all."

"Can we get through the rest of the night without talking about my failed love life?"

"Hey," she says softly. "I'm sorry. And yes, no talk about men the rest of the night." We stop at a crosswalk. "But can I just say—"

"Nope."

"You're no fun."

I let out a breath, resisting the urge to turn around and look at the bakery as if Owen will walk out of the doors next.

"You know you do need to talk about it though, right?"

"Yeah, I know." I pull at the thin silver chain around my neck. "And I will. Just…just not yet. Because when I talk about Todd I feel stupid, and I'm so tired of feeling stupid."

"You're far from stupid, Charlie."

"Thanks," I sigh. "Now let's pig out on those cupcakes, get dinner, and then go out for drinks or something."

"Oh, I'm totally up for drinks. We could go to Getaway after dinner."

Face neutral. Shoulders relaxed. Voice level.

Just like I'm in a courtroom.

"Sure."

"Sure?"

"Yeah. It was always a nice place to hang out."

"Have you been gone long enough to have forgotten who owns it?"

"It hasn't been that long since I've been here." In truth, it hasn't. Todd and I came to visit last Christmas, and the year before that we had Thanksgiving dinner at my parents'. But the trips into town were always quick, going straight to my parents' from the airport and then back again in a day or two.

There was no walking around town like this. No chances of running into anyone. Because even with Todd at my side and the big diamond lie on my finger, I was a little afraid of seeing Owen.

But it's not because I still have feelings for him or anything.

Nope. That's definitely not it at all.

~

"IT'S ALMOST SAD." CARLY LOOKS AT HER PHONE FOR A SECOND before showing me the listing for her house that just went up. "But we are just busting at the seams in that place. Five people in a three-bedroom, one-bathroom house is a challenge. I am so tired of doing my makeup while someone is pooping."

I laugh, reaching for my glass of red wine. We're eating outside at one of Eastwood's more upscale restaurants located on the main street that runs through the center of town. It's a new place, having gone in only three years ago, and this is my first time here.

"It is sad to leave your first house. How are the kids handling it?"

"Matt is excited. Libby goes through phases of excitement and then being terrified we're going to forget something when we move. I've assured her over and over we'll double-check every closet and cabinet before we make the official move. And Jack doesn't care about anything as long as someone is feeding him," she laughs. "That kid is such a little chunk."

"But he's an adorable chunk."

Carly smiles. "They're good kids."

"You and Justin are good parents."

"We try." She gives me a wink.

"Do you have a plan for the house picked out yet?"

"Of course!" She pulls out her phone and shows me the blueprints, excitedly talking about how she's going to paint and decorate. It's a welcome distraction, but I can't keep my mind from wandering back to Owen and how things could've been different if we never broke up in the first place

"Oh shit," Carly grumbles, reading the text that just came through on her phone.

"Everything okay?"

"Jack has a fever and is throwing up again. Poor kid can't get over that virus."

"Do you need to go home?"

"Nah." She waves her hand in the air, making me so thankful for my sister. She's a stay-at-home mom, totally devoted to her children, and loves them more than life itself. Just the fact that she's willing to stay out with me when she's got a sick baby at home means a lot.

"After dinner," I start. "Go home. Jack will want his mama."

"You sure you don't mind?"

I shake my head. "Not at all. It was nice getting out of the house, but this is the first time in two weeks I've done more than listen to *Defying Gravity* on repeat while chugging a bottle of three-dollar wine so I'm kinda tired."

Carly presses her lips together, smiling with concern. It's a strange look only she and our mother can pull off. "You're still into *Wicked*? I almost forgot about that phase."

"It's a great play and the music is classic."

"I'll take your word for it. How many times did you go see it?"

"Four." The first time was with Owen. Broadway is not his thing, but he knew how much I wanted to see it, so he surprised me with tickets.

"Did you go see shows a lot in New York?"

I shake my head. "I didn't really have time." And Todd never wanted to go with me. "Maybe we can go up to Chicago and see something together this summer."

"I'd like that."

We talk about Broadway shows and summer plans the rest of dinner. I get my leftovers boxed up to take home to no doubt eat later tonight, when I wake up at two AM unable to fall back asleep. Carly drives me back to Mom and Dad's, gives me a hug goodbye, and goes home to take care of Jack.

The house is quiet and empty when I step inside. Taking off my shoes, I go into the kitchen and put my leftovers in the fridge. Then I go upstairs and sink back into bed. Tulip pads into the room and jumps up on the bed next to me, letting me pet her for a minute before she bites my hand.

I flop back on my pillows, trying hard not to think. Not to feel. And then my phone rings. It's Todd, and just when I'm about to end the call and block his number for good, I decide I should answer.

Because it's time to face this shit.

Just seeing his name on my phone screen makes my heart skip a beat and anxiety to spread through me. All the food I ate at dinner threatens to come up. Swallowing hard, I grit my teeth and answer.

I don't want to be angry anymore. Maybe talking to him will bring some sort of closure…or maybe it won't. But I don't know if I don't pick up the phone.

"What do you want?"

"Charlie," he breathes. "You answered."

"Yeah. I did. So…what do you want?"

"I want you to hear me out."

Closing my eyes, I pinch the bridge of my nose. "There's nothing to hear. You cheated on me. With someone I know. I was Gemma's secret Santa at work last year and I spent way over the suggested budget because that's what I do. I'm a nice person, giving good fucking gifts to people who don't fucking deserve it."

So much for closure.

"I'm sorry, babe. I'm sorry I hurt you."

I wasn't expecting an apology if I'm being honest. By saying

27

he's sorry, Todd is admitting guilt, and that's not something I thought he'd do. "It's nice to hear you say that, but it doesn't change things." I let my hand fall to the mattress and I flop over on my side. My heart is heavy, but it's not being weighed down by pain like before. It's more like a deep sadness for what could have been, paired with the fact that I know it's time to let it all go.

To move on with my life.

"We had issues even before the cheating, you know." I never admitted that out loud to anyone, not even Todd.

"No one is perfect."

"I'm well aware. Just…just…answer one question for me."

"Of course."

"Why did you delay the wedding the first time?"

A few seconds of silence pass by.

"Tell the truth," I say. "It's not like it's going to change anything. We're over, Todd, but I think we both know we were over long before this."

"I don't want to hurt you more than I already have."

"Just say it."

"I guess…I guess it was because I wasn't sure if I really wanted to get married. It wasn't you, it was…it was me. I didn't want to settle down yet. Become a husband."

"They why did you propose?" I ask, though I could be asking myself a similar question: why did I say yes?

"I don't know. I loved you then, Charlie. Just like I still do now."

"Too bad it wasn't enough." My eyes fall shut and I'm suddenly hit with a new emotion. Am I actually happy he cheated? That this was the swift kick in the ass I needed to realize that I didn't really want to get married either.

I thought about breaking things off for weeks before he proposed. We'd been fighting a lot, and I was homesick. But then he asked, and in that moment I felt hope for us. If only I knew then what I know now.

"Can I see you?" he asks, and before he gives me a chance to answer, his phone call turns into FaceTiming. Whatever. Maybe if he looks at me as I say it, he'll get it.

"Wow," he says as soon as I come into view. "I almost forgot how beautiful you are."

"Don't do this, Todd."

"I'm so lonely, Char."

I cock an eyebrow. "Am I supposed to feel sorry for you?"

"I fucked up, okay? And I'm sorry. Come on, babe, come back to New York. Come home."

"New York never felt like home," I remind him. "And you used to get pissed at me for saying that, but it's true."

"I know…if I could take it all back I would. I was an asshole. I see it now. But, babe…" He gets up and moves into the bedroom. *Our* bedroom. Minus my stuff that I took with me when I left, it looks the same, which isn't quite as unnerving as I thought it would be.

"You look good," he tries. "Have you gotten some sun?"

"Oh, loads of it." He doesn't need to know I holed up in my childhood bedroom, hiding from the sun like a vampire.

"You always looked good in blue."

I respond with a roll of the eyes.

"And you know it drove me crazy when you curled your hair like that. I miss running my fingers through it, slipping my hand down the ends and down to your ass." The blankets rustle. "Do you miss that too, babe?"

I stare at the screen of my phone for a few seconds, hoping to God what I think might be happening isn't really happening.

"No."

"We were good together." He holds the phone back a little farther and yes…it is happening. His hand is in his pants and his lips part. Does he seriously think he can call me up and have phone sex like it'll fix anything? "Don't you miss it? The way you got me off…it was unlike anyone else."

"You're a fucking joke, Todd. I'd tell you to go fuck yourself, but it looks like you're already doing that. We are over. Don't call me again." I end the call and immediately block his number.

Dropping my phone onto the bed, I close my eyes and lie back down, wanting to retreat under the covers and not deal with anything ever again.

"Fuck," I grumble and sit up. I run my hands over my face and let out a breath. I just want to get back to normal, and I know that has to start with doing something—anything—other than lying in bed feeling sorry for myself.

Set to go grab my leftovers and eat them while I finally think about everything that happened, I go downstairs and stick the plastic to-go container in the microwave. Carly was right in saying I have to deal with this breakup sooner or later, and I can't hide here forever, even though I'm certain Mom would happily let me crash here for the foreseeable future.

Life dishes out its fair share of rough patches. You can't go around them. You have to go through them.

CHAPTER 5

OWEN

"There you go, ladies." I slide a tray of tequila shots onto the table and make eye contact with a woman who I think introduced herself as Rose. Or was it Rachel? Hell if I know. The only name that matters is mine in this case, because she'll be screaming it later tonight. "What's the occasion?"

"Oh, nothing really. We just wanted to come out and let loose a little," Rose or maybe Rachel giggles.

"You came to the right place." I flash her a grin. It's one of my go-to moves, and one that hasn't failed yet. She smiles back, eyes glimmering, and drops her gaze to my crotch. A blush comes to her cheeks, realizing that I just caught her staring.

And then she does it again.

"You let me know if you need anything else, all right?"

Rose? Rachel? Ros-chel? Whoever it is, reaches out and touches my arm, letting her fingers trail down my skin. "Oh, I definitely will." Her friends erupt in giggles and catcalls. I flip my hand over, sweeping my fingers over hers as I walk away, going back behind the bar.

"Please tell me you didn't just give away all those shots."

Logan fills two beers and sets them on the bar. "Because if you did—"

"It's coming out of my paycheck," I say in a voice that's meant to mock Logan. In reality, it's hard as fuck to mock someone who sounds exactly like you.

"They'll pay," I tell him dryly. "And then I'm taking that redhead home. Maybe the blonde too."

"I don't know how your dick hasn't fallen off from disease yet."

"Don't be jealous," I shoot back. "You're the one who decided to settle down with one pussy for the rest of your life."

"It's good pussy. And the fact that I'm, you know, in love with Danielle doesn't hurt."

I laugh and go around the bar, grabbing an empty glass on my way. I'm happy for Logan, really, I am. It was painful watching him try to cross the friendzone line, and I didn't want him to become a miserable old bastard in the years to come, beating himself up every night over what could have been.

Which isn't something I do. Not at all.

The bar gets busier as the night goes on. During the day and into the evening, we serve more food than drinks, and things shift dramatically around ten PM. I'm back at the table with Rose —I heard one of her friends call her by name—when Dean and Archer come in.

"Hey," Dean shouts over the noise. "Come over here when you get a chance."

"Awww, what a cute couple," Rose says, watching Dean and Archer find stools next to each other at the bar.

I let out a snort of laughter. "The cutest." With the promise of free shots, I leave the table and go around the bar.

"What's up?" I ask my older brother. "Hiding out from martial responsibilities again?"

"Hardly."

I give the girls at the table a wink and grab two glasses from under the bar.

"I see you're hard at work," Archer laughs. "Though I think they're looking at us."

"They are. But it's because they think you're some cute hipster couple."

Archer's brows furrow. "That's the second time this week."

I let out a snort of laughter. "I do wonder sometimes."

"Do I need to remind you I knocked up your sister? Twice."

"Fuck you. Who else thought you were a couple, though?"

Archer looks at Dean, who looks across the bar for Logan. Dean shifts his weight and meets my eye. "Charlie."

Charlie.

My Charlie? No...she's not mine anymore. I fucked things up with her and I have to live with that. What we had was perfect, and I know I'll never find anyone who compares. It's been years, and I'm still kicking myself over losing her, in pushing her away.

She wanted more.

I should have given it to her.

And now I'll never get another chance to show her I'll give her the whole fucking world.

She got a job in another city straight out of law school, and then started working at some swanky firm in New York City. But the real kicker? She's getting exactly what she wanted with someone else.

A ring. A wedding. A marriage, and a happy home, and eventually a family. Fuck, I'd give anything to go back, to be the one to put that ring on her finger. I was terrified of settling down then. I was young and didn't know how to be an adult, let alone a husband.

I was going to let her down, I was sure of it.

A million thoughts race through my head, and I want to spit out some sort of witty comeback. But I got nothing.

"What?"

"We saw Charlie," Dean says gently.

I nod, turning to grab a bottle of whiskey. "Cool."

"Cool?" Dean gives me a look. "That's all you have to say?"

I shrug and pour some whiskey into the glasses I set out for Archer and Dean. And then I drink them both down. "Yeah. I mean...her family is still here. I'm sure she comes to visit."

"She didn't look like she was just visiting," Archer starts. "And we had Quinn do a quick internet search."

"All her social media is set to private," I blurt. Dammit. "I mean, I assume so at least."

Archer just rolls his eyes. "That's not an issue for Quinn, you know. It's creepy, really, how easily she can get around that sort of stuff." He shakes his head. "But it looks like Charlie recently deleted all the photos with her and her fiancé. It looks like she's single."

"And we wanted to tell you in person," Dean finishes. Those two really could pass for a couple. "Because I think she's going to be in town for a while."

"That's fine," I tell them, swallowing my pounding heart. I was fairly certain Charlie hadn't stepped foot back in Eastwood in years. I pour more whiskey into each glass and pass them to Archer and Dean this time. "I don't own the fucking town. She can be here if she wants."

"And you're okay with her being back?" Archer asks. He's not my brother by blood, but has felt like part of the family even before he married Quinn. He was there when shit when down with Charlie and, dammit, I think he knows what I'm not willing to admit to myself.

That I'm still in love with her.

CHAPTER 6

CHARLIE

"You're up early."

I put the coffee pot back on the warmer and turn to see Mom coming into the kitchen.

"Couldn't sleep?"

"The opposite, actually," I tell her. "I slept soundly for the first time in weeks and didn't wake up exhausted. And I didn't consume half a bottle of wine in order to get me to sleep this time around."

"What led to this change?"

"Todd called." I add cream to my coffee, waiting for Mom to say something. "And we had a decent talk, well until he tried to get me to have phone sex with him." I shudder.

"You're not...you're not thinking about..."

"Getting back together with him? Oh hell no. But it did give me some closure. We fought a lot, Mom, and I can finally admit that. I never wanted to tell anyone, thinking it might make them not like Todd." I bring my hot coffee to my lips and take a careful sip. "And I should have known something wasn't right when he delayed the wedding the first time and I was kind of okay with it. And then talking to him last night...it reminded me of all the issues I was so willing to overlook, and now I just can't under-stand why I was going to do that."

I lean against the counter. "I don't miss him anymore, Mom. I'm not all that sad. In fact, I feel like I dodged a bullet, and that feels wrong. I should be sad, right? It's only been a few weeks."

"I have a girlfriend, Bonnie, who lost her husband suddenly to a heart attack. Five months after his funeral, she was going on dates again. You can imagine the scandal it caused amongst our little social group. But her heart was ready, and dating new men didn't mean she missed her husband any less. As she put it, it made her realize how short life is and how she didn't want to live out her remaining days focusing on the pain."

Mom pours coffee into a mug. "I know your situation isn't the same, but my point is to show you there isn't a right amount of time to grieve a loss. And you suffered a loss, just in a different way."

I cup my hands around my coffee mug and stare into the light brown liquid as if it's going to shift into a magic mirror and give me all the answers.

"I did," I agree. "And I never thought I'd say this out loud, but I think what upset me more wasn't that I was losing Todd, but that I'd have to tell people my life sucks. I was more worried about being embarrassed and judged than I was to lose the man I thought I'd marry."

"That's understandable, and you've always put a lot of pres-sure on yourself, honey. But it's okay, I promise you, it's okay. People mess up and make mistakes and have bad things happen to them. What matters is how you react to the event more so than the event in itself."

I nod. "Hiding out in my old bedroom is more embarrassing than being cheated on."

"You're allowed to be sad and allowed to take time to heal, Charlotte," Mom says, using my full name to drive the point home. "But you can't wallow."

"I'm done wallowing. I already left a message with Daryl about renting an apartment in town, and when Dad gets home tonight, I'm going to talk to him about doing something at the firm. I know there aren't any cases for me to take on yet, but even if I filed paperwork or answered the phone, it's better than sitting around here."

Mom smiles, tears forming in the corners of her eyes. "You've always been my strong, smart girl."

I smile back, not wanting to tell her that the two words she's used to praise me over the years were part of what made me try to tough it out with Todd. *I'm strong.* I can handle a few rough nights. Deal with the fights. Work through our issues. *I'm smart.* I don't make stupid mistakes...like agreeing to marry the wrong man.

"I just want to be happy again. Which means starting to get my life in order."

Mom sets her coffee down and comes over, putting her hand on my shoulder. "Your father always wanted you to take over his practice, you know."

"I do, and I always thought I would. I like Eastwood," I assure her. "It's not as exciting as doing real estate law in New York, but this was always my end game, and I was more than happy with it."

Williams & Beck Attorneys at Law is a far cry from the big company I worked for in New York, but it's always done well for itself. Todd encouraged me to leave the *small town law* for something bigger and better, and at the time, it seemed like he was pushing me to get the most out of my education. No one can fault him for wanting me to get a good job, but he never understood the sense of community here in Eastwood.

"That's all a mother wants, you know." Mom rubs my back and then goes back to her coffee. "For her children to be happy. Well, within reason. If you said your passion was to be in the adult film industry while selling meth on the side, I might try to persuade you otherwise."

"That can be very lucrative, you know. Though I'd probably need to get a boob job to do well in porn."

Mom laughs, shaking her head. "It's good to have you home, honey. I wish it were under different circumstances, but having you here just feels right. Like you're home."

I look out the window at the tidy but small back yard. Mom teaches art at the local elementary school, and is off for the summer. She gardens a lot, and makes weird wind chimes out of recycled materials and crystals. She's the stereotypical new-age artist, and is the exact opposite of my lawyer father.

"It does feel like home. But don't take it personally when I say I'd like to get out on my own."

Mom laughs and pulls out a stool at the island for me. I take it as my cue to sit while she makes me breakfast.

"I was your age once," she reminds me with a wink. "And I wouldn't want to be living with my parents either."

Right on cue, my phone rings. It's Daryl, the landlord from the only apartment complex here in Eastwood. We talk for a few minutes, I jot a few notes down, and then end the call.

"Well?" Mom asks, turning away from the omelet she's cooking.

"Good and bad news," I tell her. "The apartment complex is full, but one tenant is moving out at the end of next month. If I can bring the deposit by today, he'll reserve it for me."

"And are you?"

"I'm going to see if there are any nice rentals in town first. I don't need anything too big or fancy. After living in a tiny studio apartment in the city, anything over five hundred square feet will feel like a mansion."

"And with what you paid for it…" Mom clicks her tongue and turns back to the stove. "You're welcome here, you know. Having you here for the summer will be nice too."

"Yeah," I agree. "It will be."

～

"THAT'S SOMETHING YOU DIDN'T GET TO SEE IN THE CITY, HUH, girl?" I run my hand over Tulip's long fur. She's sitting in the open window, face pressed up against the screen as she watches a bunch of birds swarm around one of the many bird feeders in the back yard. We had birds fluttering by, of course, but it wasn't anything like this.

I run my hand over her fur once more and then tighten my ponytail. Stretching my arms out in front of me as I walk, I go downstairs and outside for a run. It's a little after ten AM now, and the sun is already out and shining brightly down on my face.

It makes me feel like everything is going to be okay. Which it will be. I stretch for another minute or two, turn my music on, and take off. My parents live in the downtown area of Eastwood, and these few blocks look like something out of a Hallmark movie. Most of the houses in this section of town are historic and have been carefully maintained or restored, like my parents' 1925 craftsman-style house.

I jog down the street, nostalgia filling my heart more and more with each step. Running this block used to be a routine. I've passed by these houses, over this patch of uneven sidewalk pushed up by tree roots, every morning. Now, I can't remember the last time I ran through Eastwood like this.

Eastwood is small in terms of population, but with it consisting of farmland, the actual size of the town is impressive. It won't take long before the *in town* part of Eastwood gives way to fields and farms. I slow to a stop at a crosswalk, waiting for an old Ford to rumble through the stop sign before crossing the street. I don't want to go that far today, and plan to just run up and down the same streets a few times before going back to my

EMILY GOODWIN

parents' to continue my search for a place to live so I can get my stuff out of storage as soon as possible.

My phone dings with a text, and I look down to see who's texting me. It's Marcus, who's the closest thing I had to a best friend in the city. He's an interior designer and worked on the floor below me. We coincidentally got into the elevator at the same time more than once, and then discovered that we both have a closet-addiction to Broadway shows, Disney movies and teen, TV dramas.

With us both having crazy busy schedules, we didn't have much time to hang out, but texted regularly. He's been checking in on me ever since I left New York.

Marcus: Hey lady. Haven't heard from you in days. How you doing?

Me: Much better today. Looking for apartments here so I can get out of my parents' house. I feel like things are looking up.

I exit out of my texts right as he sends me another, making a mental note to check it after my run. Inhaling deep, I cross the street and am right about to pick up the pace to a jog again when a little boy on a bike speeds out of his yard and onto the sidewalk.

"Jackson," a man calls after him. "You gotta wait, buddy."

My eyes go to the man on their own accord and my heart stops. My mouth goes dry, and I suddenly can't remember how to move my feet, despite the fact that I just ran over a mile.

He comes down the porch steps holding a tiny baby in his arms. She's wrapped in a little pink blanket and starts fussing, no doubt from him calling out to the little boy named Jackson.

If there were a lush flowerbed or even a prickly bush nearby, I'd dive right in and pray he didn't see me. I'd stay there until Jackson sped by on his bike, not wanting to risk moving even a muscle.

But it's too late, because he's looking right at me.

"Charlie?"

40

My mouth opens but no sounds comes out, though I'm pretty sure he can hear the pounding of my heart. Suddenly, the heat of the day comes crashing down on me, and I blink rapidly, trying to get rid of the dizziness.

My eyes fall shut in a long blink, and Idina Menzel's voice rings out though my earbuds, telling me it's time to try defying gravity. But it's like I already am. Because only one person can make me feel that way, like I'm floating and falling at the same time, and the shock of how strong those feelings are coming on makes the dizziness increase tenfold.

I swallow hard and open my eyes. He's coming closer, cradling the baby to his chest. She looks so tiny in his arms, and he's put on several pounds of muscle since I last saw him. Is it too late to run and hide?

Yes, yes it is. Because Owen Dawson is walking right to me.

CHAPTER 7

OWEN

Violet starts to settle down, but my heart is in my throat. Charlie is only a few yards from me, standing on the sidewalk, staring at me like she's seeing a ghost. In a way, maybe that's all I am to her.

A distant memory that's started to fade. I can only hope it's haunted her a few times over the years.

Because she's haunted me.

"O-Owen," she starts, pulling her earbuds out of her ears. It should be illegal for anyone to be this good-looking. Her blonde hair is pulled up in a high ponytail and sweat drips down her chest, disappearing between her breasts. She's wearing a pink sports bra and tight running shorts. Her body is toned and tan, and I remember all too well the way it felt under mine. "You... you have a baby?" Her eyes go to Jackson. "Or two?"

I wave Jackson back over and laugh. "No, they're not mine. You remember my brother Wes?"

She blinks rapidly as she nods. "Oh right, Dean said he had kids." Her eyes go to Violet. "She's adorable."

I give her a wink. "Now that she does get from me." I swallow my pounding heart and do my best not to fuck Charlie with my eyes. Because she somehow looks better than I remember. There's always a risk for seeing something in real life after fantasizing about it, and she does not disappoint.

She stares at me as I stare at her, as if neither of us know what to say. Because, really, what the hell do I say? I'm sorry I broke your heart years ago. I hope you're happy and got everything you deserve in life…but at the same time I really hope you're single because if I can't have you, no one else should…which is a dick thing to wish since that means you broke off your engagement?

Doesn't really roll off the tongue.

"You look good," I tell her, not caring that she knows I'm checking her out.

Her cheeks, which are already flushed from running in this heat, redden even more. "I'm all sweaty," she says, trying to brush off the compliment.

"That adds to your appeal." I flash her a grin.

"Don't," she says softly.

"Don't what? Compliment you?"

She quickly shakes her head, swinging her blonde ponytail to the side. It sticks to her neck, and she reaches up to pull it off.

"I seem to remember you liked being complimented."

She blows out a breath and hikes up one eyebrow. "Not as much as you did."

"Touché," I laugh. "And everyone likes to be complimented. Anyone who says otherwise is lying."

"Well, of course people do. It's human nature." She purses her lips and shifts her gaze to Jackson, who's riding his bike at full speed down the sidewalk, and I'm not entirely sure he'll be able to stop before he hits Charlie.

She sidesteps at the last second, moving right up against me. "Oh, shoot," she says, jumping back and Violet starts to fuss. "I didn't mean to wake her up."

"It's okay. She needs to wake up anyway. This little stinker sleeps all day and is up all night," I tell her, gently rocking Vi in my arms. Charlie's jaw tenses as she watches me for a few seconds. Then she looks away and laughs.

"What's so funny?" I ask her.

She waves her hand in the air. "It's just…just…never mind."

"Hi," Jackson says, turning his bike around. "I'm Jackson."

"What happened to not talking to strangers?" I ask him, narrowing my eyes.

"You're talking to her," Jackson quips.

"She could be some sort of psycho for all we know," I tell him with a wink.

Charlie laughs. "I might be a little crazy. And I'm Charlie. Nice to meet you."

"Charlie's a boy name," Jackson says, wrinkling his nose and making both Charlie and me laugh.

"My full name is Charlotte, but I've gone by Charlie since, well, since I can remember." Jackson just nods and pedals forward. "He looks just like Wes."

"Yeah, it's crazy how much he looks like him now that he's getting older."

"So, you're babysitting?" Charlie plays with her wireless head-phones, twisting them around her fingers.

"I am. Scarlet—Wes's wife and Violet's mother—is pretty exhausted. She's napping."

"That's…that's really nice of you."

"You sound surprised." I watch Jackson ride his bike to the corner and turn around. He's allowed to go up and down the street as long as I'm out here watching him. We have plans later to put Vi in her stroller and go to the park a few blocks down from the house.

"It's just…just…I'm not."

Fuck, I shouldn't love it when she gets flustered like this. It doesn't happen very often, making me think seeing me again is doing bad things to her just like it is to me.

Or at least I hope.

Because I've spent the last few years telling myself I'm fine, that living it up and being single is what I want out of life. That I'm over her.

And seeing her now...*fuck.*

"You look good," she says and then almost looks surprised by her confession.

"I work out." I give her a wink and she laughs, shaking her head.

"And you haven't changed much."

My cocky smile disappears from my face. I have changed. I've grown up a lot, though to be fair I still have some growing up left to do.

But I'm not the same man who told her I wasn't ready to settle down. And I've grown enough since then to realize how much of a mistake I made.

"Why change what's perfect?" I raise my eyebrows and she rolls her eyes, trying hard not to laugh. "What about you? Has the big city changed you?"

And now it's her turn to be somber. "Yes. It has."

"In a good way?"

She looks out at the street, watching a car roll through the stop sign. "I'm not sure yet."

"I heard you're getting married." I don't mean to blurt it out, but dammit, I need to know. I swallow hard and push my heart back down into my chest. I watch her face, looking for the words she won't say out loud.

But she gives nothing away, sign of a good lawyer, I suppose.

"Not anymore."

"Sorry."

"Thanks." She shrugs and turns her head down. A sharp ache hits me square in the chest. As much I want Charlie to be mine and only mine, seeing her dejected like this is killing me. I'd rather have all the heartache, all the pain and regret in the world, than have her feel even the slightest bit of it.

45

"We're going or a walk," I start. "You could join if you want. Unless you need to finish your run. Then by all means go ahead so I can watch you leave."

She shakes her head again. "I'm walking that way anyway," she confesses. "I can walk with you. It's only two blocks down and I need to get my heart rate back down."

"Then maybe being close to me is a bad idea."

"You are just as I remember."

"Is that a bad thing?"

I take a few steps back, looking back at Jackson to make sure he's slowing before he gets to the other street corner. Once he turns his bike around, I hurry up the porch steps to get Violet's stroller, grabbing it with one hand.

"It's not good or bad," Charlie answers, staying in the same spot. I get Violet situated, pull the visor up to keep her shaded, and then double-check the diaper bag, making sure I have extra diapers, wipes, and her bottle.

"You're really got this uncle thing down," Charlie comments as we start down the street.

"I'm the favorite. Don't tell Logan, Dean or Archer."

Charlie smiles and we silently go down the block, walking fast to keep up with Jackson.

"I haven't been here in years," Charlie muses to herself when we roll up to the park. Jackson ditches his bike and sprints ahead, seeing some of his friends from school. I keep walking, finding a spot in the shade to sit and give Violet her bottle.

Charlie watches us for a moment before sitting next to me. She smiles at Violet, baby-talking a hello to try and get her to smile.

"How old is she?"

"Two and a half months," I answer without having to think. "Quinn and Archer's little one is only a few weeks older."

"Aww, that'll be nice to have a cousin close in age."

I nod. "Quinn and Scarlet have become really close too. They're both obsessed with their damn cats," I laugh.

"What's wrong with cats?" Charlie hikes up both eyebrows.

"Not you too. At least Logan and Danielle have a dog in addition to their cats."

"I have a feeling I'm missing something."

"It's a bit of a running joke between us that started with Quinn being a crazy cat lady, who then turned Scarlet into one."

"And Scarlet is Weston's new wife?"

"Yeah."

"I still can't get over finding out Quinn and Archer got married. I never would have seen that coming. Well, aside from her having a massive crush on him when she was a teenager."

"She didn't have a crush on Archer."

Charlie lets out a snort of laughter. "Oh, she did big time. How did you not see it?"

I make a face and readjust Violet in my arms, sitting her up a bit so she can have her bottle. "He was so much older than her."

"He still is older than her."

"Yeah, but it's different now."

Charlie laughs and shakes her head. "All four of you were purposely oblivious to Quinn's love life back then, you know. But pretending it didn't exist didn't mean it wouldn't happen."

I laugh too. "I still like to pretend it doesn't exist. Because Archer's like a brother and she's my sister and it's a little weird."

"I think it's sweet. Oh, and I read an article a few years ago online about Quinn selling that app she developed. That's unbelievable."

"She's always been smart."

"She has. The last time I saw her she was coming back for a long weekend from MIT." It's weird having Charlie here like this. She's been gone for so long yet she fits in like she just left yesterday.

Jackson runs back over, taking his bike helmet off and drop-

47

ping it on the ground before taking off again. I grab a burp cloth and the bottle and start feeding Violet. She gets through not even half before she starts to fall asleep.

"It's really nice that you're babysitting," Charlie says again, smiling as she looks at the sleeping baby in my arms.

"I like it," I tell her honestly. "Mostly because I get to give the kids back at the end of the day."

Charlie laughs. "That is a perk. You were always good with kids, though. Probably because you're just a big kid yourself."

As much as I like sitting here talking and joking like nothing has changed, it's starting to mess with my head. Because I know what I'll be thinking about for the rest of the day.

And the night.

And tomorrow.

But worse, I know how I'll be feeling. It's all sunshine and fucking rainbows right now, but once the lights go out and it's just my thoughts in the dark, the regret will start to creep up on me. It always starts in the pit of my stomach, forming a hard knot that I have to drown in whiskey or tequila.

Yet that fucker is able to float, and will rise to the surface and remind me of everything I did wrong in our relationship. How what I thought I wanted then turned out to the be very thing I feared most in life.

Being alone, forced to watch the only woman I'll ever love move on with her life…and away from me.

CHAPTER 8

CHARLIE

"That's enough sun for now," Owen calls to Jackson about twenty minutes later. Jackson throws his head back dramatically and begs for *one more minute*. Owen chuckles and agrees, and then stands to slip the sleeping baby into her stroller.

His biceps bulge under his gray t-shirt, and the look on his face as he gently lays Violet down is doing bad, bad things to me. He really loves his niece. He actually does enjoy taking Jackson to the park. Is he a family man after all?

"Hey, Owen," a group of three moms, one of them pushing a double stroller, comes up the park sidewalk.

"Hey, ladies," Owen says back with his famous cocky grin. I don't think he realizes he does it anymore, and that smug smirk just comes naturally to him. "Nice day today, isn't it?"

The mom with the stroller bites her bottom lip and looks Owen up and down. "It's a little hot out here, don't you think?"

The other two moms make a joke about it getting hotter. Owen laughs to oblige them and the weirdest thing is starting to happen to me.

I think...I think I'm feeling a little jealous.

I squeeze my eyes closed. *Stop it right now, Charlie.* I'm not in the right headspace to date anyone. And I know better than to get back together with an ex who broke my heart years ago.

Wanting to get married and have children was what drove Owen and I apart in the first place. I wanted to settle down, go ring shopping on the weekends, and pick out baby names.

Owen didn't.

We wanted different things in life, which no one can fault either of us for. I was willing to wait for Owen, convinced he'd just need a year or two to realize that starting a family was something he wanted to do too.

I guess I was wrong.

Though, really…the joke is on me. Because here I am, in my thirties now, and still single as ever and still childless.

"Oh my goodness," one of the moms whisper-squeals as she looks at Violet. "She gets cuter every time I see her!"

"She gets that from me," Owen says and everyone erupts into giggles.

Jackson runs over, cheeks beet red and panting. "I'm thirsty," he pants, and Owen tears himself away from his fan club to get Jackson a juice box from the diaper bag. He sticks the straw in for Jackson and then rustles his hair, teasing him about being sweaty.

"Can we go swimming at Grammy's?" Jackson asks Owen as he buckles his helmet back into place.

"That's not up to me, buddy. Grammy will say yes, of course, but we have to ask your mom."

I watch Owen out of the corner of my eye, thinking that he's changed a lot. Maybe?

"Are you going to be in town for a while?" he asks me.

"It seems that way."

"Come to Getaway tonight. You can drink on the house." He turns his head, flashing that cocky grin again that makes me feel all squishy inside. "You still like sweet red wine, right?"

I nod. "Yeah, I do."

"Then I'll make sure to have some. If I'm remembering correctly, which I know I am, red wine always…" He trails off and wiggles his eyebrows.

"Owen," I start, voice edging on scolding. It'll be all too easy to fall back to old habits, and Owen would be a hard one to break. It took years for me to get over him the first time…if I even got over him at all.

Inhaling deep, I look down the opposite direction of the street.

"I…I should finish my run," I tell Owen. "It was good to see you, though."

"It usually is."

Smirking, I shake my head. No, he hasn't changed at all. "Tell your mom I said hi."

"You could tell her yourself." He adjusts the sun visor on the stroller. "Come over for dinner on Sunday."

"Your mom still does Sunday dinners?"

Owen smiles. "She never stopped. Give me your number and I'll call you."

"Owen…" I let out a breath. "That's not a good idea."

"Why not? Worried you won't be able to resist me?"

Yes, I am a little worried, actually. I narrow my eyes. "Of course not. But what's the point?"

He shrugs, getting a cocky glint in his eyes. "You never know what could happen. And if anything, we could just have sex. We were always good at that, if I remember correctly. I always pleased you. Multiple times."

I come to a dead stop, staring at him openmouthed with a *you did just not say that* look in my eyes. Then again, I'm not surprised, and suddenly heat is flashing through me. Owen is good. With his fingers. His mouth. His tongue…and holy shit, that big cock.

"You're disgusting."

He raises his eyebrows. "I did remember correctly. And you never thought what we did was disgusting before. I seem to

51

remember one particular night in vivid detail that involved you, me, and the roof of your parents' house. What you wanted me to do to you…I still think about my head between your legs while balancing two stories above the ground."

"Jackson might hear you," I hiss, getting turned on and annoyed by Owen's open dirty talking.

"Nah, he's too far ahead. Hey, Jackson, we're going to Disney World," he says just to prove his point. The boy doesn't so much as turn around. "See?"

"And if he did hear you? Have fun telling him Disney was just a joke."

He shrugs. "Then I guess I'd have to take him. Wes and Scarlet won't be going anytime soon with the new baby and all. Jackson loved going last year. And it gives me a good excuse to go on all those kiddy rides. The Haunted Mansion ride is the shit, you know."

All I can do is laugh and shake my head, which is all I've been doing since I stepped back into Owen's presence. I don't know how someone can go from making my panties melt off to then making me laugh like this. But that's Owen fucking Dawson for you…

"You didn't give me your number yet." Owen stops at a street corner, eyes on Jackson. He steps to the side of the stroller, keeping one hand on it but ready to jump forward and grab his nephew in case he doesn't stop to let the cars pass. Dammit, Owen. Stop being so attentive and caring and sexy and—*stop*.

"That was done on purpose." I stick my earbuds back in my ears. "Bye, Owen."

I take off, running down the block before I slow enough to look down at my phone to turn my music back on. My heart is hammering and sweat broke out alone my forehead as soon as I turned and ran away. I keep going, not stopping until I'm back on my parents' block.

Panting, I climb the porch steps and heft into the porch

swing. I should cool down and then stretch, but I need to sit right now and sort out my thoughts. Because they're all over the damn place. Taking my earbuds out of my ears once again, I call Marcus.

"Are you being held hostage?" he answers on the second ring.

"Yes, I am. Send me five thousand dollars," I say dryly. "Or a new pair of Christian Louboutins, which would be slightly less expensive."

"Only slightly," he laughs. "But seriously. You never call. What's going on?"

"I don't know," I confess and lean back, pressing the heels of my feet against the porch and then pushing off to get the swing in motion. "That's the issue. I have no idea what's going on. Well, I did, and then I didn't."

"Are you having a nervous breakdown or something?"

"I wish I could say that was the reason," I laugh. "I ran into my ex and was not prepared at all for it. He was holding a baby, Marcus. A little baby girl."

"Your ex Owen?" he asks, and I internally cringe over the fact that he even knows Owen's name. I could have sworn I'd only brought him up once. *Maybe* twice.

"Yes."

"He has a baby?"

"No, it was his niece and he was babysitting so his sister-in-law could nap."

"How sweet."

"Right?" I close my eyes and push the swing again.

"I still don't get why you called." The sound of a busy New York City street comes though the phone. "Unless seeing Owen is making you feel—"

"Nothing. It's making me feel nothing. I just got out of a long-term relationship. A serious one. Like as serious as you can get, well, without being married and having children. I should be upset about Todd still, right? Not about—wait. I'm nothing. Nothing towards Owen."

Marcus laughs. "You're cute when you're flustered, and I'm sad I'm not there to see it in person. I've never seen Ms. Big-shot Lawyer flustered before."

"I'm not flustered," I say, not believing it myself. "I'm a little annoyed, that's all. Owen is so…so arrogant."

"Arrogant but looks good with a baby in his arms?"

"Ugh, yes." I stand up and walk down the steps. "I need to get back to work. All this free time is messing with my head."

"Honey, maybe you should take a hard look in the mirror. Why is Owen instantly frustrating you?"

"I just told you. He's a cocky asshole. Ugh, he's seriously infuriating! You should have heard what he said to me. I cannot stand that man."

"Mm-hm. I'm sure that's it."

"Maybe I'm looking for a rebound. Is rebound sex a thing? Does it help?" I shake my head. "Never mind. I'm not sleeping with Owen."

"Can I be honest, honey?"

"Your blunt honesty is why I love you."

"I think Todd was your rebound."

"My rebound?" I open my mouth but don't know what to say. "No…no way. He was my fiancé! That's not a rebound."

"In the last two minutes, I've heard you have more passion in your voice over Owen than I did in the *years* you were with Todd. And I almost don't want to say it, but I'm going to. We all know you and Todd were over before you ended things."

"I…that's not true," I stumble over my words.

"I love you and want you to be happy. Just think about what I said."

"Fine, I'll think about it."

"And feel free to send me any pictures of that sexy man

holding a baby. You know I'm a sucker for hot guys holding babies. And puppies. Or reading or holding a cup of coffee."

"So just hot men in general?" I laugh.

"Guilty. I'm about to get in a cab, talk soon, though, okay?"

"Of course." I end the call and go inside to stretch and shower. Then I get something to eat and go back upstairs. Lying down in bed, I grab a book and plan on reading a few chapters, escaping into a fictional world and not thinking about ex-boyfriends or ex-fiancés or anything of the sort. This fictional land full of witches and sexy vampires is much more exciting, anyway.

Three chapters later and I'm feeling sleepy. I trade the book for a blanket and lie down. Mom left to go to the store and Dad is at work. The house is quiet, save for the birds chirping outside the open window. With the ceiling fan on high, things are set for prime napping time.

My eyes fall shut and I start to drift to sleep faster than I expected, slipping into a hazy dream where I'm walking through Eastwood and run into Owen again. But this time, we don't go to the park.

This time we go back to his house, which is technically his parents' since that's the last place he lived during college when we were still together. We're sitting in the kitchen and suddenly he's holding a baby again, but instead of the little blonde-haired newborn he was holding before, this baby has thick dark hair... just like he does.

Then the dream shifts and suddenly we're upstairs in his bedroom. He's on top of me, and his kisses feel just as good as before. My clothes just melt off in a way that can only happen in a dream. Owen rolls me over so I'm straddling him. I buck my hips, feeling his big cock rub against me.

"Charlie," he moans, looking into my eyes. "I've missed you."

"I've missed you too," I pant and lean down to kiss him. I grind against him, needing a release. It's been so long since I've felt anything this good.

My eyes fly open. *Oh, shit.* My hand is between my legs, and my body is still craving the release my dream didn't give. I push myself up, eyes wide. Swinging my legs over the side of the bed, I stride into the bathroom and turn on the sink, set on splashing cold water on my face.

Because having a sex dream about Owen is the last fucking thing I need.

CHAPTER 9

CHARLIE

I bring my hand up to my face, covering my nose. Mom does the same and takes a step closer to the door. She offered to help me look at rentals around Eastwood today since I didn't put the deposit down on the apartment yesterday. There are a whole three houses up for rent in Eastwood right now, and we're on house number three already.

The first was nothing more than a trailer parked in someone's yard. I'd share my propane hookup with the house, so that was an automatic no. The next house was rather large for one person, and looked promising from the outside...until we saw the water damage in the basement. Turns out it floods during bad rainstorms.

And this current house is small, tidy, but smells terribly like cigarettes and cat pee. Looks like I'm stuck with Mom and Dad for another month and a half...and that I'll be dropping off the deposit to hold my spot at the apartment complex.

Mom and I do our best not to gag as we walk through the rest of the house, which is actually cute and has potential if only it didn't smell so bad. After leaving the house, we go into town and get lunch.

As we're leaving the restaurant, Carly calls and asks if we want to go see her lot in the neighborhood today. The builders started to mark stuff off and she's excited.

"Do you want to go?" Mom asks. "I know it's not the most exciting thing in the world, but your sister is just tickled over this."

"Yeah, I'll go see it. I think it's cute she's so excited."

"Five people in her little house…" Mom shakes her head. "Plus those dogs. I couldn't have done it. The two of you took up enough room in our house." She gives me a wink. "The only downfall about older houses is the lack of bathrooms. In this new neighborhood every bedroom has a bathroom."

"That is nice, especially when the kids get older."

"Definitely. There were many mornings before school where you and Carly would be fighting over the bathroom."

"I remember. Carly took forever to do her hair."

Mom laughs and pulls her keys from her pocket. I roll down the windows as soon as I'm in the car, choking from the hot summer air. It doesn't take long before the air conditioner starts blowing out cool air, at least.

"Oh wow," I say about ten minutes later when we pull into the new development. "This is huge."

"It's really taken off over the last few years. It's nice, rather upscale houses too. You-know-who's father developed this."

"Mom, you can say Owen's name. He's not Voldemort."

Mom looks at me sideways. "All right."

Carly's lot was one of the last left in the neighborhood, and butts up to a pond with a fountain in the center. The houses are cookie-cutter without being too similar, and almost every lawn is neatly landscaped. This place looks perfect for my sister and her family.

"Hi, Aunt Charlie!" Libby comes running over to me as soon as I'm out of the car. She's four and is the spitting image of Carly. I pick her up and kiss the top of her head.

"Hey, kiddo! Are you excited to have your house go in here? I'm excited for it!" I flash a big smile, remembering Carly tell me that Libby is scared of moving. "I bet your new room is going to be perfectly pink, right?"

"Yes, with princesses!"

"Mine is going to be green," Matt says. He's two years older than his sister and is all about the jungle and dinosaurs right now.

"Oh my gosh, it's going to be so cool!" I set Libby down. That kid is surprisingly heavy for her size. "And what about baby Jack?"

"Mickey Mouse!" Libby says, raising her hands up over her head. "He's just a baby, though."

"Mickey Mouse is always a good choice." I take her hand and follow Carly through the empty lot. She takes photos of the orange flags and sends them to her husband. Libby wants to walk down the street and look at the geese by the water's edge. I go with her, but stop before we even make it two houses down.

Because of all the people in this town for me to run into— again—it's Owen fucking Dawson. And this time, he's shirtless and sweaty and pushing a lawnmower. I remember my dream from yesterday and hate the rush of heat that goes through me.

His kisses probably aren't that good anymore. And I bet he's slept with so many people he's gotten lazy in bed. Which makes sense, don't tell me otherwise.

Hoping we can hightail it down the sidewalk before he see us, I wait a beat before starting forward again, watching him turn the lawnmower around and head away from the street.

But, dammit, he sees me and stops mowing.

"Charlie," he says and my name floats off his tongue like velvet. "Are you stalking me?"

"You wish," I spit back, keeping a hold on Libby's hand.

"Then what are you doing here?"

"My sister bought the lot a few houses down. She wanted to show me."

Owen nods. "I didn't know we were going to be neighbors."

"You live here?" I don't mean to sound as surprised as I do. My eyes go to the house in front of us, thinking this place is better suited for a family of five like my sister's, not Owen.

"What, did you think I was just here mowing lawns or something?"

"No, it's just not...not what I expected."

He gets that irritatingly sexy cocky smirk on his face again. Fuck, I want to slap it right off. "So you expected things from me. Does that mean you've been thinking about me?"

"No," I say pointedly. "Not at all."

"Who is that?" Libby whispers.

"That's Owen," I tell her. "An old friend."

"We were much more than—" Owen cuts off when I glare daggers at him. "I'm Owen," he says to Libby and offers his hand to shake.

"You're all sweaty." She recoils and I laugh.

"I am. It's hot out. Are you excited to move in here?"

Libby wrinkles her nose. "Yeah, but I'm sad to leave my old house. Heidi lived across the street and we played."

Owen crouches down to Libby's level and points to a house down the road. "Two little girls live there, and I know there are a handful of other kids about your age in here. I see them up and down the street on their bikes all the time. Actually, the girl who lives right next to me just got one of those princess Power Wheel cars. It looks like it can seat two and she never has anyone to ride with her."

Libby's face lights up and I'm hating Owen more and more. Not only is he amazing with his own niece and nephew, he just made my own niece's day.

"Well," I say, tugging Libby forward. A bead of sweat rolls down Owen's chest and slowly makes its way over the ridges of his abs. He was in good shape when we were together, but he's in even better shape now. "We were going to see the geese."

"They're mean," Owen warns. "Don't get too close."

"We'll be fine."

"Bye!" Libby waves and jogs to keep up with me. I slow once I realize I'm making the poor kid run. The geese hiss and shake their heads at us as soon as we step off the sidewalk. "They are mean. That man was right."

"Geese usually are. Maybe we can bring bread or something for them next time and try to be friends."

"Okay!"

I pick up Libby and carry her down the sidewalk, moving fast and instantly regretting it. I'm sweating by the time we get back to Carly and my mom.

"Who were you talking to?" Mom asks, though by the tone of her voice she clearly knows.

"Just one of the neighbors," I say and set Libby down.

"Really?"

"Yeah. He lives a few houses down from here, which makes him one."

Mom and Carly exchange glances, but before either of them can get on me about it, Jack picks up something off the ground and sticks it in his mouth. After a moment of panic, we pull a dried-up worm from the kid's mouth and decide to call it a day. I help load the kids into the car, and right as Carly gets Jack's carseat buckled, her phone rings.

"Oh my god," she says, stepping away from the car. I watch, worried at first that something is wrong. Then I see her smile, and a minute later she comes back.

"You're never going to believe this!"

"What?" Mom asks.

"Someone just put an offer on the house. Full asking price! And they want to close as soon as possible!"

"That's amazing!" I give my sister a hug.

She puts her hand to her chest and lets out a big sigh. "I was so panicked about having to pay for two houses if the first didn't sell. This is such a—oh shit."

"You said a bad word, Mommy," Matt points out.

"What's wrong, honey?" Mom starts Carly's car so the kids don't get cooked in there.

"This house won't be ready for another few months. I know we talked about moving in with you guys to patch the time, but that was with the assumption it would take our house through the summer to sell, not the day after we put it on the market."

"We'll make it work." Mom's smile doesn't falter. "It'll be fun having us all together. And it's only temporary."

My smile, however, does falter. My situation was only temporary too, and now I'm cursing this stupid small town and its lack of rentals. My eyes go to Owen once more, and my heart skips a beat in my chest.

"It'll be fun," I flat-out lie. My parents' house is decently sized, but cramming my sister, her husband, three children, and two golden retrievers in along with Mom, Dad, me, and Tulip…we'll be lucky if we all make it out alive by the end of the summer.

CHAPTER 10

OWEN

Maybe I should get a cat.

Seriously. What the fuck is wrong with me? I shift in the chair, trying to get comfortable. I fell asleep watching reruns of *The Office* and my dream was about Charlie.

Again.

It's been a week since I've seen her, and it's not for lack of looking. Eastwood seems like a small town until you try to find someone amongst all the residents...and corn fields...and cows.

I want to fuck her. Feel her pert nipples against the rough palms of my hands as I cup her supple breasts. I want to push my cock into her tight little pussy and feel it contract around me as she comes.

That's all. Fuck her, and forget about her.

Which is what I should have done tonight. Well, not fuck Charlie. But someone else. I could have, and even got two numbers handed right to me at the bar tonight. Yet those women weren't doing it for me.

Were they pretty? Yeah.

Would they have been a good time? Yeah.

But were they Charlie? Hell no.

I think it's time I admit it to myself. After years of denying it, years of pretending it didn't matter because I liked hooking up with a different girl every night…I think it's time to—nope.

Not doing it. Not sober, at least. Stretching my arms out in front of me, I get up with a yawn and go into the kitchen, flicking the light on above the sink. I rub my eyes, stare at the dirty dishes on the counter, and then go to the fridge to get a beer.

It's way too late—or too early, depending on you look at it—to be drinking, but I have nowhere to go tomorrow and know there's no way I'll fall back asleep unless I have something to dull the pain.

Because that's exactly what I'm feeling: pain.

I fucked up. I've missed Charlie all these years and I've lived with repressed regret. I broke up with her because I wasn't what she needed and I wanted her to go find her own happiness. But I'm not the same guy, not at all.

Bringing my beer to my lips, I chug a few mouthfuls and then set the bottle on the counter. I have to show her I've changed. Give her a reason to take another chance on me. Because no one can love her like I can.

No one will please her like I have.

I want nothing else but to make her happy.

I turn on the sink and grab a rag, washing the dishes that wouldn't fit in the dish washer. I suck down the rest of my beer and go upstairs to shower and brush my teeth. Naked, I pass out in bed.

No surprise, I dream about Charlie.

"What aren't you telling me?" I narrow my eyes at my twin, able to sense that he's withholding something secret.

Logan smiles, looks out at the bar, and motions for me to join him in the office. He's sitting at the computer, and has been working on the schedule for the next few weeks.

"Danielle's pregnant."

"Shit, congrats!" I clap him on the back. "Your boys can swim!"

He laughs. "We already knew that, jackass. Don't tell anyone yet. Danielle wants to wait until she gets her first ultrasound, ya know, since the last one didn't stick."

"Your secret is safe with me. And this one is it. I have a good feeling about it."

His smile grows. "I hope so. It was really hard on her—and Mom—last time."

Danielle had an early miscarriage only a few months ago, which we were told was totally normal, yet still devastating for everyone.

"When does she go into the doctor?"

"Next week. She thinks she's already six and half weeks so we're past where we got last time."

"You're gonna give me another nephew, I can feel it."

Logan laughs. "I'd love a son. Fuck, that's weird to say."

"Don't start the dad-jokes just yet."

"I'll try my best."

It's Friday evening, and Getaway is busy like usual. I'm in a good mood, happy for Logan and Danielle. It's the first time since seeing Charlie over a week ago that I felt this good. The night is going by fast...until she walks in.

I don't know what makes me look up, but I do the moment she steps through the doors. Her hair billows around her face and it's like everything moves in slow motion, including my heart.

Charlie steps into the bar and stops, looking around. She's alone, but isn't uncomfortable. It's easy to forget she's a lawyer, that she's ruthless when she has to be and isn't afraid to find her own voice. She's wearing a black top and tight jeans and looks so fucking good. Her blonde hair is pulled up in a bun on the top of her head, and her red lipstick is making me want to kiss those lips.

She catches my eye and gives a small smile as she makes her way over to the bar

"Miss me?" I reach under the bar for a wine glass.

"Keep dreaming," she says, and I wonder if she's able to read my mind. I have been dreaming about her.

I turn and go to the mini fridge, getting out a bottle of sweet red wine. I fill up her glass and slide it over. She takes it but looks at the liquid as if there's poison inside.

"Then what are you doing here?"

"Can't a girl come get a drink?" She brings the wine glass to her lips. I swallow hard, talking down my cock. God, this woman is gorgeous.

"Of course she can. But why come here of all places?"

She takes a big drink of wine. "There aren't any other places to go after ten PM here." Setting the glass back on the bar, she looks around. "This place is nice."

"You sound surprised again. Are your expectations that low?"

She cocks an eyebrow. "Do you want me to answer that?"

I roll my eyes and shift my attention to another female customer who comes up to the bar, tits popping out of her top. She makes a point to lean over and show them off, making me think she just got them done and wants everyone to notice. The surgeon did a fantastic job, but even Ms. Designer Tits falls short next to Charlie.

My Charlie.

"Really, though," she starts, taking her eyes from me to the woman next to her. "I just need some quiet."

"You came to the wrong place, sweetheart."

"Don't call me sweetheart," she shoots back.

"What, will you sue me?"

"I would love to."

I round on her, leaning against the bar. "And I'd love to see you in a tight skirt and button-up blouse. Oh, wait. I have. Remember when you used to play sexy librarian with me? I had overdue books all the time."

"Shut your mouth," she snaps and picks up the wine, downing the rest. "I shouldn't have come here."

"Wait," I say, putting my hand over hers before she walks away. "Stay. You obviously came here for a reason."

Logan, able to sense what's going on, I'm sure, comes up behind me.

"Hey, Charlie," he says, all smiley and happy. Right. Charlie doesn't drive everyone crazy. Just me.

"Hey, Logan," she replies with a smile just as big. "I heard you got married. Congrats."

"Thanks. I'm a lucky guy. Danielle is everything I could ever want."

"That's really sweet."

Logan refills her wine glass. "And I'm sorry to hear about, uh, what happened."

Charlie watches the wine fill her glass. "Thanks. It's all for the best though, right? Gotta find that silver lining."

"Right." Logan steps to the side, handling Ms. Designer Tits, who's now freaking out a bit that Logan and I are identical twins. It happens all the time, and usually I use it to my advantage.

"You said you want quiet," I go on, studying Charlie's pretty face. "Everything okay on the home front?"

She takes another sip of wine. "Oh, it's fine. Just...busy."

"Busy?"

"My sister's house sold in record time and the buyer wanted to close as soon as possible. Which meant my sister and her family needed somewhere to stay until their new house is built."

"Which will be a few months at best."

"Exactly." She takes another sip of wine. "So right now it's me, my sister, her husband, her three children, their dogs, and my cat all crammed in with my parents. I have a deposit down on an apartment, but it won't be open until the end of next month." She brings her fingers to her temple. "It's a first world problem, I know. But my God, I've never hated my sister so much as I do right now."

I laugh. "It's rough being crammed together like that. There's nowhere else for you to go?"

She slowly shakes her head. "The three rental properties available where not cutting it. But it's fine…I just need to tough it out for another month." She drains the rest of the wine.

Charlie is in a weird situation. She's smart, probably has a decent amount of money in the bank. I have no idea what she's doing for work right now, but if she wanted to get another city job, I'm sure she would. Taking over her father's firm was always her plan…maybe that's why she's sticking around town. Her father has to be getting close to retiring.

The rentals in Eastwood are shit. They were back when I graduated from college and didn't want to live at home anymore, and they still are today. The only apartment complex here is decent enough, but isn't very large and I'm not surprised to hear it's full.

"You could come stay with me," I offer before I get a chance to fully think about it. "We both know my house is more than big enough."

Charlie looks at me, blinking. "No fucking way, Owen," she laughs. "I am not living with you."

"Why?" I rest my elbows on the bar. "What are you afraid of? That you'd get in behind closed doors and wouldn't be able to resist me?"

"Oh yeah, that's my main worry." She rolls her eyes.

"What is your main worry then?"

"That I'll get arrested for murder because living with you would be worse than living with my entire extended family."

"Ouch, that was harsh."

"Fine, I wouldn't kill you. Just do major bodily harm."

I wiggle my eyebrows. "That sounds like something I might enjoy."

"You are impossible," she sighs. "Thanks, but no thanks."

I shrug. "Why not, though? I have the space. Ever since Logan moved out, the house has seemed kinda empty anyway. Don't tell him, but I miss Dexter, his dog, more than him."

Charlie's eyes start to narrow as she looks at me. "I'm not stupid, Owen."

"I never thought you were. Not ever once."

Her hard glare softens. "I...I know. But...no. I'm not moving in with you."

"Don't think of it as moving in, more as me swooping in and coming to the rescue. You can crash at my place until the apartment is ready for you. No strings, no expectations. Though we both know you'll be crawling into my bed at night."

"Seriously?"

My tongue darts out, wetting my lips. Charlie's eyes flick down to it, and she pushes her shoulders back in a subconscious way to try to make it seem like she's holding it all together.

And maybe she really is. Or maybe...maybe she's feeling what I'm feeling too. It's a long shot, but fuck, I want to take it.

"The offer is on the table," I tell her and step away for a minute to take care of a few other customers. In the minute I'm gone, she somehow slips away and is nowhere to be seen.

Then it hits me, and I wonder what the hell was I thinking? Asking Charlie to live with me? To sleep in the room next to me. Eat breakfast by my side. Watch late night TV together like we're *friends*.

I will never be just friends with Charlie, and having her so close yet so far would hurt.

Not being about to touch her. Not hold her. Not tell her how I feel and rub her back until she falls asleep. Not being able to bring her coffee in the morning.

It would kill me. Then again, when I think back to these last few years without Charlie, I don't know how alive I've really been. Maybe…maybe I'm already dead. I haven't been living, just surviving.

And she's the only one who can revive my non-beating heart.

CHAPTER 11

CHARLIE

I can't believe I'm even considering this. I spent the night tossing and turning, thinking about Owen's words. Living with him would be stupid. He's my ex-boyfriend.

But also...he's my ex-boyfriend.

Sounds the same, I know, but I promise it's not. He's my *ex*, as in we're over. Done. The final curtain has been called. The major TV network canceled our show and no amount of protests and signatures can get us back.

I don't like to turn down any sort of challenge, and my competitive nature makes me a damn good lawyer but doesn't always lead me to make the best personal choices.

And. I. Know. This.

So why am I lying here in bed, kicking the sheets off for the millionth time, feeling like Owen is going to come out feeling like he won? That by me refusing his offer of crashing at his place until the apartment opens up, I'm admitting that I still have feelings for him?

Tulip paws at the door, wanting out of the bedroom. Internally groaning, I get out of bed and consider getting an apartment in Newport, the next town over. They'll have spaces available, that's for sure. But I start unofficial work at the firm next week, and I'm currently carless since I didn't need one in the city. Dad offered to let me drive his 1965 Mustang around town, but it hasn't been fully restored and starts to shake when it goes over thirty miles an hour, which is obviously a safety issue and can't be driven on the highway. Around town, it's fine. But getting me from Newport to Eastwood…yeah. Wouldn't happen.

I'll have to get a car before I can move out of Eastwood, and since I'm technically unemployed, I have no idea what kind of loan I'll be able to get. I have a decent amount of "oh shit" money saved in my bank account, but I don't think I'm ready to take it out just yet.

Especially when I have options.

Like put up living in this super-crowded house for another month while risking ruining the surprisingly good relationship I've had my entire life with my sister. It's really not that bad. Many people have it way worse, and I'm lucky to have a free place to live with a loving family.

We have clean water, food in the panty, and a safe place to spend our days.

I should count my blessings…and really, I do. But after living on my own and then again with Todd, which was really like living on my own since I did everything around the apartment, living with two other families is grating my nerves.

Which leads me to consider Owen's offer.

It's temporary.

It wouldn't mean anything.

He was right, he does have plenty of space.

And I'll work during the day and he'll work at night. We'll hardly see each other. Maybe it could work.

Maybe…or maybe not.

Tulip darts out of the room as soon as the door opens. I leave it cracked and get back into bed. It's nearing four in the morning and I haven't come close to falling asleep yet. At least I don't have to be up early.

I finally fall asleep when the sun starts to come up, and am woken up only an hour later to Jack pulling my makeup bag off my dresser. It comes crashing down, startling both of us.

Justin runs in after him, face turning beet red when he sees me in just a t-shirt and underwear.

"I am so sorry."

"It's okay," I tell him, gritting my teeth when I see my expensive eye shadow pallet upside down on the ground. "I was the one who left my door cracked for the cat."

Justin scoops up his youngest son and turns away. I grab my robe and quickly slip it on. My shirt is long and really, I've worn a bikini way more revealing than this.

"I'll come back and clean that up," he offers.

"It's okay," I tell him. "I got it."

Justin pries a beauty blender out of Jack's hands and hurries out of the room, closing the door behind him. With a sigh, I drop to my knees. One of my blushes is cracked, but it's one I hardly ever use since it's too red for my skin tone. The eye shadow pallet was new and thank goodness survived. I zip everything up and put it in the closet, closing the door behind me.

I throw on leggings and a bra and go downstairs for coffee, which I desperately need. Libby is having a meltdown about not wanting to go potty, and Jack is screaming because he wants to go back into my room.

It's loud and my head hurts. Rubbing my temples, I go right for the coffee pot, only to realize it's empty.

"Oh, sorry," Justin says, zooming into the kitchen. He's getting ready to go to work. "Filled up my to-go mug and forgot to put in more water. Want me to—"

"I got it," I tell him with a smile. "Don't be late for work."

"Thanks." He breezes out of the house, handing off Jack to my mom.

73

"You're up early," she says with a smile.

"Kinda hard to sleep in." I take Jack from her and make silly faces to try and get him to stop crying. He pulls my hair instead, but at least it gets him to settle down, right?

"I was clearing out the basement to make a little play area of the kids," Mom starts as she refills the coffee pot. "And I came across a box of old photos. There are some real gems in there. The box is in the living room."

I take Jack and go into the living room to look through the photos as I wait for more coffee. Sitting front and center on top of the pile is my senior prom photo. Owen's arm is around me, and he's looking away from the camera and at me.

Man, we look so young. And happily in love.

Because we were.

Jack toddles off, finding the toy bin in the corner of the room. I sit on the couch and flip through the old photos. There are more of me from high school, and as soon as I flip to a snapshot from graduation, my stomach starts to feel funny.

Oh, how I'd give anything to be that carefree again. Though I wouldn't want to go back to high school. In the photo, I'm standing in between Logan and Owen. Logan's girlfriend at the time is on his other side, and both of Owen's arms are wrapped around me. Our friends hated how affectionate we were, and that continued on through college, even when we were going to different schools.

That *I can't keep my hands to myself* phase never ended for us.

I flip through the photos, laughing when I see one of us on a family vacation from the early nineties. Mom's hair was amazingly poofy.

Suddenly, one of the dogs barks, startling me and setting Tulip off in a panic. She tears across the living room, seeking shelter under the coffee table. Chewy barrels after her, knocks over a lamp, and barks. Tulip shoots forward but is caught by Ray, the other—and bigger dog.

Tulip yowls and Ray pounces again, landing with both paws on my poor little cat. It's pure chaos for a minute, and I might have screamed a time or two. But by the time we get the dogs off Tulip, it's obvious something is wrong with her.

I'm in tears as Mom wraps her in a blanket and rushes with me out the door, speeding through town to get to the vet. An hour—and a large bill—later, I leave my cat under the vet's care.

She has a broken leg, one bite on her neck, and is battered, bruised and stressed to the max. They're keeping her under observation for a few days, and then when I bring her home, she'll have to be kept calm and away from the dogs.

But even if she's locked in my bedroom, the poor thing is going to be terrified.

"I'm so sorry," Mom tells me as I pull my seatbelt over my lap.

"It's not your fault. Carly should have trained her stupid dogs better."

"I won't agree or disagree," Mom says gently. "But even the vet thinks they were just trying to play."

"I know." I rub my eyes. "She's so little compared to the dogs."

"We'll figure something out. Maybe the dogs can stay outside during the day."

"As mad as I am at them, I don't want to stick those dogs out in the heat. Send them away to dog boot camp...yeah, that's a good idea. Carly is lucky those things haven't hurt one of her kids."

Mom, who never wants to say anything bad about either of us —even when it's obvious, shakes her head again. "I'll suggest training. The dogs could learn manners."

"They need more than manners." I'm pissed, already out a thousand bucks and I know the bill will double by the time I get Tulip back, and know I'm going to blow up the moment I see my sister.

I look out the window at the barn and small pasture behind

the vet's office. For the sake of saving my relationship with Carly, I need out of that house.

And I only have one option...which might be the stupidest thing I've ever done. Then again, I've based most of my adult life on what I *should do*. What's *right* and what *makes sense.* Todd was a Vivian Kensington while Owen was an Elle Woods, and given that we were both lawyers, it seemed fitting. It was logical. Rational, even.

Maybe it's time I throw logic out the window and trust my instincts...*and leap.*

CHAPTER 12

OWEN

"**R**umor has it you haven't taken anyone home with you in over a week." Logan unlocks the office door and looks at me over his shoulder. We just got to Getaway and are getting ready to open for the day.

"What, you're keeping tabs on my sex life now?"

"Someone has to. You certainly aren't."

"I lost count years ago."

Logan rolls his eyes and pulls out the desk chair, sitting in front of the computer. "I'm sure your lack of fucking has nothing to do with Charlie being back in town."

"Why would it?"

"Because you want to fuck her."

"Of course I want to fuck her," I shoot back. "Have you seen her?"

"She's more than a piece of ass to you."

I make a big deal out of checking the schedule hanging on the wall, even though I know it. Charlie is more than a piece of ass. She's always been and she always will be. I'd do anything to get her back. And fuck...that's exactly what I'm going to do.

"You're right," I tell Logan, who looks surprised by my confession. "I do want to fuck her, but I want more. She's single now and doesn't seem too torn up over her ex. I'm going to make her fall in love with me again. Next time I see her, I'm sweeping her off her goddamn feet."

"Easy tiger. That's not exactly something you can do in a day."

"Have you seen me? Shit, you do every time you look in the mirror. Well, the slightly less attractive version of me, that is."

Logan chuckles, and I half expect him to drop some line about how I use humor to deflect my feelings, but he's extra perceptive today and keeps his mouth shut. Leaving the office, I go to the bar, pour myself a shot of whiskey and start setting up to open.

I ended our relationship because we wanted different things. She wanted someone ready to settle down. Someone more responsible and mature than recent-college grad-Owen. And I'll be the first to admit I was a little shithead back then. I might still be, but I'm a changed man.

And I'm going to prove that to her, no matter what it takes.

Setting the last chair up, I go into the kitchen, make sure everything is good to go, and then unlock the door and flick on the neon *open* sign. It's Friday, and we're always busy on the weekends, even for lunch.

Never in a million years did I think Getaway could have grown into something this big, and Logan and I were tossing around the idea of building an addition not that long ago. Opening for lunch and dinner was a genius idea, and while I didn't like working all those extra hours at first, it's more than paid off. We still serve drinks, but this place is family-friendly during daytime hours.

We're packed, with people waiting for a table by the time seven o'clock rolls around. Logan left to help Danielle close down the bakery, and I've been ready to leave and hand the place over to Barry, one of the bartenders, but have stayed to help get through the rush.

And it's a good thing, because *she* walks in, and I swear the whole place goes silent for a moment, like the building holds its breath as she walks through the doors. Charlie makes a beeline to the bar, snagging a stool.

"I knew you wouldn't be able to resist me for long," I tell her, reaching for a wine glass.

"No thanks," she says, shaking her head at the wine glass. "I don't want anything to drink today."

"Oh, right. I forgot how alcohol makes you frisky."

She lets out a heavy sigh. "This was a mistake."

"What was?" I rest my hand on hers. She drops her gaze to it, and I feel her fingers slightly tremble before she jerks her hand back.

"You know what? The closer I get to saying it, the crazier it sounds." Her eyes fall shut, and she shakes her head at herself. "I need to talk to Jolene. She'd tell it to me straight."

"Who's Jolene?"

"A homeless lady who lives in Central Park." Her brows pinch together. "I hope she's okay."

I cock an eyebrow. "What the hell are you getting at?"

"Nothing. Forget it."

"For a second there, I thought you were coming in to tell me you want to take me up on my offer."

Charlie's face doesn't waver. "Your offer?"

"To move in until there's more room. I heard what happened to your cat. I don't have any dogs, you know."

She leans back, looking slightly horrified. "How do you know what happened to Tulip?"

"Quinn," I huff. "She basically funds the local cat rescue group on her own. She's at the vet more than anyone I know."

"More than your mom?" she asks, and a small smile starts to pull up her face. "She still has a million dogs, right?"

"Just four," I laugh. "Quinn actually does have a million cats, though."

"Cats are amazing." Her eyes sparkle even under the dull overhead lights.

"How is your cat?"

Her smile goes away and concern takes over her face. "She'll pull through. I'm lucky I was home to break up the fight."

I nod. "You are. So when are you two moving in?"

Biting her lip, she gives me a glare. Fuck, that stern look makes my cock jump. What I'd give to have her punish me right now…

"Owen," she starts, but doesn't finish her thought.

"If you're unable to resist me, just say it and I promise not to be offended."

"I can resist you just fine."

"Then use the guest bedroom for the next few weeks. It has its own bathroom. And I have no pets."

"Why don't you?" she asks as if it's incriminating not to have any.

"I'm not home much. I had a bird for a while."

"A bird?" She wrinkles her nose.

"Yeah. Someone ditched it in the cage on the side of the road. He was cool and knew how to say 'fuck' and a few other choice words."

"What happened to him?"

I lower my gaze to the bar, stomach clenching just thinking about it. Captain Morgan was a fucking awesome cockatiel. "Jackson let him out when the living room ceiling fan was on high."

Charlie gasps and brings her hand to her mouth. "Oh my God, I'm sorry."

I just shrug. "It was an accident. And as far as Jackson knows, Cap is living at the aviary at a zoo. I haven't gotten any new pets since."

Charlie tips her head up, holding my gaze for a few seconds.

"You really wouldn't mind having me and my crippled cat at your place for a while?"

"Of course not."

"If I do this—and that's a big if—it's only because I'm literally out of every single other option, and that includes screening in the back porch and living in my parent's yard."

"Well, what else would it be?" I lean a little closer. "A chance to win you back?"

"Win me back?" Charlie's eyebrows go up. "Like I'm some sort of prize?"

"Of course not. You're a strong, smart, independent woman who I've always respected. I was using *win you back* as a saying, I suppose. But I do plan to."

Charlie quickly shakes her head and looks down. "Fool me once," she says so softly I hardly hear her.

"Come to dinner with my family on Sunday. I'll show you I'm not going to fool you again. Fool around with...yes. But just fool...I'm not that person anymore, Charlie."

She looks up and I see the hurt in her eyes. It's only there for a second, and I'm not sure if she's thinking about us together in the past or her loser fiancé. The guy has to be the world's biggest dumbass to do anything to lose Charlie.

Right when I think she's going to say no, her eyes meet mine. "What time?"

"Six."

"Should I bring anything?"

I shake my head. "My mom's methods of cooking haven't changed."

"So she's still making enough food to feed a small army."

"She is, and we usually eat it all."

"You Dawsons are basically a small army." Her lips start to curve up into a smile. "And there are more of you now. Is everyone going to be there?"

"More than likely. Sometimes Wes and Archer are called into

work, but the rest of the gang will be there. I think you'll like Danielle, Logan's wife."

"It's still weird to hear you say that."

I chuckle. "It's still a little weird for me to say that. And to have him be busy with her all the time."

"You two were always close."

I shrug. "It's a twin thing."

"And you said that all the time too. I never really understood it."

Even though Charlie said she didn't want wine, I grab a bottle just in case she changes her mind. "No one but twins will. It makes it fun."

"So…I'll meet you there?"

"I can pick you up."

"Sure. That would be fine. I take it you remember where my parents live?"

My head bobs up and down. "I drive by every holiday hoping to see you changing in your bedroom window."

She purses her lips. "That happened once, and—oh my God. You took a picture!"

I was nineteen at the time and mostly took the photo to show her how visible she was from the street. But also, because I was nineteen and making mature decisions every day, of course.

"And it's printed as a poster and plastered to the ceiling above my bed. Along with some of the other nudes you sent me over the years."

Charlie just stares at me, and I wonder if she's thinking how weird it is to be that close to someone, to share something so intimate as naughty photos, and then to just break up and never see each other again.

"I think Logan might have stolen one of my favorites, though."

"And which one is that?" she asks dryly, crossing her arms over her chest.

"Remember when you were a sexy Bo Peep for Halloween?"

"Oh my God, no!" Her eyes close as she laughs. "We were what, juniors in college then? I have no idea why I thought that was a good costume. Actually, I might still have it in my parents' basement. I have a few bins of crap down there."

"Wear it to dinner Sunday."

She laughs once more, reminding me how much I miss hearing that sound. And the way her eyes crinkle just a bit when she's laughing. Reaching out, she takes the wine from my hand and pulls out the rubber stopper. She pours a bit in her glass and then looks around once more.

"This place is amazing. I can't get over how busy it is."

"Thanks, and you should see it tonight. Fridays and Saturdays are crazy."

"Maybe I'll come by sometime with Carly. When I'm speaking to her again." She takes a sip of wine.

"I can imagine things being a little tense since her dogs attacked your cat."

She nods. "They didn't do it maliciously, but still…" She lets out a sigh and turns back to me, biting her lip. She's probably thinking that crashing at my place is a bad idea. And if that's the case, I'm going to show her just how good bad can be.

CHAPTER 13

CHARLIE

I changed my outfit three times. My first dress made me look way too much like a stuffy lawyer. The second showed an indecent amount of cleavage. And the third? It's a simple red sundress that matches my lipstick.

Not that I care how I look for Owen or anything.

Smoothing my hair back that keeps blowing in my face from the wind, I lean back on the porch swing and look out at the street. It's weird, living back home with my sister and parents. I'm a responsible adult, yet I almost felt compelled to tell everyone where I was going.

Mom knows I'm going out, but that's it. She doesn't need to know the small details, and it's not like I have to ask permission. If they knew I was going to see the entire Dawson crew? It wouldn't matter, because nothing is going to come from this. It'll be nice to see everyone. They were a big part of my life for a long time, and it'll be nice to catch up. Too bad I don't have better news about myself. Though until a few weeks ago, things were going pretty damn well.

Feeling like a teenager again, I hop up when I see a black pickup truck slow to a stop in front of the house. Years ago, I'd run down the sidewalk and leap into Owen's arms. My heart flutters at the thought, remembering in vivid detail just how amazing Owen used to make me feel.

Like I was on top of the world, because I was his whole world.

"Hey," I say, opening the passenger side door before Owen has a chance to even take off his seatbelt.

"Hey, Charlie." He runs his eyes over me, not even caring that I can see he's obviously checking me out. "You look good."

"Thanks."

"What, no complimenting me back?"

I pull my seatbelt over my lap. "I don't want to lie, now would I?"

Owen laughs. "I miss this."

"What?"

"Your sass."

I look out the window, biting the inside of my cheek. Owen does look good. He's wearing a t-shirt and jeans, and his hair is messily styled in a way that looks way too sexy for anyone to be able to pull off. And now I'm remembering him all sweaty, body glistening in the sun as he pushed the lawnmower up and down his yard...

"What's your mom making for dinner?" I ask and fiddle with a strand of my hair.

"Don't know."

"Are you sure I shouldn't have brought something? My own mother would scold me to know I showed up at a dinner party without anything."

"It's just dinner. Not a party."

"You know what I mean."

"There's a good chance it's going to be hot dogs and hamburgers on the grill, so don't worry." He takes his eyes off the road for a second to look at me. "And when I bring you home, should I go inside and get your stuff?"

"My stuff?"

"To take back to my place."

Twisting my hair around my finger, I watch the landscape pass us by. "We'll see."

"I'll convince you tonight."

I turn to look at Owen, not sure if his confidence is annoying or sexy. Heat rushes through me, settling between my legs with a quiver. Narrowing my eyes. I sink my teeth down against my lower lip. I can handle whatever Owen throws at me. I think. I hope. I'm not interested in dating or even hooking up.

"You won't convince me, but go ahead and give it your best shot."

~

THE CENTURY-OLD FARMHOUSE LOOKS EXACTLY THE SAME. IT'S strange how the sight of it brings up a maelstrom of emotions.

Sunday dinners spent around the table.

Sneaking up the creaky old stairs and into Owen's bedroom, which he shared with Logan for a while. When Weston moved out, Logan took his room, leaving Owen and I with way too much privacy.

Holiday time split between my own family and Owen's.

There was so much promise. So much hope in a future together. I look at Owen and wonder what things would be like if we'd never broken up. Would he have eventually turned around? I didn't demand a ring or a baby. All I wanted was a promise of a future together, to get serious about the next phase in our lives, and look for a place of our own to put down roots.

Owen didn't want any of that, and at the time, it felt like a betrayal. Like I wasn't enough for him. It haunted me for years, wondering where I'd gone so wrong. What I could have done differently to be enough for him. Looking back now, I can see that we were just too different of people.

The truck bumps along the gravel driveway, and Owen parks

next to a Tesla.

"Whose car is that?" I ask.

"Archer's."

"Ahh, right. He's a doctor."

Owen takes off his seatbelt. "Quinn still makes more than him."

I can't help but smile and feel a little warm and fuzzy inside. One thing all the Dawson boys take seriously is looking after their baby sister. For a time, Quinn kind of felt like a sister to me too. I can't even remember the last time I've seen her, and now she's married with two kids.

Time goes by so fucking fast...until shit hits the fan and your own life is scattered to the wind all around you.

Smoothing out my hair once again, I get out of the truck and follow Owen around the house. We enter through the garage, and a brigade of dogs comes barking as soon as we step into the house.

"Easy," Owen tells them, but his voice is lost under the scrambling of paws and excited barks. A large German Shepherd comes barreling over, nearly knocking Owen to the ground in his excitement.

"Dex!" Owen drops to his knees and lets the dog get up close and personal for a few seconds. "You're getting fat," he tells the dog, who's now lying down for a belly rub. "This is Logan's dog, Dexter."

"He likes you."

"Logan got him back when we were both at the house. He's used to me."

"Owen?" Mrs. Dawson calls. "Is that you?"

"No, Mom," Owen calls back. "It's a burglar, and I've secretly befriended all five dogs over the course of a year just so I can sneak in unnoticed."

"Oh, well, good. Feel free to take any of the junk in the attic while you're burglarizing the place."

Owen gets back up, brushes dog fur off his lap, and goes through the rear entrance and into the kitchen. I follow behind, heart racing a little faster than I expected. Quinn and two other women, who have to be Scarlet and Danielle, are sitting at the island counter. Quinn is nursing the newborn I saw with Archer, and a gorgeous blonde woman I'm guessin to be Scarlet is holding baby Violet, who I recognize right away by the shock of blonde hair on her little head. Cascades of blonde waves fall around Scarlet's face, and even though she's sitting, I can tell she was one of those lucky women who lost all the baby weight right away without even trying.

A brunette is sitting next to her, and I'm guessing that's Danielle, Logan's wife. She's pretty as well, and is talking and laughing about something with Quinn. Seeing the three of them there together makes me feel a little out of place, which isn't something I was expecting to feel.

Because it means I want to fit in. Again.

Quinn looks up, about to say hi to Owen, and then sees me. All it takes is a split second of total shock on her face to let me know Owen didn't tell anyone he was bringing me.

"Charlie?" Quinn's eyes go wide.

"Hey," I say with a small wave. "I take it you had no idea I was joining you for dinner."

Quinn keeps staring at me like I'm a spirit who might disappear into the night if she takes her eyes off me. "No, he didn't." A second later she rapidly blinks and turns to Scarlet.

Mrs. Dawson, having heard my voice, rushes through the kitchen. She too stops dead in her tracks, looking from me to Owen and back again. Then she takes me in her arms, wrapping me in a big hug.

"It's been years!" she exclaims, releasing me. "I heard you were back in town but I didn't know if I'd see you."

"Yeah, I'm home now. For a while at least."

"Owen!" Mrs. Dawson steps to the side. "Why didn't you tell

me you were bringing someone? I have to add another place setting to the table."

"Don't go to any trouble," I start, but Mrs. Dawson waves her hand in the air.

"It's no trouble at all. It's this one who's in trouble."

Owen zeroes his eyes in on me, giving me a *punish me later* type of smirk. "I wasn't sure if she'd actually come," he admits.

"Come in, come in," Mrs. Dawson says, waving me into the kitchen. "Dinner is almost ready. Do you want anything to drink? I just opened a bottle of red wine."

"Yeah, that'd be nice," I say though my head is screaming at me to avoid alcohol at all costs. Because being back here in this familiar house with the family I loved so much is pulling on my heart strings.

"Danielle, Charlie. Charlie, Danielle," Owen introduces. "And this is Scarlet, Wes's wife."

"Nice to meet you." I sit in the barstool Owen pulls out.

"So, how have you been?" Quinn starts, readjusting her baby at her breast. "I don't even remember the last time I saw you."

"It's been a while. And I've, uh, been good. Well, until recently."

"Yeah, I, uh, heard. I'm sorry."

It takes a lot to unnerve me or make me feel inadequate. Being a female in a male-driven profession toughened me up fast, and I've always been more or less confident in who I am. The Dawsons aren't judgmental people, and I can't see Wes or Logan marrying anyone who'd sit here and make me feel bad.

"Thanks. Better I got out now, right?"

"What did happen between you and your ex?" Owen asks.

"Owen," Quinn scolds. "That's rude."

"It's fine." I push my hair back. "He, uh, cheated on me with his assistant," I blurt it all out fast, like ripping off a Band-Aid. The truth will come out sooner or later, and things can get twisted when spread through the rumor mill.

"Ugh, I can't stand cheaters." Danielle shakes her head, speaking with enough emotion to make me think she's dealt with it in the past too. "I'm sorry."

"Thanks. Though really, I'm fine. I probably should have broken up with Todd months before, but you know how it is when you're in a familiar routine."

"The guy is an asshole," Owen says. "Anyone willing to lose you is a fucking idiot anyway, but cheating? I'm sorry."

"Thanks." I bring my hands into my lap, feeling uncomfortable.

"His name is Todd?" Owen asks with a smirk.

"Yes."

"Haven't you seen any early 90s movies? The assholes are always named Todd."

"That is true," Quinn agrees. "Or Brad. Avoid the Todds and Brads from now on."

"I plan to avoid everyone for a good while," I say.

Mrs. Dawson brings me a glass of wine. "Are you back in Eastwood for good then?"

I take a sip of wine. "I'm not too sure. My dad has always wanted me to take over his firm, and one of the lawyers there is retiring soon, so it's kind of good timing to move back permanently and start work."

"Your dad is Joseph Williams?" Scarlet asks.

"Yeah, he is."

"He's a good man," she tells me with a smile. "He helped us a lot with getting custody over Jackson."

I smile back. "Not all lawyers are bad."

The sliding doors leading from the breakfast nook to the patio open and Logan comes in.

"I thought that was you." He gives me a hug. "I didn't get a chance to talk to you at Getaway. Shit, it's been a while. How have you been?"

"Uh, all right," I say, not wanting to repeat everything. "It's nice to be back. And congrats again on getting married." I look at Danielle. "Both of you."

"Let's go say hi to the everyone else," Owen says and stands up. "Get it over with." He holds out his hand for me to take. Swallowing hard, I take it and let him help me pull me to my feet. We go outside on the patio where Mr. Dawson is grilling. Dean, Archer, and Weston are playing with Jackson and Emma. I'm introduced to Kara, Dean's wife, who's sitting in the sun reading a book. She's polite enough, but it seems a little weird that she's out here instead of being inside with Quinn and the others.

With only ten minutes until dinner is ready, Owen slowly walks over to a shaded glider near the pool. I sit across from him, watching the kids run around the yard. Emma is trying so hard to keep up with Jackson and keeps falling in the grass. She pops right back up every time, laughing.

"Feels good to be back, doesn't it?" Owen pushes the glider forward.

"It feels familiar."

"But good?"

I shift my gaze from Owen to the growing corn in the field behind the yard. "I'm just trying to get back on my feet," I remind him. "Just...don't."

"Why not?"

"I don't want to go down this path again," I say softly. "My heart's been through enough."

"I'm not that guy anymore, Charlie." His brow furrows. "I promise you, I'm not."

I let out a breath and shake my head. It shouldn't matter. I don't want to get into a new relationship, let alone go back to an old one. But then something strange happens. My mouth opens, but the words don't come from my head. They come from my heart.

"Prove it."

CHAPTER 14

OWEN

I will prove it.

 I'll prove it a thousand times over and over again.

I'm a changed man. The kind of man Charlie needs. The kind she's always needed. I told her anyone willing to let her go was an idiot, and I'm the biggest one of all.

"I remember you," Jackson tells Charlie as we walk into the house for dinner. "You're not sweaty now."

Charlie laughs. "Not yet. If I stay out here long enough I will be."

"We could jump in the pool."

"I didn't bring a swimsuit."

"Sometimes I go in in my underpants," Jackson tells her.

"I like that idea," I say, nudging Charlie with my elbow. She laughs and shakes her head.

"Maybe another time," she tells Jackson.

"Are you Owen's special friend? Scarlet was Daddy's special friend for a while. First she was my nanny. Now she's my mom."

"We're just regular friends."

For now. I grab a tray of hamburgers from the grill, helping Dad bring in the food. A few minutes of chaos follow as everyone loads up their plates, pours themselves drinks, and sits around the table.

Dad is the last one to join us at the table, and comes over carrying copper mugs, passing out Moscow Mules to everyone but Quinn, who can't drink since she's breastfeeding Arya.

I don't catch it right away, but then I remember Danielle is pregnant. Other than Logan—of course—no one else knows, and they want to keep it that way until Danielle gets things checked out by the doctor.

Danielle, who's sitting next to me, looks across the table with a bit of panic at Logan. If she refuses to drink, it'll be the first thing people ask her. Everyone knows they've been trying for another baby.

She picks up her mug and brings it to her lips, pretending to take a sip. Mom says grace and then we all start eating. I pick up my own drink and suck it all down. Charlie watches me out of the corner of her eye but doesn't say anything.

Most days, I eat pretty healthy. Why put all the effort into working out when your nutrition sucks? But some days, like today, I'm just lazy. I had breakfast while watching TV and snacked the rest of the day, and came here with an empty stomach.

Sucking down a drink isn't a good idea.

I take a big bite of my burger and then grab Danielle's drink, trying to surreptitiously swap out our mugs.

"Thank you," she whispers, slowly moving her mug onto my placemat. I think we pulled it off.

"How's your cat?" Quinn asks Charlie. "I saw her at the vet when I stopped by to check on a litter of kittens from the shelter."

"She's doing as well as she can be. She's eager to get up and move around again."

"Poor thing. She's very pretty. We don't have any long hair cats."

"Don't even think about it." Archer puts his arm around Quinn. "Unless you want me to get a motorcycle."

"No way. Those are dangerous."

"Wait," I say as I feel the vodka start to hit me. "If Quinn gets more cats, you get a motorcycle?"

Archer chuckles. "That's the deal. Actually, let's go look for long-haired kittens."

Quinn narrows her eyes, trying to act like she's mad at Archer. "I'd worry too much about you."

"You shouldn't risk your hands," Dean tells him.

"Right," I quip, looking at my brother. "That's your favorite part, right? Wait, I mean second favorite."

"Hilarious," Dean deadpans.

"You're a surgeon, right?" Charlie asks, sticking her fork into her salad.

"Right. I do general surgery."

"I would see riding a motorcycle as an unnecessary risk then too."

"Thank you," Quinn tells her. "I agree. Scraping up your hands aside, you have too much to lose."

"You sound like my mother," Archer laughs. The conversation shifts from one subject to another, and by the time we're almost done eating, I've finished my drink and the refill Dad got for Danielle.

It doesn't feel like I've had that much until I stand up and realize I'm pretty buzzed. Which is fine.

But then we move onto dessert and Dean busts out a Mason jar of moonshine he got from one of the guys on the construction crew. He pours everyone but Quinn—and the kids, of course —a shot.

"I don't think I want to try this," Charlie laughs, apprehensively sniffing the shot glass in her hands.

"Me neither," Danielle sets her glass down.

"You've had it before," Dean tells her. "And liked it. I got a second jar for you and Logan."

"Oh, uh, thanks." Her face starts to turn red. I've never wanted a baby or got anyone pregnant. I can only imagine how much it would hurt her and Logan to find out they were expecting only to lose it again, and I understand completely why they don't want to tell the whole family out of fear they might have to go through everything all over again.

So I do the only thing I can think of. Down my shot and reach for Danielle's.

"That is good." I set the empty shot glass down. "Strong, but good." Fuck, I'm so fucked. I can see Charlie looking at me again, and I do my best to act like I'm super interested in the last bit of food left on my plate.

Danielle gets up to help Mom with the dessert she brought from her bakery, and Logan catches my eye from across the table. He gives me a curt nod, thanking me for taking Danielle's drinks and saving her from having to explain why she's not drinking. Dean pours us all another round, skipping Danielle this time since she's not at the table, and that third shot goes down a lot smoother than the first.

The moonshine hits me right as I'm digging into my chocolate cake. Leaning back, I let my fork fall to the plate and reach for my water instead. Moonshine isn't supposed to be drank like shots.

I'm drunk.

Things move in a bit of a blur after that. Everyone else eats dessert and Logan comes up with an excuse to take me outside. I do my best to hold it together, but it's obvious I won't be able to drive Charlie home.

I told her I changed, but as far as she can see it, I'm just the same as before.

CHAPTER 15

CHARLIE

Owen closes his eyes in a long blink, and picks up his keys from the breakfast table. I don't know why I even entertained the thought of coming here with him. That he might be different than before.

Changed.

More mature.

Not getting stumbling-through-the-kitchen-drunk at a family dinner. And stealing drinks from Danielle? What the hell was that? I snatch the keys from his hands before he can even say he's good enough to drive us home.

"Get in the car," I snap, narrowing my eyes. I turn and plaster a smile on my face so I can thank Mrs. Dawson for dinner. My heart is in my throat, and I fear I might throw it up on the floor at any moment.

Because it felt so good to be back here.

To be around this amazing family...and Owen.

Sitting there with the Dawsons, seeing them all married and happy and with babies...it gave me a stupid sense of hope. It brought me right back to college and beyond, when Owen was all

I needed, and I thought—without a doubt—that we'd be married with babies of our own not long after graduation.

He was everything to me.

My first kiss. My first love. We lost our virginity together, but it was so much more than that.

Owen was my world.

If only I was his…

"I'm okay," he says, but doesn't try to take the keys back from me.

Ignoring him, I turn. Quinn is right there, telling Emma to put her shoes on. She looks over my shoulder at her brother, and her brows pinch together with concern.

"I'll take him home," I tell her before she has to ask.

"Are you sure you don't mind? He can come back with us. Or stay here."

I shake my head. "I don't mind. And I kind of want to get home to check on Tulip."

"Your cat, right. Don't blame you there." She bends over and helps Emma slide her feet into her shoes. "Don't judge him," she blurts, looking up at me. "He's not usually like this, and I think he's nervous being around you again. He won't admit it, but we all know he's still in love with you."

Her words break my heart even more, because it reminds me how much I love this family. They believe in each other one hundred percent and will do anything for each other.

"If things were different," I start, looking down at Quinn. Things have changed so much. She used to be like my little sister, and here she is, with her life together and living her dreams, giving me advice.

"It was so nice to see you again," Mrs. Dawson says as she comes into the kitchen. It's a welcome distraction. We hug, I thank her for dinner, and then she sends us off with two large plates full of leftovers.

Owen stumbles out of the house behind me, and it's all I can do not to peel the foil off the plates and smear the food all over the front of Owen's truck. It's not entirely his fault. I mostly blame myself for giving him the chance to show me he changed.

And then disappointing me.

My mind goes back to what Marcus said, that Todd was my rebound after Owen. I didn't put any merit in it before, but the hurt that I'm feeling right now is making me think that he was right after all.

Until the end, things with Owen were perfect.

Easy.

He got me, and I got him.

I didn't have to put on a show for him. Didn't have to get dressed up. Hell, I didn't even have to shave my legs.

And Owen always made me feel like I was enough. More than enough, really. We loved each other so, so much, and I thought love was enough to get us through anything.

How did we fall apart?

Looking behind me, I watch Owen drunkenly struggle to get out of the gate without letting any of the dogs out. The question of how we fell so far still haunts me, because for the life of me, I cannot figure it out.

We were happy.

In love.

The sex was good. *Really* fucking good.

Why wasn't I enough for him? Maybe I dodged two bullets. Owen never grew up and Todd is an asshole.

Maybe I'm destined to be alone for the rest of my life.

And I'm fine with blaming Owen for that. He ruined me. Gave me unrealistic expectations that even he couldn't fill in the end. I open the passenger side door and wait for Owen to stumble his way across the gravel driveway and into the truck. Slamming the door, I force myself to take a deep breath. I'm mad at myself more than anyone else.

I get in, move the seat up, and put the plates of leftovers on Owen's lap.

"Hold onto these. If they fall, I'm not cleaning up your truck." I pull my seatbelt on and slowly back out of the driveway. Logan and Danielle come out of the house in somewhat of a rush, and it almost looks like Logan is flagging me down.

I put the truck in drive and it lurches forward, surprising me with the pickup. The last truck I drove was Owen's, and that was back in college.

"Charlie," he starts, turning to look at me. His eyes are bloodshot but are also glossing over. I don't think it's from the alcohol, but I don't want to give him the chance to sway me.

Because if anyone can, it's him.

"Just...just don't, Owen." My own voice catches in my throat, and I lean forward, turning on the radio. Synced to Owen's phone, his music automatically gets pulled up. He listens to the same stuff he did when we were together, and I love and hate that about him.

I skip past three Def Leopard songs, another by Motley Crew, and am surprised when *Defying Gravity* comes on.

"Seriously?" I turn, taking my eyes off the road for a split second. He has his head resting against the window as he clutches the plates of leftovers.

"It reminds me of you," he mumbles, and my eyes instantly fill with tears.

Damn you, Owen Dawson.

❧

"We're at your house," I say, putting the truck in park in the driveway. Owen sits up, blinking. "I'll walk you in. I don't want to be responsible if you stumble, fall, and then die of exposure from the heat or anything."

Owen doesn't say anything. He blinks and undoes his seatbelt.

99

Holding the plates of leftovers in one hand, he gets out and slowly walks up the driveway, using a keypad to open the garage doors. I stay a few feet behind him, watching to make sure he gets in the house okay.

Going against my better judgement, I follow behind. Just to make sure the plates get put in the fridge and he gets himself water. The moment I step inside the kitchen, I'm shocked. Because this does not look like the kind of house I'd expect Owen to live in.

The kitchen is clean and impressive, with a huge island counter decorated with three apothecary jars full of fruit. The biggest jar is in the center, and the lemons inside of it set a theme for the rest of the decor. Nothing is over the top, but the little pops of yellow amongst the white and gray color scheme in the kitchen is Instagram-worthy.

The kitchen opens into a living room, and the same colors are carried throughout that part of the house as well. The TV is obnoxiously large, giving me Owen-vibes, but everything else looks like it was copy and pasted right off of Pinterest.

It even smells good in here. But looks mean shit, obviously. Owen's house is perfect for a family, but he's obviously not.

He takes his phone out of his pocket, sets it on the island counter, and mumbles something about having to use the bathroom. Taking the leftovers, I go to the fridge and find a place to fit them in.

His phone rings, and I look over my shoulder to see who's calling. It's Logan, and I'm sure he's wondering if Owen made it home okay. I silence the call and then get a big glass of water for Owen.

I care more than I should, but I'm also a little curious to look around the rest of the house. Crossing through the kitchen, I set the water down on a glass coffee table in the living room. I gather my hair up in a ponytail and pull a hair tie off my wrist as I look around.

There's a two-story foyer right when you walk in through the front door, with a formal dining room on one side and another room, set up as an office, on the other. Things are neat and tidy, and I can't get over how impressive and flawless the decorating is.

"You can go," Owen slurs, coming out of the bathroom. "And I'm sorry."

"It's…it's…it's nothing I shouldn't have expected," I sigh.

"It's not, though," he starts, eyes looking heavy.

"Sit down." I motion to the couch. "I got you some water. And Logan called, probably to make sure you're not drowning in your own vomit or something."

Looking dejected, Owen nods and plops down onto the couch. I take a lingering look at him and then leave, not saying another word. My heart is in my throat, and I wish I could cough it up, getting rid of it once and for all. That thing has let me down over and over again.

I'm smart. Rational. I can see both sides to every story, and am able to look at arguments with an unbiased opinion. It's what makes me a good lawyer. I get my clients as well as those we're opposing, giving me a leg-up on whatever case I'm working.

Is it sad to say I miss it? That I'm craving a good argument in front of a judge? I need a win in life right now, because I'm feeling like the biggest loser. And not in a good way.

CHAPTER 16

CHARLIE

"Sorry, sweetpea," I tell Tulip, who's pathetically meowing by the bedroom door. "You can't go out there. We're both stuck in here."

I open my laptop, set on watching a movie and passing out. I just got back from taking Owen home, and his big truck is parked out in front of the house. It's only a matter of time before someone asks me about it, and I'll have to reiterate my story about how Owen is still the same carefree—or careless—boy he was back when we were together.

Not even ten minutes into the movie, someone knocks on the door.

"You decent?" Carly asks.

"Yes," I tell her. She opens the door, and one of the dogs dashes in before she can grab her. Tulip limps under the bed and my heart about falls out of my chest. Fuck, we need to get out of here. Maybe I'll rent a room in the only bed and breakfast in Eastwood. It would still be cheaper to live there for a month and a half than it would be to rent my NYC apartment for a week.

"Sorry," she says, shoving the dog into the hall. "Owen is here."

"What?"

"He's at the door, asking for you."

"Owen?" I repeat. He was borderline passed out when I left. There's no way he pulled himself together to get here already. And I have his truck. "Are you sure?"

"I think so."

Shaking my head, I close my laptop and get up. Carly opens the door, ready for the dogs this time. We both make it out without further traumatizing my poor cat. Someone is in the foyer downstairs, and from behind, he does look like Owen. But the second he turns, I know it's Logan.

"Hey."

"Logan…hey. What are you doing here?" I go down the last steps.

"I was hoping to talk for a minute."

"Uh, sure. Is everything okay?"

"I'm hoping it will be." He gives me a smile, and I motion to the porch.

"Is Owen—"

"He's sleeping, but he's fine."

"Good." I step onto the porch and close the door behind us. "I see he's the same as ever."

"He's not. Danielle is pregnant," Logan tells me.

"Oh, wow. Congrats. That's exciting!"

"No one else knows yet. She had a miscarriage a few months ago, so we're not sharing the news until she gets an ultrasound this time. Owen knows, though."

"That's why he drank all her drinks."

Logan nods. "Danielle is a fan of booze. The first thing my mom would have asked if she saw her not drinking was if she was pregnant. They know we've been trying since she lost the last baby."

I mess with my hair, tightening and then loosening my ponytail. "That was…was annoyingly noble of him then." I blink, not sure how to process everything. "And I'm so sorry to hear about your loss."

"Thanks. It was really hard on Danielle, which is why she's being so cautious now."

"Oh, I totally understand. Well, not totally since I've never been pregnant, but I can only imagine."

Logan nods. "Don't give up on him yet." He pats my shoulder and looks at the car. "Danielle's not feeling well, so we're going to head home, but I wanted to at least let you know why he seemed like a raging alcoholic tonight." He gives me a smile that almost mirrors Owen's cocky grin. "Maybe a second chance is on the horizon?"

I laugh. "Fat chance. What we had…" I shake my head. "It was a once in a lifetime kind of thing."

His eyes go to the car, looking at Danielle through the window. "Well, you never know."

"Sure," I say, not wanting him to press this anymore. My resolve is crumbling, and I'm desperately reaching and picking up broken pieces from the ground. I loved Owen with everything I had. More than I loved myself. Way more than I loved Todd.

I can't risk being hurt by him again.

"And I won't say anything about the baby," I tell Logan as he takes a step toward the porch steps. "Congrats again. I'll keep you guys in my thoughts."

"Thanks." He smiles. "We have a good feeling about this one."

"You'll make a good dad," I tell him and mean it.

"It's kind of scary to think about, but thanks." He dashes down the porch steps, going around to the driver's side of his car. Danielle gives me a little wave as they pull away from the house, and I'm left there feeling bad for jumping to conclusions. But does this mean Owen really has changed?

I suppose there's only one way to find out.

"Was that Owen?" Carly asks as soon as I open the front door.

"That was Logan."

"They look so much alike."

"Well, they are identical twins," I laugh.

Carly glances into the living room, where her kids are watching a movie. "Did you ever get them mixed up and accidentally sleep with the wrong twin?"

"You've watched too much cheap porn."

"So you're saying yes, that did happen? Or maybe you really knew all along but went with it anyway?"

"Cheap, badly written porn."

"Ohhh, or maybe you did them both at the same time!"

I roll my eyes and laugh. "No, no, and no. I don't think they'd be into incest in that way."

"But is it really?"

"Stop reading the Jamie and Cersei fan fiction, please."

"Hey, I haven't read any of that in like a year," she laughs. "But what did Logan want?"

I shake my head. "Nothing important."

"If you say so." Giving me one last look, Carly goes into the living room to tell her kids it's almost bedtime. They protest and I dash up the stairs before I get caught in the crossfire. I like being the cool aunt but won't go against Carly's parenting. She's an awesome mom, and one day those kids are going to realize it.

Back in my room, I change out of my dress and put on comfy shorts and an oversized t-shirt with Disney villains on it. After washing off my makeup, brushing out my hair, and brushing my teeth, I get back into bed to finish the movie. This time, I make it another ten minutes before I close my laptop again.

I don't know if Owen needs his truck in the morning. Or if he's feeling sick right now.

"Stop it," I tell myself, knowing I'm trying to come up with excuses to go see him. Putting my head in my hands, I rub my eyes and think about him. Of his deep brown eyes. His perfectly messy hair. The ripples of muscles over his chest. His abs. That sharp V on his waist...

"I need help," I tell Tulip and flop back on the bed. Wrestling with the desire to go drive back to Owen's, I get up and slip out the door. I trip over one of the dogs in the dark hall.

"Sorry," I say, not sure which one I tripped over. They look exactly alike in the daytime. It's impossible to tell them apart at night. Nevertheless, the dog follows me downstairs and into the kitchen. I grab a bottle of wine from the fridge, pull out the stopper, and put it to my lips.

I chug just enough to prevent me from driving anywhere.

"There," I say, satisfied with my inability to go over to see Owen, though the wine is going to make me want to even more. I put the bottle back only to take it back out again and carry it upstairs.

Tulip tries to dash out of the room when I go back in. Poor cat. I hate that she's been confined to one room...and that her litter box is on the other side of my nightstand. It's only temporary. We'll get through this.

I settle back into bed, drink wine from the bottle, and fire up the movie again. I'm feeling sleepy when one of the dogs paws at the door, startling me. Tulip growls, which makes the dogs start whining. I assume they'll settle down in a few minutes.

They don't.

By the morning, everyone is cranky and annoyed by the dogs barking. Carly brought them into her room, which is when the barking started...and never stopped. How the dogs didn't run out of energy is beyond me.

Dad grumbles throughout breakfast and Mom gives him the side eye the whole time. I'm going into the office with Dad this morning, and refill my coffee twice before I'm dressed and ready to go.

"Hey, Dad?" I ask as we head out of the house. Heat creeps up the back of my neck, making me feel like a teenager. "Can you pick me up from Owen's house? I, uh, need to drop off his truck."

Dad stops short, turning and raising one eyebrow. "Why do you have Owen's truck?"

"I, uh, went to dinner at his parents' last night and drove myself home."

"Yeah, kiddo, I can pick you up." Dad looks at me for a few seconds. "You know, I always liked Owen." He starts forward again, and what he doesn't say screams louder than anything just spoken.

But it doesn't matter, because Owen and I had our chance and it didn't work out. Trying again will only end in heartache.

CHAPTER 17

OWEN

Groaning, I roll over and open my eyes. Did I just imagine that or did the—yep, the doorbell did ring, and now it's ringing again. Tossing back the covers, I get up. My mouth is dry and my head hurts.

Fuck, I'm getting old. I haven't had a hangover in a while, which is almost impressive considering how much I drink. But chugging moonshine like tequila shots...never again. Plowing my hand through my hair, I make my way out of the master bedroom and down the stairs. Someone is standing on the porch, and I'm not in the mood for whatever it is they're selling. Usually, I ignore solicitors until they go away, but this morning I feel like telling them ringing the doorbell around eight AM is fucking rude.

Not caring that I'm only wearing boxers—I plan to just crack the door open anyway—I unlock the front door. Instead of an old guy in a suit asking if I've found Jesus, Charlie stands before me.

"Hey," I say, blinking in the sunlight. She's the last person I expected to see standing on my porch this early in the morning.

"Owen. Hi." Her eyes sweep over my body, reminding me I'm only wearing boxers.

"Miss seeing me half-naked in the mornings?" My lips pull up in a smirk.

She purses her lips and holds out my truck keys. "Those days are long behind us."

"They don't have to be." I open the door all the way and inch toward the door frame. "And about last night," I start.

She holds up her hand. "It's okay. Logan stopped by and told me why you were drinking Danielle's drinks. There was probably a better way to go around it, but it was nice that you were trying to help her out."

My heart does a weird flutter thing inside my chest. "Was that a compliment?"

"Yeah, I guess so. Still doesn't change anything, but at least I know you're not a raging alcoholic or something."

"I'm only a raging alcoholic when I think about how much I fucked things up between us. I miss you, Charlie." The words come out like vomit and the look on Charlie's face isn't much different that if I upchucked all over her expensive-looking shoes.

"Owen." Her eyes go to the ground and she shakes her head. "I can't do this, okay? Not with everything else I have going on."

I swallow hard, feeling like I might actually throw up now. If she says the words, it's over. Or at least that's how it feels. I'm not an *all hope is lost* kind of person. I usually get what I want. I refuse to give up until I do.

Charlie is no exception.

I can't make her love me, but I can try my damnedest.

"Well, whenever you're ready then, Charlie. I'll wait."

She hands me my keys, blinks tears out of her eyes and nods. "Take care of yourself, Owen."

I hate how that sounds like a goodbye.

"Charlie," I blurt. "Wait."

She stops mid-turn and looks back into my eyes. Sunlight reflects off her shiny blonde hair, which is pulled away from her face with a black headband. She's dressed like a lawyer today, and while her pencil skirt and blouse are very office-appropriate, she looks like she could have sauntered off the set of a naughty librarian adult film. I'm only wearing boxers and can't risk my mind going to the gutter. It'll be too obvious that she's turning me on.

"Yeah?"

"Can we try dinner again? Come here and I'll cook for you."

Her face doesn't show any emotion, but her eyes glimmer in the sun. "You cook now?"

I chuckle. "I do live on my own."

"I thought your mom sent you leftovers every day," she teases.

"She would deliver me meals twice a day if I let her."

Charlie laughs. "She's a good mom."

"She is. So dinner tonight?"

"Not tonight. I'm really tired already."

"The day just began."

"I know." She pushes her hair over her shoulder. "My sister's dogs are going to be the death of me. Well, not really, but quite possibly my cat."

"My offer still stands. You're welcome here. As a friend."

She smiles. "I'll keep that in mind. Thank you, Owen. I, uh, I…" She runs her eyes over me again and a slight flush covers her cheeks. "I need to go. I'm working with my dad today."

"Have fun lawyer-ing."

Her smile widens. "I actually will. I'm really looking forward to going back to work and arguing with people."

She's joking, but I can only imagine how it would feel to get your ass handed to you—legally, of course—by someone like Charlie. I bet when she walks into a courtroom, her opposition sees her as easy, as nothing more than a pretty face. And then the Pitbull in her comes out.

She's always been like that, standing up for what she believes in, and she doesn't back down or get shaken. Her sweet disposition makes her unsuspecting, and those who go against her are often not prepared.

Including me.

I had no idea how fast I'd fall for her. How deeply I'd love her. How she'd become my whole moon and stars and reason for living.

Until she was gone.

"I'll see you later," she says, and I like that much better. It's not a goodbye, yet I'm still not sure I believe her. Watching her dash down the driveway and into her Dad's Lexus, I don't step back inside or close the door until she's out of view.

I go into the kitchen, turn on the coffee pot, and find something to eat. I don't have to work today and should go back to sleep. My head still hurts, my stomach is unsettled, but I'm starting to think it has less to do with the booze and more to do with the feeling that I'm never going to have another chance with Charlie.

I need a leg up. Do some sort of grand romantic gesture. She said she wants me to prove to her I've changed, and I'm going to do it. Taking my coffee onto the screened-in porch off the back of my house, I watch the water from the fountain in the pond rise and fall.

Trading my coffee for my phone, I text Quinn to see if she's awake. As soon as she replies, I call her.

"Are you okay?" she answers.

"Yeah, why?"

"You never call this early. You're never *awake* this early."

"Charlie just left."

Quinn gasps. "She stayed the night?"

"No, she brought my truck back to me after driving me home and then taking herself home last night."

"Ouch. That wasn't your finest hour. Are you sure you're okay?"

"Yeah, don't worry about that. But I have a favor to ask."

"I'm not building you a sex robot."

I laugh. "How'd you know that's what I wanted? Can you make it look like Charlie?"

"Gross, Owen."

"Dean said you were able to look at Charlie's social media accounts even though she has them all set to private. Could you possibly look at them again?"

"I can, but why?"

The sunlight reflects off the water, blinding me and making my eyes water. "I want to get her back, Quinn. And I'll do whatever it takes to prove to her I'm not the same guy I was before."

"So, having your little sister internet stalk her is your answer?"

"Technically, yes. I mean no. I invited her over for dinner and was hoping she posted about a restaurant or a meal she liked or something so I could make it for her."

"That's actually pretty sweet. And yes, I'll look through her profiles. She accepted my friend requests so it takes the creep factor way down."

"Thanks."

"I'll text you if I find out anything. I hope this works. You two were so good together."

"We were. And we will be again."

I end the call, finish my coffee, and get up to go to the gym. Working out always makes me feel better. I mostly lift but decide to hit the cardio today to burn off steam, which ends up leaving me feeling like shit after waking up hungover.

I go home, shower, and fall asleep in bed watching TV. I wake up to a text message from Quinn, saying Charlie's posted about some fancy pasta dish from the same restaurant a few times. Quinn went so far as to find a "copycat recipe" of the sauce for me and sent a bunch of wine pairing suggestions.

She's the best little sister I could ask for.

I reply with a thanks and then get up. I try to devote one day a week to getting shit done, and it's usually on the day I don't work. Then the house is somewhat cleaned, groceries are stocked, and my laundry is done and, well, not folded and put away if I'm being honest. But at least the clean pile is separate from the dirty, right?

Going the extra mile today—because the house needs it, not because I'm distracting myself from thinking about Charlie—I strip my bed, put on fresh sheets and then dust and vacuum my room. I do the same to the guest room. There are two more bedrooms upstairs, but one is set up like a game room and the other is rather empty and is just used for storage. It was staged as a little girl's room when this house was the model home for the neighborhood, and the walls are still a pale pink with an accent wall of polka-dot wallpaper.

Impressed with myself and how clean the house looks, I go downstairs, finish my laundry, and then wash dishes. I never understood when people wanted to downsize so they wouldn't have so much housework to do, but now I get it. This house is meant for a family of four or five and has a full, partly finished basement that Logan and I converted into a theatre room the year before he moved out.

I'm mostly in the kitchen, living room, and bedroom. I don't know the last time anyone even sat at the formal dining room table, and I don't do too much work at home in the office. I've considered selling this place before, though since Logan and I bought it together, it would only be right to split the profit with him.

We got a good deal on it since our dad built it and it was a model home for a few years before we moved in. People trampled through here during several Parade Of Homes events, resulting in nicks and scratches on the walls as well as one huge scratch in the hardwood in the foyer. To this day, we have no idea how that happened, and I've successfully kept the mark hidden under an area rug.

The rest of the damage was cosmetic and has been fixed, and this house is too much space for me and me alone. But I like it here and it's home, and I suppose in the back of my mind I held onto the hope that I'd settle down and start a family of my own as well. Though I knew there was only one way that was happening.

There was only one woman in this whole fucking world I want to spend the rest of my life with, and she's—

Texting me right now?

I glance down at the preview of the text that just popped up on my phone. It's from a number with an area code I don't recognize. I unlock my phone at record speed to read the rest of the message.

Unknown: Hey, Owen. It's Charlie. I ran into Quinn on my lunch break and got your number from her. Do you still want to do dinner?

I read the text three times, not sure I'm believing what I'm reading. Inhaling deep, I type out my reply.

Me: Yeah, I'd like that. What time do you get off work?

Three little dots pop up right away. I stare at the phone, heart in my throat, as I wait for her to reply. I'm pathetic, I know, but this woman gets under my skin without even trying.

Charlie: I can be there around six-thirty. Can I bring my cat?

Me: Is that code for a sex-thing?

Charlie: We're having dinner as FRIENDS, remember? And no, it's a "my sister's dogs won't leave the cat alone" thing.

Me: I don't mind if you bring the cat.

Charlie: Thank you so much.

Me: You can thank me later.

Charlie: Don't make me change my mind.

She sends an eye rolling GIF after that, which I top with a crazy cat lady meme. A laughing emoji comes through after that, and then nothing. Assuming she went back to work, I spring back into action, cleaning the rest of the house as fast as

I can. I need to go to the grocery store, and I have no fucking idea what some of these steps in the recipe Quinn sent even mean.

I spend about half an hour watching YouTube cooking videos and then rush out to buy what I need to make dinner. With a full cart, I pass by the wine on my way to the register and grab three bottles of the red wine Charlie likes. At least that hasn't changed. I remember the first time we snuck wine from the pantry at my parents' house.

We were sixteen at the time. Dean, who's two years older than me, was away at his first year of college and Weston was deployed. Logan was at his girlfriend of the time's house and Quinn was at a friend's house for the night. And the best part was my own parents were away for the weekend.

We'd been dating for well over a year at that time but hadn't slept together yet. Charlie was scared of getting pregnant and wanted to wait. As much of a horny teenager as I was, I knew back then she was worth waiting for.

It was supposed to happen that night. In our teenage minds, everything was perfect...until we drank the wine. Charlie had never had a drop of alcohol before and being tipsy freaked her out. She wanted to call her sister and have her take her home, confessing everything to her parents.

Somehow I was able to convince her to just lie down with me, and instead of getting laid for the first time, she fell asleep in my arms, snoring loudly. I can still feel the pins and needles in my arm when I think about how it fell asleep only fifteen minutes after she passed out, but I didn't want to move and disturb her. Maybe it's a weird memory to cherish, but to this day it's stuck out in my mind.

The next morning, when she woke up and felt silly for getting so scared about being drunk, she thanked me over and over for being so comforting to her. Her friends were impressed I didn't try to take advantage of her, which was a little sickening to hear.

That shouldn't even be a concern. Guys should never take advantage of a woman like that.

Charlie was my world, my everything, and I wouldn't have done a single thing to hurt her. Well…until I broke up with her.

If—no *when*—I get her back, I'm never, ever letting go.

CHAPTER 18

CHARLIE

I t's just dinner.

Everyone has to eat. It's a basic human function, and talking with Owen is harmless. Because that's all we're going to do. *Talk*. So what if seeing him standing at the door this morning in nothing but boxers got me all hot and bothered. It doesn't matter. And if I divert my thoughts, I almost forget how good his cock felt inside of me.

How the sex was good almost every single time. How Owen took his time with me. Was more concerned with pleasing me than enjoying it himself.

Our first time was painful, and I didn't realize how well-endowed Owen was back then since I'd never seen another penis before. We had sex for the first time together after our senior prom—cliché, I know.

It hurt, probably only lasted five minutes, and had me freaked out for a week that I was pregnant. I didn't want to get pregnant in high school, but once I was in college, everything was fair game, and once we started, we couldn't stop.

"All right," I tell Tulip, dropping down to the floor. The bedroom door was open when I got home, and after a moment of panic that I was going to find Tulip's dead body chewed up and bloody on the floor, I found her shivering in fear under the bed. "You get a little break from the dogs. I know you don't like new places, but at least nothing will chase after you."

Not wanting to drag her out and hurt her broken leg, I end up moving the bed to get to her, and carefully put her in the designer pet carrier I bought back when I was working in New York. I enjoy fine things, and don't see anything wrong with indulging yourself every now and then if you can afford to do so.

There were several other female lawyers at my firm, one closer to my age and the others all older than me. They were all about designer suits and having the latest trends. I thought I was fashionable until I moved to the city, and was quickly reminded that "designer" meant different things to the girl from some small town in Indiana and someone living in New York.

I made good money at my job there, more than enough to indulge, and it still sickened me a bit the first time I bought a two-thousand-dollar purse. But then I got compliments on it from the girls at work.

The next month I bought a three-thousand-dollar one.

I shake my head, not having time to bring up every stupid thing I did in the past and feel regret and shame. No, I'll save those thoughts for when I'm lying in bed at night trying to sleep. Memories from high school and college will come rushing back too, I'm sure, and I'll regret that stupid answer I gave in my psychology class all over again.

"It's not a long drive, at least." I gently pick up the carrying bag and go down the stairs. I packed myself an overnight bag with the intention of driving past the bed and breakfast on the way home from dinner.

There was one room open as of this morning, and it's not like Eastwood is a happening place. I can't see it filling up, and just one night away from barking dogs will do Tulip and myself some good. Plus, everyone at the house will be thankful for a night of peace.

Setting the carrier on the passenger seat of Dad's old Mustang, I pull the seatbelt over and loop it through one of the straps, just in case. Then I fire up the engine and drive to Owen's house.

It's just dinner.

Everyone eats.

Owen eats. I eat. Owen was really good at eating—stop it.

It's just dinner.

Pushing my shoulders back, I make a promise to myself right then and there that no matter what Owen throws at me, I'm not going to bend. There's no point, even though having him bend me over sounds like a good time.

Wes and Scarlet are pushing a stroller down the sidewalk, following behind Jackson on his bike. They wave as I drive by. I wave back and feel a tug on my heart. It's one thing to resist Owen, but damn him for having such a nice and welcoming family.

I turn on the radio, only able to get the local country station to come on. Singing along with Luke Combs, I roll down the window and welcome the warm breeze through my hair. The drive to Owen's ends too soon, and I have to repeat my *it's just dinner* mantra over and over in my head.

I didn't plan on coming. I know better than to put something tempting in front of me. But then I ran into Quinn, who did such a good job of talking Owen up I'm starting to seriously suspect her of witchcraft. The next thing I know, she's giving me his number and I'm agreeing that dinner and catching up would be nice since I didn't really get to do it Sunday.

It made sense at the time. It doesn't make sense now. I put the car in park and kill the engine. If she's not a witch, then she's a Jedi who can pull mind tricks. Yes, that has to be it. Because something starts to build inside of me as I look at the perfectly manicured lawn. I blink and now I know a curse has been put on me because I see a flash of Owen standing on the covered front porch, a baby in his arms again.

Shaking my head, I make a mental note to burn sage or throw salt or whatever it is I need to do. Because I can't let Owen hold me spellbound.

The wind picks up right as I walk up the steps to the front porch. The smell of rain blows in over the horizon. It's fresh and reminds me of home. I pause before going up the last step to turn my head and feel the breeze in the air. There's something else in it, a slight electrical charge that promises a storm.

It sounds weird, I know, to say I can sense storms like that. But it's been scientifically proven that some people are more sensitive to the change in pressure and the electrical charges in the sky. I've always been one of those people, and bad storms give me terrible anxiety.

Growing up in the Midwest should have made me accustomed to bad storms. It should have taught me that tornadoes are inevitable, and as long as you're smart and know how to hide, you'll be okay.

But instead it left me with an almost panic-attack like reaction that makes me want to throw up, cry, and run around screaming at the same time. Yes, I'm thirty years old and scared of storms. Call me pathetic if you will.

Though technically, thunderstorms are okay. I enjoy them, really…as long as there's no threat to my roof being torn off and my house turning into that one infamous barn scene from *Twister*.

I go up the last step and ring the doorbell, readjusting Tulip's carrying case on my arm. She's a small cat but is surprisingly heavy when she's being carried like this. Only a few seconds pass before Owen opens the door.

He's wearing a gray t-shirt and dark jeans. His hair is messily styled and the perfect five-o'clock shadow covers his strong jaw line. Light from the setting sun reflects off his chocolate eyes, and his whole face brightens as he smiles at me.

"Hey, Charlie. And Tulip."

"Hey," I say back, hating that I find it kind of cute that he remembered my cat's name. "I have her stuff in the car."

"Her stuff?" he laughs, stepping aside to let me in.

"Yeah, a litter box and food and water bowls."

"Glad you came prepared." He takes Tulip from me, and I dash back to the car to grab Tulip's bag. I'm tempted to bring my overnight bag in with me, giving myself permission to stay the night here.

And by stay the night I mean have sex with Owen.

I shake that thought right out of my head, telling myself I don't remember what his thick cock looks like. I have no recollection of that vein that runs down his shaft or the way his balls feel in my hands.

Owen shuts the door behind me once I'm in the house, and the smell of whatever he made for dinner wafts through the house.

"Dinner smells amazing," I tell him, taking off my shoes. It's a habit of mine to take off my shoes as soon as I'm inside a house. Owen isn't wearing any, and I hate how something as meaningless as shoes can cause me so much stress. Take them off or leave them on?

Once I went to a party in college and was the only one who took off their shoes. I didn't realize until halfway through—dammit. I'm doing it again. I'll save that random embarrassing story for another day, waking me from a dead sleep or something

"Hopefully it tastes as good as it smells." Owen sets the carrier down and bends over, unzipping the top so Tulip can get out.

"She can't jump," I tell him. "Her front leg is broken."

"Awww, poor girl." He gently takes her out and to my surprise, she doesn't hiss at him. I think she's so shocked and upset to be somewhere new again she's not even reacting. Or maybe she just likes him.

"Thanks again for letting me bring her. Those dogs want nothing more than to play with her until she's dead. She's getting up there in age, and I worry about what the stress will do. And I know, I sound like a crazy cat lady. But with my work hours and living in an apartment, a dog wasn't really an option. Plus she's a nice cat."

Owen chuckles and sets Tulip on the area rug in the foyer. "It's okay. I like both cats and dogs. Cats are easier."

I nod in agreement and then set up Tulip's stuff in the bathroom downstairs. I wash my hands and meet Owen in the kitchen. The table in the breakfast nook has been set, and I'm almost afraid to look and see how much—or little—effort he put into this.

I don't want candles and wine.

But I hope for more than a frozen pizza and cans of pop.

What I get is a perfect mixture of both. There is a bottle of red wine on the table, but there aren't any candles or even flowers.

"Is that chicken tetrazzini?" I ask, looking at the dish on the table.

"It is," he tells me and pulls out a chair for me to sit. "Do you like it?"

"I love it!" I take a seat, mouth watering as I look at the pasta in front of me. Owen takes a seat across from me and pours us both wine. The last thing I need is anything clouding my judgement, but dammit, this red goes so well with the pasta.

"I've never made it before," Owen confesses. "So if it's not good, let me have a redo another day."

My fingers wrap around the stem of my wine glass. "Is that your way of saying you purposely sabotaged dinner to get me to come over again?"

"It wasn't, but now I'm wishing I'd thought of that." His eyes flash and that grin takes over his face, fanning the old flames that

I'm trying so hard to stomp out. I take a drink of wine, fully knowing how flammable alcohol is.

"That dress looks good on you," Owen tells me as he starts to dish out dinner. "You always liked fruit patterns."

My eyes go do to my dress. It's an off-the-shoulder white dress, with a pattern of printed lemons on it. My heart jolts in my chest, and a weird sensation takes me over. It's been so long.

We've put years between us.

And even more miles.

Yet every little thing comes rushing back right to the surface. The love we had for each other. The way we knew each other better than we knew ourselves.

The pain.

The absolute heartache.

Crying until my eyes were so red and swollen I had no tears left.

"I do, and I don't really know why. Though, right now lemons are kinda trendy. Pineapples still are too, which I like. They're cheerful," I supply with a shrug. Owen puts a big serving of chicken and pasta on my plate, and I take a piece of garlic bread from the bowl in the center of the table.

Swallowing down another mouthful of wine, I set the glass back on the table and tell myself it should stay there the rest of the meal.

"This is amazing," I tell Owen after I've taken a few bites of my pasta. "It tastes just like something I'd order back in the city."

"Do you miss it?" he asks.

"The pasta? Or the city?"

"Both."

"If I can have this at least once a week," I start, using my fork to point to the food on my plate. "Then no, I wouldn't miss the pasta. And the city…not at all. It wasn't for me. I'm not a city person."

"No, you're not. Though I suppose you get more cases and more interesting ones at that in the city as opposed to here."

"Oh, for sure. It's a lot faster paced and so much more competitive there too. I kind of miss that, but the city can be hard to live in. Not everyone is terrible like some movies make it out to seem, but I did work with a few of the most entitled, stuck-up people I've ever met."

Todd included.

"You're home now. You can breathe easy."

I take another bite of pasta and nod. "So, other than the bar, what else have you been up to these last few years?"

"That's pretty much it. We put a lot into Getaway to get it started, and then again recently to turn it into more of a bar and grill instead of just a bar."

I nod, feeling like this conversation is contrived and I'm pretty sure I've already asked him this.

"How is it at home with everyone under one roof?"

I reach for my wine again. "It's a struggle, and I feel bad saying that."

"Why do you feel bad?"

"It reminds me how privileged I am when I'm complaining about how hard it is to live in my parents' three-thousand-square-foot house with clean water, air conditioning, and a fully stocked fridge."

"Good point. But you're allowed to recognize that it's not easy as well. It doesn't make you a bad person."

"Yeah, I know. I still feel bad complaining about it, though."

"You could just stay here and you won't have to feel bad," he suggests.

I cock an eyebrow. "Nice try."

"I really don't see the harm in it. I have no dogs to terrorize your cat. And my bedroom is down the hall so when you change your mind in the middle of the night, I'm only a few yards away."

"I'm not changing my mind. *Been there, done that* fully applies to us, Owen. It was fun while it lasted, but it's over."

"It can start again." He leans forward, dropping his eyes to my cleavage. "Don't tell me you don't miss it."

I swallow hard and somehow that damn glass of wine ends up in my hands again. "Miss what?"

Smirking, he runs his eyes over me and I know I just asked the worst possible question. The next best thing to having sex with Owen is hearing him describe it to me.

"You think I haven't enjoyed sex since we've been together?" I blurt and take another gulp of wine. "I have. Multiple times."

"And I have too. Many, many times. Yet no one compares to you, Charlie."

Dammit, Owen. I glare at my wine, which is almost empty, and set it back down. Owen refills my glass, and my body is reacting to memories of him. Owen was my first and only for so long. It took me a long time to get back into the dating world after we broke up, and my next sexual encounter is something I actively work to repress.

My friends convinced me a one-night stand was all I needed to get Owen off my mind. So we went out, I got drunk, and I went home with someone. The sex was good, but once I sobered up and realized what I did, I was totally that girl who cried after sex.

"Tell me then, was Todd as good as me?" Owen's top teeth sink into his bottom lip for just half a second. It's playful and sexy, and I honestly don't know if he's aware of exactly what he's doing or not.

"He was good enough for me to accept his marriage proposal," I retort, and the words fall flat. Dammit. It sounded much better in my head. I shove a forkful of pasta in my mouth to keep me from saying anything more.

Todd and I had a good sex life at first. Kind of. There was a lot of pounding and him fumbling around my vagina, not quite able to find my clit without me guiding his fingers. And then he'd rub it too hard or too fast, but hey, he got the job done most of the time.

"I suppose I should apologize," Owen goes on, and that cocky grin shouldn't turn me on like this. "I set you up for disappointment."

"You're awfully full of yourself for someone who'd only slept with one person at the time."

He picks up his own glass of wine and takes a drink. "You're saying I didn't satisfy you then?"

I exhale heavily, shaking my head. And there's that magic wine glass appearing in my hands again. "Life is about more than sex, you know."

"Oh, I do. Sex just makes everything better."

Rolling my eyes, I focus on my food. Maybe I should sleep with Owen. Get it out of my system. I'm an adult and can hook up with whoever I want. I look across the table at Owen, feeling the wine start to hit me and make me think having sex is a good idea.

And then a weather alert on both our phones go off, warning us about a severe thunderstorm.

"So," I say and change the subject. "Has Danielle been to the doctor yet?"

"She goes tomorrow."

"That's exciting. I hope everything is good."

"Me too. That's going to be one good-looking kid at least. Hopefully he'll look more like his uncle than his father."

I look up from my food to see him smiling. "You guys share like ninety-nine percent of the same DNA, right?"

"According to science we do."

"So your kids and Logan's kids will technically be cousins, but they'll be as related as siblings?"

"Maybe?" Owen's shoulders rise and fall in a shrug. "Archer

would know, though I suppose it doesn't matter until I have a kid of my own."

"Do you want kids?" I ask carefully, twirling a noodle around my fork.

"Yeah, I do," he replies with no hesitation. "I want to have a family, Charlie. And I'm ready for one. I told you, I've changed."

I let out a shaky breath, feeling my resolve crumble. A loud clap of thunder rattles the windows, and it reverberates deep within my soul.

"Have you changed?" he asks carefully, and I know what he's asking. He wants to know if I still want to get married and have babies. I haven't changed much in that aspect. Starting my career was important to me, but I always imagined I'd do both. It wouldn't be easy, but I've never been one to back away from a challenge.

"I have," I say quietly, right as another boom of thunder sounds above us. My stomach flip flops, both from the storm and the direction our conversation is going. Owen, sensing my discomfort, gets up and brings a cake over to the table.

"You still like red velvet cake, right?"

Swallowing my emotions, I force a smile. "Yeah. I do."

"Good. Because I do too."

He serves me a slice once I've finished my pasta.

"So tell me," I say as I stick my fork into the cake. "Has there been any good drama in Eastwood lately?"

"Tons. Owning a bar gives me prime people-watching vantage points. Remember Lizzy Mitchel?"

"Yeah, she was such a stuck-up bitch in high school."

Owen laughs. "She's having an affair with a much younger man."

"Ohhh, that is good drama. And I didn't even think of that, but you're right. Bars are the place to be to witness drama and hear gossip."

127

"The sad, lonely, and desperate are good for business," he says with a laugh. "Do you talk with anyone from school anymore?"

I shake my head. "I lost touch with most of them during law school. I'm friends with Annabeth on Facebook, and Cheryl and I follow each other on Instagram. It's kinda weird when I think about it. We were so close then. What about you?"

"Logan and I still hang out with Jake and Tom."

"How are they?"

"Pretty much the same as they were in high school. Tom got married two years ago, though."

"It is weird how you grow up and go your separate ways," I say.

"That's one of the good things about having a twin. It's like a built-in friend I can't get rid of."

I laugh and take another bite. He tells me about more drama he's witnessed over the years as we finish dessert. Once we're done eating, I help him clean up the dinner dishes. We get along well, and being together feels natural. I don't realize we've slowly been washing the dishes for nearly an hour until I look at the clock, surprised to see how late it's gotten.

"I should get going," I tell him, drying my hands on a dish towel. "I have to work in the morning."

As if it's right on cue, a huge clap of thunder rings out, making me jump. Lighting flashes and heavy rain falls down. The power flickers twice before the whole house goes black. Silence fills the dark, and I let out a shaky breath.

"Maybe you should stay." Owen turns on the flashlight on his phone and sets it upside down on the counter. "At least until the storm passes."

"Yeah, good idea." I turn around, squinting in the dim light for my own phone. It's still in my purse, and I take it out to check the radar. The worst of the storm is yet to come, and it makes my stomach tighten just looking at the yellow and green on the map.

Wind howls outside and the siding on the house groans in protest.

"If it's not safe for you drive, you can stay here," Owen offers. "As a friend, of course."

I look up, swallow hard, and open my mouth to tell him no. But something strange happens again, and this time, nothing comes out. I snap my jaw shut and stare into his brown eyes, unblinking.

"Charlie?"

CHAPTER 19.

OWEN

"Charlie?" I repeat, watching her eyes glaze over. She's deep in thought, but I have no idea what she's thinking about. Is she still scared of storms? She used to be terrified of them.

"Sorry." Shaking her head, she looks down at her phone. I follow her gaze, watching the radar move across the screen. It looks bad. She definitely shouldn't be driving. "I'm just...I'm really tired."

"I have a guest room and an extra toothbrush if you need it. I can loan you some clothes too." I tip my head a bit as I look her up and down. "You always looked good in my white t-shirts. With no pants, of course."

She doesn't smile, doesn't roll her eyes. The lack of response troubles me, making it hard to read her. "I actually have clothes in my car."

"Preparing to stay the night with me, I see. I knew you couldn't have resisted for long."

She looks up with a glare. Now there's that sass I was missing. "I was going to grab a room at the bed and breakfast in town."

"With your cat?"

"She's quiet. I could have snuck her in."

130

I laugh. "I like this naughty side, Charlie."

"Shut up," she quips.

"I'll grab your bag for you," I offer.

"It's pouring rain, you'll get soaked."

I shrug. "I'll take my clothes off first and then will towel off."

Her mouth falls open again, but she quickly recovers. "Let's hope you don't get struck by lightning then. Because I'm not dragging your naked body back inside."

"You'd leave me out there and cause a spectacle for the neighborhood kids?"

"Oh, I would. It would be a lesson in what type of stupid shit they shouldn't do."

Chuckling, I pull my shirt over my head only to push her buttons. "Is your car locked?"

"Of course."

Grabbing her keys, I run out through the garage to get her overnight bag from the car. I am soaked by the time I get back inside.

"Thank you," she tells me, taking the bag.

"I'm going to change."

"What happened to getting naked?"

I cock an eyebrow. "Is that an invitation?"

"You wish. Do you have any candles or anything?"

"Yeah," I tell her, wiping my arms dry with the dishtowel from the counter. "In the cabinet next to the sink. There's a lighter in there with them."

I rush up the stairs to change and come down to find a few candles placed around the downstairs.

"I can do you one better." I kneel down in front of the fireplace, opening it up and rearranging the logs inside. I haven't used it in months, and it's going to get hot in here fast, but at least we'll have some light. It takes a few tries, but I get a small fire going.

"Now what?" she asks, sitting on the couch with a bottle

of wine.

"You're asking me how to entertain ourselves in the dark during a storm?"

"Owen," she scolds. "No."

"Your loss."

She mumbles something that I can't quite make out. An agreement, maybe? Moving away from the fireplace, I look at the light dancing over Charlie's face. It's not right for one person to possess so much beauty, both inside and out.

"I have an idea."

"That involves keeping our clothes on," she presses.

"Prude," I tease and go to the closet next to the downstairs bathroom. Pulling out a stack of board games, I take them into the living room.

"It won't be as much fun with just the two of us, but it's something to do. Unless you think this is lame."

Her smile lights up the room brighter than the fire. "No, not lame at all."

～

"I HATE MONOPOLY," I GRUMBLE, WATCHING CHARLIE MAKE IT RAIN with all the fake money she collected after she won the game.

"Don't be a sore loser."

"I spent the last two hours losing. I'm sore."

She waves pink bills in my face and leans back on the couch, laughing. "It's late." Yawning, she pushes herself forward and starts putting the game pieces away. "Taking a mini leave from work was boring, but I very much enjoyed sleeping in."

"I do too."

"Right. You were never a morning person."

We pick up the game and she stands, eyes going to the window. The storm quieted down and I wonder if she's thinking about leaving. It is late, though, and the power is still out. Eastwood has a lot of the older power lines that get knocked out during windstorms. It wouldn't surprise me if the way into town was temporarily blocked off anyway.

"I should get up to bed."

"Me too. I work tomorrow as well, but I don't have to be in until the evening at least."

Her eyes meet mine and our gazes linger. Everything inside of me wants to go to her, to pull her close and feel her heart beating up against my chest. But instead, I step aside and let her pass. She picks up her cat and her overnight bag, and heads toward the stairs.

Using my phone for light, I follow her upstairs and show her the guest room. Then I go back down, put out the fire, and look around the living room.

Charlie is here.

In my house.

In my bed.

Well, one of my beds. I've never wanted anything more, but she's not just a physical temptation. I drag my ass into my own room, brush my teeth, and sink into bed. My hand falls to my waist, fingers brushing over my cock. I'm not going to hide in my room and jerk it like a teenager, but fuck, I'm getting turned on just thinking about Charlie in that white dress. The sleeves rested off her shoulders, and more than once while she was laughing and leaning forward to move her game piece along the board, one sleeve slipped down a little more.

The regret for letting her go eats me alive, churning my stomach and filling it with bile. Having her so close yet so far hurts more than I expected, and I need to figure out my next move to make her fall in love with me.

Though, really, I know there's no one move that'll sweep her off her feet. I hurt Charlie. Broke up with her when she thought I was going to offer her more. I told her I didn't want to be with her when really I didn't want to let her down. Back then, I saw it as merciful to let her go, thinking she'd move on to bigger and better things.

The only way to get her back is to prove to her that I really have changed. That this time, I *will* be not only the man she wants, but the one she deserves. Rolling over, I tuck my pillow under my arm and close my eyes. It takes a while, but I eventually drift to sleep...until another weather alert goes off on my phone.

This time, I shoot up, squinting at the glowing screen as my eyes adjust. It's a tornado warning. One touched down in Newport and the storm is far from over. I pull up the weather radar and let out a breath of relief. The storm can circle back around at any moment, I know, but for now, it looks like the worst is going to miss us.

Still, I get out of bed and walk down the hall to the guest room. I crack the door open, not wanting to knock and wake up Charlie in case she's still sleeping.

"Hey," I say quietly, seeing her sitting up and looking at her phone. "You got the alert too?"

She nods and looks up. Even in the dark, I can see the fear in her eyes.

"Are you still scared of tornadoes?" I ask, stepping into the room. I shut the door so the cat doesn't get out.

"Terrified."

"I think it's going to miss us."

She nods again, pulling her lips around her teeth. "Hopefully."

"Want me to sit with you? We can go into the basement if that'll make you feel better too."

"If the sirens go off, I'll go down. And yeah...I'd, uh, I'd like if you sat with me."

Crossing the room, I sit on the opposite side of the bed. Charlie puts her phone down and leans back against the pillows.

"Do you think it's pathetic I'm still scared of tornadoes?"

"No," I tell her honestly. "They are scary. You can't do anything to prevent them or stop them. All you can do is hide."

"Exactly. And the energy gets me all jittery." She holds up her hand. "I'm shaking."

I take her hand in mine, lacing my fingers through hers. "It's okay. Try to go back to sleep, if you want. I'll listen for the sirens."

"Aren't you tired?"

"Not really. I closed down the bar a few times last week. My sleep schedule is always fucked up."

"That would mess with you, I guess."

She swallows hard, looking over me and out the window. It's pitch black out there, and the rain comes down in sheets. Thunder and lightning tear through the sky, and the windows rattle. Charlie squeezes my hand a little tighter.

"Bad storms tended to break up before they got into the city," she says. "We had storms, of course, but no tornadoes."

"We won't have one tonight either." I give her hand a squeeze and settle down next to me. She's still shaking, and it's killing me not to comfort her more. Pulling the blankets back up to her shoulders, she wiggles a little closer. I don't know if it's on purpose or if she's trying to get comfortable.

Heart hammering, I pull my hand from hers and rest it on her waist. The blankets are between my hand and her body, yet it sends a jolt through me. She moves closer again, and this time I know it was intentional. She rests her hand on top of mine and slits her eyes open, looking up at me.

"Thank you, Owen."

"Of course," I whisper back. Her blonde hair is a mess around her face, and I turn off the light on my phone. The storm rages around us, but Charlie is safe in my arms. Her breathing becomes slow and steady, letting me know she fell asleep.

It's innocent and platonic, and I'm hit with the memory of holding Charlie while she slept off her first drunk experience. I'm working hard to tell myself that this doesn't mean anything, yet I know this will be a new favorite memory of mine...even if it doesn't lead to anything.

CHAPTER 20

CHARLIE

Owen's arm is still around me when I wake up. The first light of dawn is shining through the window. I can tell it's going to be a sunny day already, vastly different from last night. The power is back on, and the air conditioner is pumping the room full of cool air. The ceiling fan is on above me now too, chilling my skin. I was hot last night and only covered up with a thin quilt. Owen stayed outside the blankets and didn't cover up at all.

Inhaling deep, I feel Owen's fingers press against my body. My eyes flutter shut again, and I want nothing more than to roll over and slip my arms around him. How easy it would be to fall back into his arms and ask him to never let me go.

But I can't, because I know better. Besides, I'm not at a good point in my life to start something new...even when what we had isn't new at all. Owen's embrace used to be my favorite place to be. It didn't matter where we were or what was going on around us. As long as we had each other, everything felt okay.

Carefully twisting so I can see him, I move my hand and my fingers brush over his shoulder. His skin is cold from being under the fan and not having any blankets. He's just wearing boxers, and his messy hair and innocent face as he sleeps is making me all sorts of conflicted.

I want this.

But I shouldn't.

It feels good when it should feel wrong.

Being here with Owen makes me feel like the years apart were just a blur and we can go back to the day we broke up and pretend it never happened.

But we can't.

So much life happened between breaking up and where we are right now. I've grown and changed and messed up and made more mistakes than I can count. I'm sure Owen's tale is no different.

Moving carefully so I don't wake him, I reach down and pull up the thick comforter I'd discarded at the foot of the bed and pull it up, covering us both up. In his sleep, Owen slips his arm farther around me, spooning his body against mine. My heart leaps into my throat, and for some reason, tears fill my eyes.

Why the hell am I getting emotional?

Is it because Owen was sweet and kind and thoughtful and it's making me realize how much I miss this? How I'm fairly certain I'll never find someone else who gets me like he does? Or how he didn't mind at all that I came over here like a crazy cat lady and set up a litter box in his pretty spotless house?

Nope. Definitely not any of those.

I nestle my head back into the pillow and rest my hand on top of Owen's. I don't have to get up for another few hours, and I'm going to enjoy every minute of this. Because I'm *not* getting into bed with Owen again.

"You awake?" Owen whispers.

I almost say yes but don't want to ruin the moment. So instead, I respond to his voice by pretending to be asleep and snuggling a little closer. Owen exhales and slides his other arm

EMILY GOODWIN

under me, pulling me close to his chest. He rests his head against my face, lips brushing over the flesh on my cheek.

In the back of my mind, logic and reason are screaming at me. I'm in bed, all snuggled up with Owen. What. The. Hell. Am. I. Doing?

We didn't have sex. We didn't even kiss. He came in here to comfort me, not try to get in my pants. I'm all caught up in my emotions right now because I'm still in bed, tired and comfy, not wanting to move. But once I'm up, dressed, and dealing with some of the county's pressing legal issues, I'll come to my senses.

But until then…I turn and bring one leg up, hooking it over Owen's.

Motherfucker. This is bad. Really bad. But holy shit does it feel good.

⁓

MY ALARM WAKES US BOTH, AND I SIT UP, UNTANGLING MYSELF from Owen's arms to silence it. Groaning, Owen rolls back over and kicks the blankets off his body.

"Do you have to get up already?"

"Yeah, I do." I run my hands through my messy hair. The sun is up now and the room is full of bright light. I swallow hard, and fight my urge to admire every ridge of muscle and every pound of flesh that makes up Owen's body. I set my phone down on the nightstand. "Thank you, Owen, for last night."

"I didn't even do anything." He rolls over, propping his head up with his elbow. "But if you have a few minutes, I can do something you'll thank me for."

I know he can.

"I'll pass."

"Your loss."

Dammit, he's right.

"Really, though," I start and get out of bed. I'm wearing a tank top and sleeper shorts. It's comfy, a little revealing I suppose, and might be sexy if it wasn't covered in smiling avocados with little stick arms and legs. These might have been marketed for teen girls, but I thought they were way too cute to pass up. "Thanks. For letting me bring Tulip and then for, uh, holding me like a child during the storm."

Owen smiles. "You're welcome. And you can leave the cat here. She's quiet and can't really get into anything with that cast on. It won't bother me at all, and she won't be tormented by the dogs over here."

"You really don't mind?"

He shakes his head. "Does she need medication or anything?"

"Yeah, but I'll give it to her before I leave and then again when I get off work. You sure you don't mind?"

Owen's smile widens. "Not at all. And it gives you a reason to come back over, so I see it as a win for me. Now only if it'll storm again," he laughs.

Laughing too, I shake my head. "Dinner was nice. Playing a game was nice."

"Nice enough to do again?"

I should say no. I know I'm weak right now and fighting temptation. An alcoholic shouldn't go to a bar. A gambler should stay out of a casino.

And I should stay far, far away from Owen Dawson.

"We'll see," I tell him and let out a breath as I turn, grabbing my bag and going into the bathroom to shower and get dressed. Forgoing washing my hair, I twist it into a bun on the top of my head and get in the shower.

I wash up quickly and then get out, wrapping myself in the towel. Pausing by the door, I listen to see if Owen is still in the bedroom. I don't hear anything, but that doesn't mean he's not in bed sleeping again. I get dressed, pull my hair into a sleek bun, and put on just enough makeup to look put together.

Owen isn't in the bed when I step out of the bathroom. The

139

bed has been made, which surprises me for some reason. I set my bag on the foot of the bed and look around for Tulip. The bedroom door is open, and while she can hobble around just fine, I do worry about her on the stairs.

Going into the hall, the smell of coffee and bacon hits me, making my stomach grumble. I find Owen in the kitchen, still only wearing boxers and making breakfast. Tulip is sitting on a folded blanket on the floor by him, eating little crumbled pieces of bacon.

"You still like creamer with a splash of coffee, right?" Owen asks, opening a cabinet to get a coffee mug.

"I need two splashes now. I'm old and need the caffeine."

Smiling, I take the mug from Owen and go to the coffee pot. "What about you? You used to not even like the taste of coffee before."

"I still don't. I guess I'm old too. I need caffeine just as much as you do."

I fill my mug halfway and then go to the fridge to get the creamer. Owen has caramel-flavored creamer, which will do just fine. I go to the table and sit, sipping my coffee.

"Hungry?" he asks, turning around with a plate filled with toast, eggs, and bacon.

"I usually don't eat breakfast, but I'm not turning that down."

"How do you not eat breakfast?" He sets the plate down and goes back to the stove, dishing up his own breakfast. "It's the most important meal of the day. I'm starving when I wake up."

"Mornings used to be busy for me. I'd get up, run, and then barely have time to shower and get ready for work. I used to put more effort into my appearance," I admit. "Appearances meant a lot to the people at my old firm."

"You always look good."

"To you."

"To anyone with eyes." He sits across from me at the breakfast table. "Why would you want to work somewhere like that? Doesn't sound like the Charlie I knew."

My stomach starts to feel a little unsettled, because it's true. "It was a good job," I start.

"You mean good-paying job."

"Well, yeah. I made a lot of money at that firm, even as a new lawyer. But honestly…" I let out a breath and look out through the sliding glass doors that lead to a screened-in back porch. "Honestly I'd take a pay cut and less stress any day."

"What was stressful? The job or the people you worked with?"

"The people. I loved my job and the thrill of a good case."

"Did you represent mobsters or something?"

I laugh. "You've watched too many cheesy TV shows. I did real estate law, which can be just as cutthroat as anything you see on TV, actually."

"You won't be bored here?"

"That's to be determined, I guess. Though there's more going on here than you'd expect. There's no shortage of divorces happening, as you can guess since you've seen the infidelity firsthand."

He laughs. "Very true. For a small town we have no shortage on the drama either. You'd be surprised at what a few shots of tequila can bring out in some people."

"I'm not that surprised, actually."

"So you're staying here in Eastwood."

"Yeah," I say, and relief floods through me as soon as I say the words. I hadn't decided for sure what I was going to do. "Though I'm not entirely sure how working with my dad for a few years will be."

Owen chuckles. "I love my family but couldn't work with them. Though Dean and our dad get along fine, so it's possible."

"I'll have my own office too so it's not like we'll be stuck in the same room."

"That should help."

"Oh, it will."

"I bet you look hot sitting behind that big executive desk. At least that's how I imagine you." He gives me a smirk and then lets his eyes fall shut. I always thought it was unfair how long and thick his eyelashes were. "I see you now sitting there, with your hair twisted up in a bun. The top buttons on your blouse undone…and that tight skirt. You're going to see a huge influx of guys needed legal counseling, you know."

"Owen, stop."

"Buzzkill." He opens his eyes and looks at me. "And come on, it's not like you don't know how good you look."

"That's not what I'm talking about."

"So you admit you know you're hot."

Shaking my head, I pick up a piece of bacon. "Impossible," I mutter under my breath.

"What's impossible?"

"You."

He holds my gaze for a beat, smirking. "You always liked a challenge."

Dammit, Owen. I do like a challenge. But right now the challenge is resisting you.

CHAPTER 21

OWEN

I lie back in my bed, trying to get comfortable. Something is missing, so I grab another pillow and stick it in the stack behind my head. Holding onto the thickest one, I roll over onto my side and try to get comfortable.

But no amount of pillows or blankets is going to help.

Because I know exactly what's missing. *Charlie.* I haven't slept so well, haven't felt so peaceful and comfortable, as I did last night with her in my arms. It would have felt better if she were naked, but I'll take what I can get for now.

It won't be long until she's back in my arms sans clothing. I'm sure of it.

Maybe.

At least I hope so.

Why is my confidence wavering? The better question should be why is she resisting me like it's easy to do?

Tulip meows from the hallway, and I look up to see her limping into the bedroom. I get out of bed and scoop up the black-and-white cat, gently putting her on my bed. She starts purring and rubs her head against me.

"Are you going to help Charlie fall back in love with me?" I

143

ask her, running my hand over her fur. Letting out a deep sigh, I roll back over and try to fall asleep. It's going to be a late night at the bar and—shit. Charlie needs to get back into the house and I didn't leave her a key or tell her the code to the alarm system. I'll be at the bar when she gets off work.

I flop over again and kick the blankets down. Tulip growls and goes to jump off the bed. I catch her at the last second and help her down. I don't want the cat to hurt herself, and I know how devastated Charlie would be if anything else happened to her cat.

After tossing and turning and pushing away the deep feelings of regret and fear that Charlie means what she says and doesn't want to give things another go, I get up and get dressed for the gym.

Dean and Archer are finishing up their last set of weights when I walk in. This is the only gym in Eastwood and is usually busy. Every once in a while, I'll show up at the same time as one of my brothers, and even rarer are the times when we all get here together. Logan and I used to go together almost daily, finding it almost fun to have an accountability partner.

"Hey," Dean says, exhaling heavily as he lifts the weights up. "I heard Charlie spent the night with you last night."

"Way to cut to the chase." I move over by the leg press. "And how the fuck did you hear that? She only left about half an hour ago."

"I had to drop something off at one of the construction sites and saw her car. So she did spend the night?"

"Yeah. She did," I say and Dean and Archer exchange glances. "But it wasn't what you're thinking. Unfortunately."

"But she stayed the night with you."

"I invited her over for dinner and she stayed so she wouldn't have to drive in the storm. In the guest room. Alone."

"You didn't try to make a move?" Archer looks at me skeptically. "Or did she flat our reject you?"

"No one rejects me," I spit out and then shake my head. "No, I didn't make a move."

"You must really like her then."

"We have history," I say, and leave it at that. I start my workout, mind drifting to Charlie the whole time, of course. I stop by the law firm on my way home from the gym to give Charlie a key to get into the house.

The firm is downtown, in one of the historic buildings along the main road that goes through Eastwood. The building is three stories high, and Charlie works on the top floor. I go up the stairs, stopping on the second level when I step into the office.

"Hi, welcome to Williams and— Owen?" the secretary cuts off. She peers up at me over the top of her glasses. "That is you, isn't it?" Her top teeth sink into her bottom lip, and it takes me a second to place her face. Mostly because I didn't see much of it that night.

She came home with me from the bar one night and I fucked her from behind. And then we had sex again that morning. I always lead my escapades with making it clear things are no strings. I never want to lead anyone on, and I never wanted anything more from anyone anyway.

The closest I've come to dating since Charlie and I broke up was Meredith James and the three months we spent naked in bed together. She'd just gotten a divorce and wanted to make her ex-husband jealous, which I was happy to assist with. Then I started feeling sorry for her and unwelcome feelings started to form. She'd been treated like shit and put up with it for five years.

She got back together with her ex after we broke things off.

"Yeah, it's me." I flash the secretary a smile, needing to look down at her badge to recall her name. "How have you been, Amy?"

"Oh, you know. Same old, same old." She tugs at her shirt, moving the collar down to expose more cleavage. "What can I do for you?"

"Is Charlie here?"

"Charlotte Williams?"

"Yeah. I suppose she goes by her full name when she's working. Is she in?"

"She is. She's upstairs in a meeting with a client, I believe. I can buzz you in up there if you'd like. There's a lobby right outside the elevator to wait in."

"That would be great."

"Are you in some sort of legal trouble?" She bats her eyes. "You have that bad boy air about you."

My first reaction is to flirt back with her. It usually gets me what I want while giving whoever is flirting with me what they want in that moment. "Bad? I'm the devil." I smirk, wink, and walk past her desk to the elevator.

Amy lets out a deep sigh and picks up the phone, calling up to the third story to let me in. The old elevator shakes on its way up, and the doors hesitate just long enough to make me think I'm stuck before they finally open.

Charlie is sitting in the lobby, leaning back on a leather couch and looking bored.

"Owen," she exclaims, sitting up so fast she almost slips off the couch. "What are you doing here?"

I step out of the elevator, not wanting to get in that thing again. I wouldn't say I have a fear of elevators…just a fear of getting stuck somewhere. But if Charlie were with me, I might purposely jam the door or something.

"I forgot to give you this." I pull the key out of my pocket. "I'll be at Getaway by the time you're done here."

Her eyes go from mine to the key and back again. "Right. Tulip is at your house." Charlie doesn't move, but instead pulls her arms in closer to her body. "I'll, uh, I'll stop by on my way home and take care of her."

"You can stay," I offer. "I won't be home until two or three, depending on how easy it is to clear out the bar."

"You really don't mind?" She's asked me if I mind a dozen times. She knows I don't. She's trying to convince herself that she *shouldn't* mind.

"I wouldn't have offered if I did."

Taking a tentative step forward, she holds out her hand. "Maybe I will."

I put the key in her hand and close my fingers around hers. Stepping closer, our hips touch and Charlie's eyes flutter shut. Lips parting, she tips her head up, looking right at me when she opens her eyes.

I bring my other hand up and rest it on the small of her back. My heart skips a beat in my chest and I swear Charlie's starts to beat faster too.

"I miss waking up with you in my arms," I whisper, bending my head down so my forehead rests against hers. She brings her free hand up and rests it against my chest, splaying her fingers.

"I'm sorry," she says back so quietly it's hard to hear her.

"Why are you sorry?"

"I'm sorry that it won't happen again. It can't, Owen."

"Why not? We're good together, Charlie. We always have been." I pull her tighter against me, until my cock is up against her pelvis.

She takes in a shaky breath and balls my shirt in her hand. Her eyes fall shut again and her jaw tenses.

"We haven't always been good." She pushes away, and not having her against me is like someone ripped my oxygen mask off and I can no longer breathe. "If we were, we wouldn't have broken up." She turns the key around in her fingers.

"I made a mistake," I blurt, heart in my throat again. It won't take much for it to come tumbling out, bloody and bruised on the floor.

Charlie's eyes get glossy. "I know you did. And now I'm trying really hard not to as well."

CHAPTER 22

CHARLIE

The door to the conference room opens behind me. I whirl around, blinking back my emotions. I've been out here waiting to come in and be briefed on the case. Jack Richards, our client, is old and sexist and "didn't trust a woman" to do his legal work. Being old and sexist is exactly why he's a regular client.

"I need to go," I tell Owen. Closing my fingers around the key, I walk forward trying to block Owen from my dad's point of view.

"Owen Dawson," Dad says, and I know I'm too late. "I haven't see you in years. How have you been?"

Gritting my teeth, I step into the conference room and let go of everything else around me so I can focus on the client and case at hand. In New York, I specialized in real estate law. Here, I'll be more of a Jack-of-all-trades when it comes to counseling clients, and right now I want to tell Jack Richards he's a big bag of dicks and deserves to be sued for firing a flat-chested cashier from his store after telling her she should consider getting breast implants. But I also like to win, and I know that my strong desire to win every case comes from a subconscious need for control.

There is no controlling Owen Dawson, and that freaks me out enough on its own.

I know you can't control another person. Hell, I wouldn't want to have that sort of control. It'd be wrong and weird and would go to my head. But knowing what's going to happen—to an extent—it's always been my safety net.

Going back to Owen's place tonight…I have no idea what that will bring. He says he's changed and after last night I'm starting to see it.

"Are we going to get started or what, sweetheart?" Jack grumbles.

Narrowing my eyes, I look down at him. "I am not your sweetheart. I will be your lawyer once Timothy retires, and you will treat me with respect. Yes, I'm a woman, and yes, I am younger than you, but I graduated with honors and spent the last few years representing some of New York's biggest real estate moguls in court. And my record? It's impressive. Very impressive. I'll show you the numbers if you so desire to see them, but trust me when I say I'm good. I like to win." I put my hands on the table and lean forward.

"We both know you are guilty as hell. What you did to those women makes you a grade-A scumbag. But like I said, I like to win and I hardly ever lose." I hold Jack's gaze for another second.

"Then what's the problem?" he asks, getting a little flustered.

"The problem is that there's two sides to every lawsuit. Two teams, if you will. I haven't signed onto anything yet." I push off the table and straighten up, crossing my arms. "I am just a silly woman. Maybe I'm better suited to go and represent the other party?"

Jack's face pales and he leans back in the chair, swallowing hard. The door opens again and my dad walks in. He warned me that Jack was a crotchety old coot.

"How are things going in here?" Dad asks.

I tear my eyes away from Jack and look at Dad, smiling. "Perfect. We're ready to start."

～

THE KEY SITS ON MY DESK, SHINING IN THE SUNLIGHT LIKE SOME sort of demonic beacon. If I pick it up, the Devil himself will be summoned. Biting my lip, I reach for it, snatching my hand back at the last second.

I don't want to summon him.

Don't want to get the offerings ready.

But if anyone can make you bend your will, it's the Devil himself.

"Charlie?"

Blinking rapidly, I grab a pen from my desk and put it to my notebook, pretending to be writing notes. All that comes out is the letter "O" followed by a "w".

Dammit.

"Hey, Dad! What's going on?"

"I wanted to see how you're doing after talking to Jack Richards."

"Really?" My brows go up. "Dad, I told you, I'm used to worse people than that."

"Fine," Dad sighs, relenting much easier than I thought. "I wanted to know why Owen Dawson was here this afternoon."

"Tulip is staying at his house," I blurt the first thing that comes to mind. "So the dogs don't get after her."

Dad's head moves up and down slowly, and I fear for his judgement. I'm an adult yet I still crave his approval.

"Okay," he says and doesn't press. "So should I tell Mom to set your place at dinner tonight?"

"Yes," I insist. "I'll be home for dinner."

"Just dinner?" Dad smirks. "Spoken like a true lawyer. Just be careful, honey."

"I am being careful," I promise, and Dad just smiles once more before closing the office door. My eyes fall shut and I let out a deep breath. I feel like I almost got caught.

But why?

My phone buzzes before I can dive in to my own head too deep. Pushing my hair back, I grab my phone from my desk and see a text.

Marcus: Hey, hun. Haven't heard from you in a while. Everything okay?

Me: I think so. Maybe?

Marcus: You don't sound so sure. What's going on?

Me: Owen. That's what's going on. And also, what's not going on.

Marcus: Did you sleep with him?

Me: Not yet.

I hit send without thinking and immediately wince.

Me: I mean no. I won't. I can't.

Marcus: Sounds like you want to. I stalked him on Insta. Just do him.

He sends a slew of fire, eggplant, and heart-eye emojis after that and I set my phone back down. I push the chair away from my desk and spin it around, blowing out a slow breath. I'm bored here and I wish I could distract myself with work and not get stuck on memory lane, remembering all the good times with Owen.

Planting my hands on my desk, I close my eyes. I'm tired and want a nap, and I'm definitely not going back to Owen's for the night. Because his body against mine when he came into the office this morning didn't feel good.

And I certainly didn't react to his touch.

Or crave more of it.

Getting up, I go into the break room and get some coffee. Then I spend the rest of the morning going through case files and updating my dad's computer. I take my lunch right at noon, and since I didn't have a chance to make anything this morning, I head downstairs to go into town and find something to eat.

"Hey, Charlotte," Amy, the firm's secretary says as I pass by.

"Hey! How are you?"

"Good. So how do you know Owen Dawson?"

"We're, uh, friends." I adjust my purse over my shoulder.

"Friends, huh? We were *friends* before too." She gives me a wink.

"No, it's not like that."

"I won't tell if you don't tell."

Shaking my head, I move closer to her desk. "How long ago were you two, uh…"

"Friendly?"

"Yeah."

She shrugs. "A couple of months ago." Biting her lip, she drags one finger over her collarbone. "Best night of my life."

I do my best not to shudder. "I'm sure it was."

"Oh, it was. I mean, have you seen the guy?" she laughs.

I laugh too and then turn to leave. I knew Owen had gotten quite the reputation around Eastwood, but I didn't think it would bother me. Because things can only bother you when you care about them.

~

"Where were you last night?" Carly looks up from the Barbie house and narrows her eyes.

"With a friend."

"You have friends?"

"Hah." I sit on the floor and take off my heels. "I might have one or two left in this town."

Libby hands me a doll. "Play birthday party with me!"

"For a few minutes," I tell her, taking the Barbie.

"Was this friend tall, handsome, and has a name rhyming with Smowen?"

"Smowen? Really?"

"That's not a word, Mommy," Libby says pointedly. "Did you have a sleepover with that man with the ducks?"

Carly snorts a laugh. "Ducks, right. That's what you were doing wasn't it, sis. Looking at his ducks."

"They are geese and yes, I did stay there. But mostly so Tulip could get some peace and quiet and also because it was storming and you know how I'm still scared of storms."

"You don't have to be scared of storms." Libby pats my hand. "Thunder is just God bowling."

"Right." I smile and nod. "I'll remember that next time."

"Honey, do you want a snack?" Carly asks Libby, who nods. Waving me into the kitchen, Carly grabs my arm and pulls me around the fridge. "You slept with Owen! What? I mean, not that I blame you, but what?"

"I didn't sleep with him," I press. "He invited me over for dinner and by the time I went to leave, it was pretty late and storming. He offered up the guest room for me, and I was more or less alone the whole night."

"What the hell does that mean?"

"It means, he came in and sat with me when the storm was at its worse. He knows I'm scared of storms."

"And he didn't try to make a move?"

"Nope. He was a perfect gentleman." My heart swells a little when I say the words out loud.

"That's pretty sweet, actually."

"I suppose."

"It's irrefutable evidence or whatever you lawyers would call it. Are you going back tonight?"

"Tulip is there, so I am, but I'll probably come back home."

"Wait, he's babysitting your cat too?"

"Yeah. He doesn't have any pets and said it's not a big deal."

153

"Sounds like he's really trying." She opens the fridge and takes out a bowl of grapes.

"He tried before." I pick a grape off of the bunch and pop it in my mouth. "Do you remember how I barely survived our breakup?"

"I do. You kind of went all Bella Swan and didn't eat or sleep or shower."

"I was not that bad, but I'll admit, I felt like my heart had been literally ripped out of my chest. But what hurt even worse was coming home later that year, still just barely surviving, and hearing about how Owen had slept with half of Eastwood."

"I remember that too. You drank all the wine I'd been saving for Easter dinner."

"I still don't like Merlot because of that." Letting out a deep breath, I break off a few more grapes, watching Carly cut a few in half to give to Libby. "That hurt cut deep, though, knowing how easily he was able to move on. I didn't so much as look at another guy for over a year."

"Did you ever think that was his coping mechanism?"

I look at my sister incredulously. "You're defending him?"

"No, not at all, and if it was his coping mechanism, it's kind of piggish, but that was a long time ago."

"People don't change."

"No, not really. But they grow. Just look at you."

"I'm pretty much the same person I was in high school."

Carly laughs. "Physically, you really haven't aged much, which is totally unfair. I mean, look at how perky your boobs are and you have no stretch marks."

"I haven't had three kids, either."

"But what I'm saying is, look at how far you've come. You moved to New York, Char. That's huge!"

"But now I'm back."

"Right, because you were mature enough to put your pride aside and admit the city life wasn't what you wanted. I know how hard quitting your job and coming back home was. And we both know you could have moved to a new part of the city, gotten another fancy job, and lived your life fairly confident you'd never run into Todd again."

What she's saying is true. You can blend in like the best of them in the city, and I'd already been approached by another firm about joining them.

"All I'm saying," she goes on, "is that I like having you back in Eastwood, and part of me wants you to get back together with Owen so you have a reason to stay. And I want you to be happy too. He made you happy once."

He did. But he also broke my heart into a million tiny pieces.

CHAPTER 23

OWEN

There's no way Charlie is going to be at the house. I pull into the neighborhood with my heart beating faster and faster the closer I get to home. I want to hold her again, to see her pretty smile and sparkling eyes.

The garage lights illuminate the front of the house, and to my surprise, that old Mustang is parked in the driveway. My heart leaps and I have to talk down my dick. It's late and I'm sure she's sleeping. She'll be up and gone by the time I wake in the morning, and it'll be like she wasn't even there.

I pull into the garage, kill the engine, and grab the pizza and bag of fries and onion rings. Every once in a while, we're left with a ton of food at the end of the night. We offer it up to the staff for free, and depending on what kind of food is left, we take it to a homeless shelter.

Balancing the bag of fries and onion rings on top of the pizza box, I unlock the door and step inside, the house is dark and quiet, and I silently move through the mudroom and into the kitchen, setting the food on the counter. Tulip, meowing softly, limps into the kitchen. I pick her up and get a few pets in before she growls. I really don't get why people like cats so much.

I run up the stairs to change into clothes that don't smell like the bar. The guest room door is open but Charlie isn't in bed. I pull my shirt over my head, strip out of my jeans, and pull on sweatpants. Then it's back downstairs to look for Charlie. She's not in the living room either. Did I miss her upstairs? Maybe she was in the bathroom?

But the bed was made. I'm right about to go back up and look when I see the door to the screened-in porch is open. Stepping out, I see Charlie huddled up on a lounge chair. There's a book on the floor next to her. She must have fallen asleep reading. It's a little chilly tonight, so I grab another blanket from the living room and go out onto the porch.

The boards creak softly underfoot, and I pause, not wanting to wake her up. Light from the porch lamps illuminate her face, and the gentle steaming from the fountain in the pond fills the night air, muted slightly by a chorus of crickets. Falling asleep out here is easy to do. It's quiet and peaceful, though probably not the safest.

The door exiting the porch has a lock, but it's one that would be easy to bust through. I don't keep anything valuable out here, even though the crime rate in Eastwood is low. You never know, and I'd rather not have to call Wes and report that something was stolen. Charlie seemed to have a similar train of thought and pushed a chair up against the door.

Smiling, I drape the blanket over her. She lets out a soft moan and pulls the blankets tighter over her shoulder, rolling over to her side. The lounge chairs are comfortable to sit in and, well, lounge, and I've taken a good nap or two in them before. But sleeping all night...that can't be comfortable.

Her hair is in her face and I want so bad to tuck it away. I want to run my fingers through it and put my lips to hers. Tearing my eyes away, I go back into the house. The porch is right off the kitchen, and I pull down the kitchen window's blinds before turning on the light so it doesn't bother her.

I grab a water bottle from the fridge and open the box of pizza.

"Owen?"

"Hey, Sleeping Beauty."

She rubs her eyes. "I didn't mean to fall asleep out there."

"Were you hoping to make it out of here before I got home?"

She laughs. "I was, but now that I know you brought home pizza, I'm glad I stayed." Crossing the room, she grabs a slice and joins me at the table. "I actually told Libby she could have my room tonight. She's sharing a room with both her brothers and it's a tight fit. How was work?"

"Busy, which is good. Two of our regulars got into a fight."

"Sounds more exciting than my day."

"Missing the hustle and bustle of the city already?"

She shakes her head. "Not really, but I do enjoy challenging cases. And I will miss going up against asshole men who see me as less because I'm a woman and then I get to tear them limb from limb. Metaphorically, I mean. In the courtroom."

God, this woman is perfect. "I'd love to see you in action, and I don't mean that sexually for once."

"Thanks. It's kind of funny to say I love conflict in that sense. Well, mediating conflict." She takes a bite of pizza. "This is good. It's from Getaway?"

"It is."

"I have been missing out by not going. Are those onion rings?" She opens the bag. "And French fries? Score!"

It's three AM and we're pigging out on junk food. I never thought this would be a perfect night, but it is. I want more of this...and more of Charlie.

"How's she doing?" I ask, looking at Charlie's cat.

"She's back to her old self today. I think being away from the dogs is all she needed. Thank you again for letting her stay." She grabs an onion ring. "And save the crazy cat lady jokes."

"I was going to make a pussy joke instead."

Charlie pops the onion ring in her mouth and shakes her head. "I should have seen that coming."

"Pussies and coming...you're basically forcing my hand, Charlie." I toss the crust of my pizza back in the box and get another piece. "Unless you're trying to give me a hint of what you want to do later." I wiggle my eyebrows.

"I told you, that's not happening."

"You would enjoy it."

She swallows hard and reaches for a napkin. Wiping her hands, she gets up and goes to the fridge to get a drink. She's wearing the same PJs from last night, and while the smiling avocado print makes me think the clothes were meant for a teenager, they sure look good on Charlie. My eyes go to her ass, tight yet still supple. She's not wearing a bra, and I can see the faint outline of her pert nipples through the tank top when she turns around.

"I'm sure I would," she quips. "And you would too." Twisting the cap off the water bottle, she shakes her head and blows out a breath. "But we just can't, Owen. It's not a good time for me, and I'm pretty sure I know how this would end."

"With you screaming after you come for the third time."

She tenses, but not from discomfort. She's thinking about it too, remembering how good we were together.

"Talking like that...don't. Just don't."

"Why? Am I getting you all hot and bothered and you're going to have a hard time resisting me later?"

Her eyes narrow and part of my brain yells at me to shut up. Yet for some reason I can't, and all the frustration and regret has to come out somehow. Being a smartass has always been my thing, and yeah, I know deep down it comes from some sort of place of insecurity, that using humor and deflecting my feelings is a way of coping with the shit I don't want to cope with.

Though right now, *coping* Charlie is exactly what I need.

"Thanks for the pizza. I'm going to bed."

"I'll leave my door open."

Charlie grabs one more piece of pizza and takes it upstairs. I finish eating, clean up a bit, and then start to trudge up the stairs. I stop halfway up only to turn around, go back down, and set out a to-go mug and program the coffee pot to go off at seven AM for Charlie in the morning. She's probably going to have a hard time falling back asleep and will be tired in the morning.

I shower, fall into bed, and close my eyes, ready to pass out. I'm tired and should fall asleep easily, but I don't. My mind drifts back to Charlie, and my heart hurts once more. I'm still in love with her. I've always been in love with her, and I know I always will be.

CHAPTER 24

CHARLIE

I braid my hair as I walk down the stairs. I couldn't fall back asleep after going to bed last night, and finally drifted off about an hour before my alarm went off. I hit snooze twice and then just shut off my alarm, waking fifteen minutes later in a panic. Luckily, I washed my hair last night. It's long and thick and takes forever to dry.

I secure a hair tie around the end of my braid and throw my blonde locks back over my shoulder. The house is quiet, and Owen was true to his word last night: he did leave his bedroom door open. I looked in when I walked down the hall, seeing him in all his glory sprawled out on his stomach on his mattress.

He sleeps naked, like he always has, and the sheets were barely covering up his ass. The sight of his naked body sent a jolt through me, awakening every single nerve in me. Physically, there's no denying that Owen is a gorgeous man. He's tall and fit, with deep brown eyes, full lips, and a strong jaw that's always covered in the perfect amount of stubble.

I know he works out, and I've seen the protein shakes and supplements in the panty. Still, it's not bloody fair for someone to be in that good of shape when they bring home pizza and French fries several times a week. I run because I like it but also because my family has a history or heart disease. Also, I like to drink wine and eat sweets. Instead of cutting things I enjoy out of my diet, I'd rather add in working out to balance the scale.

The smell of coffee fills the kitchen. Owen isn't down here making me breakfast this morning, and he rarely gets up this early. He told me himself. Did he change the timer on the coffee pot so it would be ready for me? There's even a mug out on the counter, ready to go.

It's sweet and thoughtful and makes me smile. I pour myself a cup and go back onto the screened-in porch to drink it. Tulip limps out after me, looking pitiful. Though her spirits really have come back up. I feed her and give her her medicine, and then fill up my mug once more to take with me to work.

Going into the office at the front of the house, I open the top drawer to look for a paper and pen to write Owen a little *thank you for the coffee* note. There's not much in the top drawer other than an unopened package of gel pens, a box of paperclips, and a stapler.

Not wanting to open the new package of pens, I move to the second drawer. This one isn't nearly as organized as the last, and I pick up a large envelope to see if there are any pens underneath it.

I assume it's sealed—my mistake. Photographs fall out, scattering across the hardwood floor.

"Oh shit," I mumble and crouch down to pick them up. My throat catches when I turn the first one over, looking down at Owen and my smiling faces. We can't be any older than sixteen in this photo. We're at the drive-in theater, and Logan and some girl are in the background behind us.

I shouldn't pry. I shouldn't look to see what other photos are in the envelope…but I do have to pick up the rest that spilled out.

The next is also of us, out on the town with friends. I stick it back into the envelope, trying hard not to let my heart override my head. I've seen firsthand what that can do to people, and more specifically, to me.

The third photo I pick up is just of me. I remember Owen taking this one, back when the camera on his phone was impressive with its colored yet grainy photos. There's only one more photo that fell out, and I bite my lip as I pick it up and flip it over. It's another one of us, and I don't know how to process this.

Owen has a secret stash of photos of us from our childhood. Is it sweet? Creepy? A sign that he might be a hoarder or can't let go of the past?

Or that, like me, he hasn't been able to move on either?

There are a bunch of loose pens in that drawer. I grab one, put the photos away, and go back into the kitchen to write a note on a napkin.

Owen-

Thanks for the coffee. See you tonight.

-Charlie

I don't know if he's working tonight or if he'll be here when I get done at the firm. But I do know I'm going to need some new clothes...and Libby would really love to have space to keep her dolls away from Jack, who grabs them by the hair and pulls off their shoes. Again, I know our issue of all being crammed into one house isn't really an issue at all when I think about how bad others have it. But if I wasn't there taking up another room, it would give my sister and her family a bit more breathing room.

Leaving the note in front of the coffee pot, I look around the tidy kitchen and smile. Maybe staying here for a few more weeks won't be that bad. As long as I don't go doing something stupid.

Like Owen.

"Charlie!"

I turn and see a brunette woman waving at me from behind

the counter of the bakery. It's Danielle, Logan's wife. I stopped in during my lunch break, and this place is packed.

"Hi," I say, waving back. I'm behind two people in line, and Danielle steps out, motioning for me to come over by her. "How are you feeling? I mean, how are you doing?"

"It's okay. I know Logan told you. And very good." She smiles, making me think she got good news from the doctor. I don't know her well enough to ask about a private manner. "We invited everyone over for dinner tonight to tell them the news. I'm not sure if Logan's talked to Owen or not yet, but I'd love if you came as well. No pressure or anything if you don't want to," she adds quickly.

"Thanks, and yes, I'd love to come. I don't know if Owen's working or not tonight, though. I, uh, didn't ask."

"He's opening this morning and then Logan was able to get someone else to take the rest of his shift. I help manage the schedules still," she explains. "That's how I met Logan, actually. I used to bartend."

"Oh, nice. I didn't know that."

"So you and Owen met back in high school?"

"We met way before then, actually, but we, uh, started dating then." My throat starts to feel a little tight. What the hell is wrong with me. I'm level-headed, able to keep my cool even when I'm freaking the fuck out on the inside. Whatever anxiety or fear or jitters I'm feeling never surface. Now I'm fumbling over words and my nerves are physically manifesting.

And I have no idea why I'm getting nervous.

Maybe more like *unnerved*, and there's only one person who can do that to me.

"What do you want?" Danielle asks, and for a brief moment, I think she's asking what I want with Owen. Then I realize she's looking at the display cases of sweets.

"Cupcakes," I say, swallowing down the lump in my throat. I need to get it together. I'm going back to work to meet with a new client, and this time, he's all mine. Since Timothy is retiring in a few months, there was no point in starting work with someone new.

"Any particular flavor? We have like a dozen options. I'm all about the red velvet ones with sprinkles right now."

"Yeah, those sound good. Do you make them?"

"No," she says with a laugh. "I'm no baker. Which, I know, sounds weird since I own a bakery. It was my grandmother's dream to run her own bakery, and when this place went up for sale last year, we decided to buy it mostly to keep it running, but as a business venture. I have this whole five-year plan to start new businesses in the area."

"That's awesome."

She shrugs. "Thanks. Gotta put that Yale degree to use some-how, right?"

"You went to Yale?" My eyebrows go up. "That's impressive!"

"It's not as impressive as it sounds, even though I suppose it is." Shaking her head, she goes around the counter and puts four cupcakes in a box for me.

"How much do I owe you?"

"Oh, nothing at all. It's on the house."

"Really? No, I can't."

She presses her lips into a smile. "Well, you could pay for it with a favor."

"Huh?"

"Sorry," she says with a sigh. "I'm not good at this. I need Quinn. Or Scarlet. Yeah...Scarlet is the professional."

"I have no idea what you're talking about. What is Scarlet a professional of?"

"She's out of the business now. We want you to go on a date with Owen."

"You too?"

She tips her head. "Who else wants you to?"

I shift my weight, fingers pressing into the sides of the pink cupcake box. "And I appreciate how much you all care about Owen. I still care about him too, but in a different way. Going on a date…I just…I don't know if I can handle it."

Danielle's expression softens. "I don't really know what happened between you two. Logan's only told me so much, and I don't think even he knows the whole story. I do know that Owen is a great guy and we all want him to be happy. You seem to make him happy, but if it doesn't make *you* happy too, then it's not fair and I'm sorry for trying to push you two together, even though I suck at it."

Her words hit me, and I can't really deny that Owen makes me happy. "It's hard trusting someone who hurt you," I admit.

She gives me a sympathetic smile. "I know. I won't keep you any longer. Enjoy the cupcakes, and I hope to see you tonight."

"Thanks again." I weave my way through the crowd, chewing on the inside of my cheek the whole time. Bright sunlight streams down on me as I walk down the block and back to the firm. I do plan on eating one of these cupcakes as I fill out the paperwork necessary to officially hire me on at the firm now that I have one client of my own.

The rest of the afternoon goes by fast, and I swing by the house for more clothes before going back to Owen's place. Libby has her dolls all set up in my room. That girl has more Barbies than anyone I know, and Mom dug mine and Carly's old dolls out of the basement for her to play with as well. She has about a dozen of them tucked into the bed, and a few others are sleeping on the floor, covered with wash cloths and hand towels as blankets.

Coming back here and kicking her out seems a little selfish. After all, I have a place to stay and the two nights I've spent at Owen's haven't been bad at all. I grab enough clothes to last me three days, toss the bag in my car, and drive to Owen's.

He's outside doing yard work again, and Lord have mercy,

he's shirtless and sweaty again. I park along the street, grab my bag, and get out.

"Hey," I call with a wave. My heels click as I walk up the driveway, and Owen straightens up, turning away from the weeds in the landscaping he was pulling.

"Hey, Charlie." He wipes sweat from his brow with his arm. "Have a good day at the office?"

"I did, actually. I have my first official Eastwood client now."

"Fun. Is he a big crime lord you're going to defend?"

"Hardly. And you know I can't talk about things. Lawyer-client privilege and all."

"Ohh, so this guy has a record a mile long then."

I laugh. "I kind of wish, but no. Just someone who's taking a stand against someone wrongfully suing them. Our case is strong and I'm sure we'll settle out of court."

"You almost sound disappointed."

"I do like going to court."

"Logan called," he starts. "Everything looks good with their baby and Danielle's farther along than she thought, so they're telling everyone tonight. Do you want to go over with me for dinner?"

"Yeah, that'd be nice. Is the whole crew going?"

"I don't think Archer is going to make it. You know, I used to think it was bullshit how much doctors got paid until I saw how much Archer works."

"And they're in school forever."

"You went to school for a long time too."

"True," I laugh. "Though not all lawyers make a lot of money. People seem to think so, but most earn a pretty average salary. And that's not to mention the student loans most of us graduate with." I hold up my hand to shield the sun from my eyes. "I got lucky getting hired at such a swanky firm right out of law school. I was able to pay off my loans."

Owen picks up a clump of weeds from the decorative stones and starts to walk toward the house.

"What time is dinner?" I ask, falling in step with him.

"About an hour from now." He motions to one of the houses under construction down the street. "Or whenever Dean's done over there."

"Good. I have time to change."

"And I have time to shower and get something to eat. I'm starving."

I go inside. Pulling my hair out of the tight braid it's been in all day, I massage my head with my fingers for a minute. Wearing my hair like this makes my head hurt, but I was too tired this morning to do anything other than braid it.

I take care of Tulip, move her into the screened-in porch so she can watch the birds, and then go upstairs to change and do my hair. I quickly curl it, needing to mostly smooth out the frizzy waves left from my messy braid, and then put on a yellow sundress.

Owen is in the kitchen, going through the fridge. He looks up when I walk in, and his eyes slowly run over me.

"You look stunning," he tells me, and I quickly dismiss his compliment.

"It's just an old dress." That I've only worn in the store when I tried it on. "And my hair is a mess." I couldn't get it to look this effortless again if I tried.

"Well, you look good. Really good." He closes the fridge.

"I got cupcakes today." I go to the counter and open the box to show him. "I ate one at work, but I saved the rest for you."

"Thanks." His face lights up with a smile. "Want so share one?"

"I never turn down sweets." He grabs a plate and two forks and goes onto the screened-in porch. "You seem to like it out here."

"I do." I flick on the overhead fan, feeling the heat of the day hit us as soon as we step out. "And Tulip does too."

Owen smirks. "I have a really good crazy-cat lady joke right now."

"No pussy jokes anymore?"

He laughs. "I can always come up with one."

"I'm sure you can *come up* with one."

"I think you're trying to make a sexual joke and failing."

"I am," I laugh and sink my fork into the cupcake, getting mostly frosting. "I'm going to have to run miles to burn off two cupcakes."

"I'm sure there'll be more tonight. Danielle will bring something from the bakery, and you know my mother. She's always baking, and I think she knows why we're all going over, so it wouldn't surprise me if she spent the day making baby-shaped cookies or something."

"Baby-shaped cookies would be a little terrifying."

"And it would be weird to bite their heads off."

"Just a little." I look at Owen and smile.

"I overheard some new drama today."

"Ohhh, do tell!"

"Last year, Danielle busted some guy for cheating on his pregnant wife. Now his ex-wife is dating his brother."

"Sounds like the start to a juicy romance novel."

"I was thinking more like a remake of the Jerry Springer show."

I laugh and take another bite of the cupcake. "True. I can only imagine how awkward family get togethers would be."

"Right?"

I take one more slice of the cupcake and push the plate to Owen. He finishes it, and we get up to head out to Logan and Danielle's house, which is on the outskirts of town.

"That's Quinn and Archer's place," Owen says as we drive past a huge white house.

"Holy shit."

"Right? You should see the inside."

169

"You did say she had a lot of cats, so I'd like to."

Owen chuckles. "You'd get along well with her."

"It's been so long since I've seen her, it's weird seeing her all grown up now. She seems to have really done well for herself. I know it's been a while, but I'm still proud. She felt like my sister for a while there."

Owen doesn't say anything back, which isn't like him. His jaw tenses and he focuses on the passing country road. Other than the radio playing, it's silent between us the rest of the way to Logan and Danielle's farmhouse.

Dexter the German Shepherd is playing fetch with Jackson when we pull up. He gets excited the second he sees Owen and bolts over, jumping up and trying to lick Owen's face. Owen crouches down, hugging the dog, and my ovaries threaten to explode.

What is it about guys and dogs that's so damn attractive?

"Hi, Charlie!" Jackson calls, picking up a slobbery tennis ball.

"Hey, Jackson." I smile at the boy and then wave to Scarlet, Quinn, and Mrs. Dawson, who are on the wrap-around porch with the other children. Jackson throws the ball and Dexter takes off after it. Brushing fur off his shirt, Owen steps behind me. His hand lands on the small of my back, fingers pressing softly into my skin. I stiffen and he jerks his hand down.

"Sorry. Habit," he mumbles and keeps his eyes locked on the house in front of us.

"I'm so glad you made it," Mrs. Dawson comes down the steps and gives me a hug. "I didn't realize just how much I've missed you until you came around again."

"It is nice having another blonde at the table," Scarlet jokes and looks down at her baby. "It'll be a while until this one has much hair."

"We blondes need to stick together," I laugh. Owen says hi to his family and goes right into the house to find Logan.

"Do you want anything to drink?" Mrs. Dawson asks. "I brought sangria."

"No, I'm fine for now, thank you. I'll have some with dinner."

"Can I smell your glass?" Quinn asks, making a face before laughing. "I miss drinking."

"You'll drink again soon enough," Scarlet tells her. "I think it's amazing you're able to stick with breastfeeding. After two months I just couldn't do it anymore."

"I only nursed my first two," Mrs. Dawson says. "I attempted to with the twins but couldn't keep up. And they turned out fine."

"That's debatable," Quinn quips. "Though I did okay for myself. Don't feel bad about it, Scar."

Scarlet smiles and blinks rapidly as if she's trying to keep from crying. This must be a sore subject for her, and seeing Quinn and Mrs. Dawson come to her defense and make her feel better reminds me even more how much I loved being part of this family.

CHAPTER 25

CHARLIE

"Do you need help with anything?" I ask Danielle, going into the kitchen to get a glass of sangria. So much for waiting until dinner, right? Danielle is standing at the oven, stirring sauce to pour over enchiladas.

"Oh, you don't to do anything," she tells me.

"I know I don't, but I don't mind, either."

"I feel bad inviting people over and putting them to work."

I laugh. "I offered, but I totally understand. Though I haven't invited people over in a while. My apartment in New York was so small. We could hardly fit guests over."

"So those roomy apartments you see on TV are all a lie, right?"

"Totally. Well, the lie would be how regular people afford them. I loved the area I lived in. It was close to Central Park and to work, but holy shit it was expensive."

"The whole east coast is crazy expensive."

I pick up the pitcher of sangria and fill up a wine glass. "Oh right, you said you went to Yale."

"I did, and before that, I was born and raised in Connecticut. I have to say I like it here much better."

"I do too."

Danielle turns off the burner. "You don't miss it at all?"

I shake my head. "Not really. I miss being challenged at work, but I'm sure once I get more clients here I'll come up against some hard cases."

"You do not look like a lawyer."

"That's a compliment, right?" I ask with a laugh.

"I think so. I'm stereotyping, though Elle Woods didn't look like a lawyer either and she turned out to be one of the best."

"I might have identified with her a lot as a kid."

"She's not a bad role model," Danielle laughs. "Sorry if I was weird earlier."

"You weren't," I assure her. I look out through the kitchen window, watching Owen run across the yard in an attempt to get a kite up in the air for Jackson. He's so good with his nieces and nephews. I bring my glass of sangria to my lips and suck down a mouthful or two.

"What do you need help with?" I ask Danielle.

"Uhhh," she moves away from the stove. "The table needs to be set."

"I can handle that." I take one more gulp of sangria and set the glass down. "What cabinet are the plates in?"

"The corner one."

I step around Danielle and open the only corner cabinet, pulling out a handful of plates. I take them to the table and then go back for more. Everyone but Archer is here, and I have to stop and count to see just how many we need. I'm starting to feel a little drunk as I count out. That's eleven adults, right? And then two babies, one toddler, and Jackson.

"The kids have their own table," Danielle tells me as she puts the enchiladas into the oven. "Well, just Jackson and Emma. Arya has a highchair and I don't think Vi is big enough to even sit in one yet."

"It's neat that they're so close in age. From what Owen said, Quinn and Scarlet are good friends."

"Yeah," Danielle says with a smile. "They are."

"Do you hang out with them too?" I ask a little apprehensively as I pick up my sangria again.

"I do. They were friends before I came into the picture so sometimes I feel like an outsider, but it's never from them. It's all me putting that persona on, if that even makes sense."

"It does," I tell her. "I used to know everyone so well. It's a little weird being out of the loop."

"Right. You and Owen dated since high school."

I nod and open the silverware drawer. "Quinn used to feel like my own little sister. Archer was like a brother. And to come back and find them married with kids…" I shake my head and laugh. "Makes me realize how much I missed."

"Does it make you want to get back in the loop?" she asks carefully as she sets a timer on the microwave.

"Actually, it does." I pause for a second before taking the silverware to the table. I look outside again, seeing Owen lying in the grass as Emma tackles him. Dexter runs around wagging his tail, and three horses graze out in a pasture behind them. Everything is so picture perfect I'm not sure it's even real.

So I do the logical thing and gulp down the rest of my sangria.

I finish setting the table and then fill glasses of water and set them at each place setting. Scarlet comes in, saying Violet needs a diaper change. I hold her once Scarlet's done changing her diaper so Scarlet can go to the bathroom.

"She's giving me baby fever and I don't even have a boyfriend," I tell Danielle as I look down at Violet's precious little face.

"Right? She's such a good baby too. I can only hope—" She cuts off when Mr. and Mrs. Dawson come into the house, followed by Dean, Kara, and Quinn, who's holding Arya.

"Do you need any help, dear?" Mrs. Dawson asks Danielle.

"No, but thank you. Charlie helped me, and it'll be about ten more minutes until the enchiladas are cooked through."

"Should I call in the boys?" Mrs. Dawson asks.

"Sure. I'll heat up the rice," Danielle says.

"I'll make margaritas," Quinn offers, handing off Arya to her mother. She gets distracted when a fat orange cat comes running. She sits on the ground to pet the cat, and I leave the kitchen to go onto the back porch so I can call the guys in.

Owen sees me as soon as I step out. His eyes lock with mine and he raises his hand in a wave. Jackson throws a football at that very moment, and Owen pretends to let it hit him hard in the chest, knocking him over onto the ground. Jackson erupts into giggles, and little Emma toddles over to try and pull Uncle Owen back to his feet. Logan scoops her up and spins her around, and Weston steals the football, running away with it before Jackson can even see.

It won't be long before Violet and Arya are big enough to play with their cousins, and soon Danielle and Logan's baby will be here. Everyone is living out their dreams, and it's not that I'm jealous, because I really care about the Dawsons and want them all to be happy...but I am a little jealous.

Owen broke up with me because he didn't want to settle down and get married. He didn't want to have kids or a family or the responsibility of being a husband and father.

But I wanted all that.

Yet I don't have it.

Maybe it's not him that needs to change, but me.

"Dinner's almost ready," I call, leaning on the porch railing. Birds chirp loudly and a slight breeze rustles the leaves on the tree line surrounding the pasture. I didn't see Owen living in a house fit for Wisteria Lane, and I never thought Logan would end up living on a farm as picturesque as his parents'.

"Time to go in," Dean tells Emma, who starts to throw a fit. Owen says something to Logan, and Logan smiles and flicks his eyes to me. Weston picks up Jackson by the feet, hanging him upside down. The boy screams and laughs, and my heart feels so full watching the Dawson boys play with these kids.

Going back inside, Quinn practically shoves a margarita in my hand.

"Want to smell this one?" I ask with a laugh.

"I already did. I might have tasted just a tiny bit of one too. Like, not even a sip but more like stuck my tongue into it."

I wrinkle my nose. "Hopefully not mine."

"Nah," Scarlet says, twisting around in a bar stool. "It was mine. Doesn't bother me, though it should, right? I mean, it sounds disgusting."

"You love me." Quinn wrinkles her nose and smiles, and I catch Danielle watching them. I remember what she said about feeling like an outsider, and suddenly I feel a lot more connected to Danielle than I thought I would.

I'm not a shy person. You can't be a good lawyer if you're shy. I can assert myself into any situation, but in social situation where it matters, I find myself more or less reserved. And while Danielle seems to be absolutely perfect for Logan, I can see how it would be hard to assert yourself into a tight-knit friendship like Quinn and Scarlet's.

Maybe we could be frie—stop it. Don't even go there.

Because I'm not taking things any further with Owen. Been there, done that, and it ended in heartbreak so severe I hardly survived it.

～

I GRIMACE WHEN I TAKE A DRINK OF THE MARGARITA. QUINN seemed so proud of herself for making enough for everyone, though, so I suffer through another mouthful. Owen steps up behind me, and I almost expect him to put his hand on my back again.

Hell, I *want* him to.

"So, we were going to wait until after dinner," Logan starts, wrapping one hand around Danielle. The enchiladas aren't quite done yet, and we're all crowded in the kitchen, eating chips and salsa as we wait. "But..." He looks at Danielle and smiles.

"I'm pregnant!" Danielle blurts, eyes filling with tears. Everyone erupts in happy cheers, and Logan holds up the ultrasound pictures.

"You're eight weeks?" Quinn gasps. "How the hell did you keep this a secret? I told everyone before the pee was even dry on the stick."

"Gross, sis," Dean mutters.

"I knew like a day after conception," she taunts, and Owen laughs. "Archer is just that goo—"

"Oh, honey, congratulations!" Mrs. Dawson pulls Danielle into a hug. "We were hoping this was why you invited us over." She lets Danielle go and wipes tears from her eyes. Mr. Dawson claps Logan on the back.

"Told you one day Dad would be happy you knocked someone up," Owen says, making everyone laugh.

Owen comes back over by me, still smiling. He's genuinely happy for his twin, and seeing him care so much makes me feel an attraction to him I've been trying to deny. I gulp down another mouthful of the margarita. It does not taste good at all, and I'm wondering if I can dump it down the drain without anyone seeing.

I turn to do just that when Quinn asks if I want a refill. Giving her a begrudging smile, I take my drink to the table.

"This is really gross," I whisper to Owen as he slides into his seat next to me. He takes the margarita from me and takes a sip.

"That is so strong. Did Quinn make this, by any chance?"

"Yeah, she did."

"There's probably three shots of tequila in that."

"No," I silently exclaim and then laugh. "I already had a glass of sangria and I just gulped most of this down!"

"You're gonna be drunk," he teases.

I shrug and take another sip. "As long as you're driving, I don't see what's wrong with that."

He chuckles and reaches forward, taking a strand of my hair between his fingers. It's something he used to do before, and would usually lead to me biting my lip because I knew it drove him crazy. We'd slowly move our heads together until his lips crashed against mine.

My breath hitches and Owen's lips part. His eyes lock with mine and he twists my hair around his finger. Heart hammering, I lean in a little closer, getting lost in the darkness in his eyes. Then I blink and turn away.

What the hell am I doing?

Clearing his throat, Owen drops my hair and picks up his fork.

"Have you thought of any names yet?" I ask, needing to distract myself from Owen.

"I like Orissa if it's a girl," Logan says. "It's a from a book series I like."

"Orissa?" Mr. Dawson's eyebrows push together. "Isn't that a city in India?"

"Only you would know that, Dad," Quinn laughs. "It's a little weird, but I like it."

"Says the girl who named her daughter Arya," Owen says under his breath, and Quinn shoots him a look. I elbow him and he laughs. "I'm joking. Arya is a badass, and the name, I'm sure, will be fitting."

"Thank you," Quinn says with a pressed smile.

"Owen is a really good name for a boy," Owen goes on. "It's a strong, masculine name, and he will be destined for greatness."

"I'd make sure to avoid that one then," Weston says and we all laugh.

"We haven't come up with a boy's name we agree on yet." Danielle looks at Logan with a smile. "There's so much pressure with picking a name."

"Just don't use Todd or Brad," Owen quips and I give him a pointed look.

"These are really good," I tell Danielle after I take a bite of my enchilada.

"Thanks. I got the recipe from my grandma's cookbook. I might not be the best baker, but I can follow simple recipes at least."

I don't realize just how drunk I am until I stand up after finishing everything on my plate. I sway on my feet, and Owen, who just got up as well, puts his hand on my shoulder to steady me. I should be worried about how far gone I am, but all I can think about is how warm his skin feels against mine.

He takes my plate from me and carries it into the kitchen. I still have a bit of sangria left in my glass, so I take it and join the girls in the living room. Owen helps Logan clean up the dishes, and I take a spot on the couch where I can see him loading the dishwasher.

Quinn and Scarlet are making plans to meet up at the farmer's market this week and then go meet Danielle for lunch since she's working at the bakery. Dean's wife, Kara, who I think is a teacher by the sounds of it, agrees to hang out with her sisters-in-law but doesn't seem too happy about it.

"Are you able to meet us for lunch too?" Quinn asks me. "We'll be downtown."

"I think so. I don't really have a set lunch break, and I only have one client of my own so far, so I'm pretty free."

"Great!" Quinn smiles and looks at Scarlet, who's about to say something. Weston catches her eye and shakes his head. She purses her lips and narrows her eyes at him in a playful glare, but she doesn't say whatever she was going to. She and Quinn want to set me up with Owen, I know.

And maybe I am way too drunk because, right now, I wouldn't mind.

CHAPTER 26

"You know how you asked me if I missed the city?" Charlie rests her head against the seat and looks out the car window, watching farmland pass us by.

"Yeah?"

"I miss one thing right now. Guess what it is."

"Easily accessible strip clubs?"

She lets out a snort of laughter. "Oh, totally." She's drunk, and it's fucking adorable. "Take-out."

"Take-out strippers?"

"No," she laughs and hits my arm. "Take-out food. I could really go for some fried rice right about now."

"How are you possibly hungry?" I ask, chuckling. "You had two pieces of cake."

"Are you judging me?" She straightens up and tries to look like she's mad, or more like she thinks she should be mad.

"Not at all. I never judge you, Charlie."

Her expression softens. "I know. You never have. Thank you."

She turns back to look out the window and I take my eyes off the road for a second to admire her beauty. Her hair is down, blowing in the wind from the open window.

"You don't happen to serve orange chicken and fried rice at Getaway, do you?"

"We just took that off the menu," I joke.

"Why'd you do that?" She twists back around in the seat, eyes wide.

"I'm joking, Charlie. It's a bar and grill. We've never served Chinese food there."

"You should. Because it's good."

"Maybe I'll bring it up with our head cook. Don't hold your breath, though. And if you want fried rice that bad, I can make you some. I don't know how to make orange chicken, but find me a recipe and I'll try."

"You'd do that for me?"

I'd do anything for her. Making her food is nothing, and I'd go to the ends of the earth to make Charlie happy. "Of course. Because now that you're talking about it, fried rice does sound good."

"It does. It so does." She's quiet the rest of the way home, making me think she fell asleep. She might have dozed off a bit, but perks up when we pull into the garage.

"It's so dark."

"I closed the garage door," I laugh. "It cut out most of the fading sunlight."

"Oh, right."

"Need help getting out, drunky?"

"I'm not drunk and no, I don't." She tries to open the truck door before it's unlocked. "I knew that was locked."

"Sure you did. Just don't bang the door into the wall."

"I'm not a child."

"But you're drunk."

She glares at me. "Like you're one to talk."

"Oh, I'm not. Not at all. And I know I need to be reminded of simple shit when I'm drunk too."

Carefully opening the door, she gets out with grace. It's

impressive really, since her heels are several inches tall and it's a bit of a drop getting out of this big truck.

"Well, I don't." She leans in to talk to me and hits her head when she goes to close the door.

"Oh, shit." I get out and rush around, finding her with her hands on her head. She's laughing, but for a split second I think she's crying.

"Fine. Maybe I do need help."

I take her hands in mine, and push her hair back. "You might have a bruise in the morning."

"Nah, I don't bruise that easily." She lets out a breath and rests one hand on my forearm. I'm still cradling her face in my hands, pretending like I'm looking for more damage.

She shuffles closer. "Everything look all right, doctor?"

"Yeah," I say, breath hitching. "I should probably look you over in the light just to be sure."

"And naked too, right?" She giggles and wiggles her eyebrows.

"That would be the responsible thing to do. Make sure you don't have a serious head injury that requires immediate medical attention."

She runs her hand down my arm and slips her fingers through mine. "I had fun tonight."

"We literally just ate dinner."

"I like to eat food."

I reach past her and shut the passenger side door. "I noticed."

"I feel like that could be an insult."

"No." I shake my head. I don't even know what I'm saying. Because I don't know what's going on. Charlie is drunk and now I think she's hitting on me. Maybe? Fuck. All I know is that I want her. Bad. We go into the house and Charlie still hasn't let go of my hand. "You still want that fried rice?"

"Nah, I'm just thirsty now."

I bet you are.

"What do you want? Plain old water would do you some good."

"You know what else would do me some good?"

I take my hand from hers and turn on the light. "I can think of a lot of things."

"I'm sure you can." Her eyes meet mine and there's no denying the lust in her eyes. She wobbles as she tries to undo the buckles on her shoes. Worried she's going to tip right over, I take a hold of her shoulders.

"Thanks." She gets one shoe off and plants her foot on the ground. I keep a hold of her just in case. Back with two feet on the ground, she doesn't need me to help her anymore. I slowly run my hands down her arms. Charlie inches closer, and her tongue darts out, wetting her lips. My cock jumps, and my body reacts on its own accord. I bring one hand to her waist, feeling the curve of her hip, and pull her to me.

She doesn't object. Doesn't pull away. My heart lurches, and I bring my other hand to her, slipping it around to her back. I splay my fingers against her and step in. Charlie's lips part and she tips her head up, looking me right in the eye. I move my gaze from her eyes to her lips, and then down to her breasts. Everything about her is beautiful, and everything about this is familiar.

She feels so fucking good in my arms. This is where she was meant to be, and where she should have been all along. I never should have let her go, and now that she's back...something feels wrong.

Because she's drunk.

Charlie wraps her arms around my shoulders, and my self-control goes out the window.

"Owen," she whispers and stands on her toes.

"Charlie," I whisper back and lower my head, so that my forehead rests against hers. She tightens her hold on me, and I can feel her heart hammering away just as fast as mine is. Her breasts are crushed against my chest, so soft and so warm. She inhales, and tips her head up.

I don't think. Don't give myself a moment to hesitate. I part my lips and kiss her. The world stops spinning the moment her lips press against mine. A soft moan escapes her lips and she kisses me back. Heat rushes through my body, and my cock jumps. She presses her hips against mine, wanting to feel me get hard against her. It always turned her on to know she was the one making my cock hard.

I slip my tongue into her mouth and bring one hand to her hair, tangling a handful around my fingers. Desperation erupts between us, and we stumble back into the kitchen, tripping over each other's feet. I pick her up and set her on the kitchen counter. Charlie parts her legs and welcomes me between, bringing her hands up to my face as we kiss.

I move my mouth from her lips to her neck and she tosses her head back, dropping one hand to my pants. She fumbles with the button on my jeans but gets it undone. I reach around and find the zipper on her dress. I start to pull it down when she grips my shoulders with one hand, leaning back and bunching up her dress with her other.

Cock hard and aching to be inside of her, I pull away just to catch my breath. She tastes just as good as I remember, if not better. Licking my lips, I go back for another kiss, and Charlie hooks her leg around me. I wrap her in an embrace, pulling her as close as I can, needing to feel every inch of her against me.

She grabs the hem of my shirt and tugs it up. I step back and raise my arms over my head, letting her pull it off. She tosses it on the floor and runs her eyes over me, biting her lip. Fuck, she's so hot. Eyes shimmering, she flattens a hand over my chest and puts the other on the back of my neck, bringing me back to her.

I put my lips on her, kissing the breath out of her before moving to her neck again. I trail kisses over her collarbone as I work on the zipper again. I pull it down in a swift movement, and the thin straps of the dress fall over her shoulders, revealing her perfect tits hidden behind thin, purple lace.

I cup one in my hand, feeling her pert nipple against my palm. She groans and pushes herself against me, widening her legs.

"I want you, Owen."

Fuck. "I want you too, Charlie." I caress her face with my hands, putting my lips to hers again. I step in, and she wraps her legs tightly around me. Still kissing her, I bring my hands down and pick her up. The house is dark and I'm more than a little distracted. I bump into the table on my way to the stairs, but none of that matters.

All that matters is Charlie, and she's in my arms with her dress gathered around her waist. My shirt is off, my pants undone, and I'm so fucking turned on right now. My cock needs to be inside of her, and my heart...my heart is longing for something else.

I'm in love with Charlie and want her to love me again. I want us to be happy together, to be inseparable again. I don't want her to wake up and regret this in the morning.

Charlie kisses my neck, lips going right to the spot that sends tingles through me. Her teeth nip at my skin, driving me absolutely crazy. She hasn't forgotten a single thing when it comes to pleasing me.

Motherfucker. It's already going to be hard to let her go. It *is* hard, trust me. Really fucking hard and begging to push inside her tight little pussy. I need it. She wants it. What's the harm?

I stub my toes on the first stair. Charlie reaches out behind her, feeling for the wall to help guide us upstairs. We're making out again as we fall onto my bed. Charlie shimmies out of her dress and I move back on top, fitting right between her legs. She rakes her nails up over my back, pressing in just enough to hurt so good.

"Charlie," I start but can't pull myself away. My lips are on her neck again, and this time I'm kissing a trail down her collarbone and over her breasts. My hands slip underneath her, and with deft fingers, I unhook her bra. She reaches up and slowly pulls the straps down, teasing me. Hungrily, I watch her pull her bra off. It's dark in the room, only illuminated by the streetlight coming through the window.

I bury my face between her breasts and she curls her legs up. Her hands land on top of my head and she starts to push me down, guiding me to her pussy. My heart speeds up even more, and precum beads at the tip of my cock. I want more than anything to pull off her panties and lash my tongue against her clit, over and over again until she's coming hard on my face.

But I shouldn't.

Not like this.

Not when she's drunk.

I want Charlie, my Charlie, and having her like this isn't right.

"Charlie," I pant, pushing myself away with more self-control than I knew I had. "You're drunk."

"And you're not, loser."

"No, I'm not." I squeeze my eyes closed and flop over onto the mattress next to her. If I stay on top of her, I'm going to go right back to where I was before.

"What's wrong?" She moves onto her side. "You...you don't want me?"

"That's just the thing, Charlie. I do want you. I want all of you. I've wanted you since the day we broke up, and I'll never stop wanting you."

"Then have me."

"I can't believe I'm saying this, but I want more than just sex. You're drunk, and until tonight, you've made it very clear you didn't want to hook up." I sit up and open a drawer on my night-stand. I pull out a white t-shirt and hand it to her. "If you want to have sex when you're sober, believe me, I will be all for it. I will fuck you in any and every position you can possibly think of and then at least a dozen new ones after that. I'll go down on you until you're so overcome with pleasure you're squirming against my face and pushing me away. And then I'll hold you until you fall asleep and we'll fuck just the same again when you wake up."

Her lips part and she pulls the shirt up to her chest.

"But only when you're sober." I turn back toward her and cup her face in my hands. "I care about you too much to let you do something stupid, even when that stupid thing is me. I've wanted to have sex with you since I saw you, but this isn't how it was supposed to happen."

My throat starts to feel tight, and I rest my forehead against hers again. She keeps my t-shirt over her breasts with one hand and brings the other to my face. Her mouth opens and a small breath comes out instead of words.

My resolve is weak right now, and I have to remind myself she's drunk. She might tell me she cares too, and that she's been resisting this whole time and it took until tonight to realize that she wants me too.

That she misses me just as much as I miss her and she couldn't keep the truth from me after a few drinks, but she's glad it's out now. That she loves me and will still feel the same way in the morning so we might as well fuck now so we can do it again once the sun comes up.

But she doesn't say anything at all.

CHAPTER 27

OWEN

"You...you should get some rest," I tell her, forcing myself to break away. I help her pull the t-shirt over her head and then untuck the sheets. She nestles down into the covers and reaches for me.

"Will you stay with me?" she asks, brows pinched together. "I'm not too drunk to know I like having you with me."

"Of course." I kiss her forehead and get up to get her water. My cock is still hard and throbbing against my jeans. Charlie is in my bed, wearing my t-shirt, and was all too willing to have sex.

I turned her down.

Hell has frozen over.

Pigs are flying.

I guess there's a first for everything.

But I meant what I said. I care about Charlie too much to let her be a drunken hook-up. Burying my cock deep inside of her, feeling her pussy contract around it as she comes...fuck, I'm getting even harder just thinking about it.

I want to fuck her.

But I want to love her more.

I awkwardly go down the stairs and grab a water bottle from

the kitchen. Charlie is almost asleep when I get back into the room. Setting the water on the nightstand next to the bed, I go into the bathroom, turn on the shower, and strip out of my clothes.

I grab my cock as soon as I step into the shower. All I have to do is think back to a few minutes ago, to the way Charlie felt up against me...the way she tasted, to get myself off. Coming brings me physical relief, but I'm still painfully unsatisfied.

Hot water streams down on me, and I stay in the shower for a few more minutes just to calm myself down. I almost had sex with Charlie and I stopped it from happening.

Do I hate myself?

Are things going to be fucking awkward in the morning? She'll leave, I'm sure.

"Fuck," I mutter and turn off the water. Maybe I should have slept with her. At least I would have had one last time before she left for good. I dry off, brush my teeth, and then go back into the bedroom. I didn't bring any clothes into the bathroom with me, so I wrap the towel around my waist again, shut off the bathroom light, and wait a beat before opening the door to let my eyes adjust to the dark.

Charlie is still in my bed, and has rolled over onto her back. Her blonde hair is strewn about her face, and she has one hand up resting on the pillow above her head. She looks so peaceful and so innocent.

I did the right thing by not sleeping with her, even though it hurts. Letting out a sigh, I cross the room, put on a pair of boxers, and get into bed.

"Owen?" Charlie grumbles, not opening her eyes.

"Yeah, it's me."

She wiggles closer, feebly reaching for me. I move in next to her, taking her in my arms. Her head rests on my chest and she hooks one leg over mine.

"Thank you, Owen."

∿

FOR ONLY THE SECOND TIME IN MY ADULT LIFE, I WAKE UP WITH A woman in my arms who I hadn't had sex with the night before. And for the second time, the morning is nearly perfect.

"Careful," I tell Charlie, who sits up fast. "You're probably going to feel last night."

Blinking, she looks at me and then down at herself.

"No, not that kind of feel," I tell her.

"I know," she grumbles and puts her head in her hands. "I remember everything." She flops back down onto the pillow and turns to face me. Her cheeks redden. "Thank you, Owen."

"For what? Taking care of your drunk ass?"

"For refusing to sleep with me."

"That's a first, isn't it?" I smile.

Charlie reaches her hand out and takes mine. "It is."

I suck in a breath and lace my fingers through Charlie's. "I meant what I said last night."

Charlie takes her other hand and runs it through my hair. "I know." She pulls her lips over her teeth and snuggles little closer. "And I did too."

"You want to have sex?"

She laughs. "I do—"

I pull her onto me and put my lips to hers. Charlie laughs and moves so she's on top of me, head resting on my chest.

"Not right now. I kind of feel like I might puke if I move too fast. Oh, shit!" She sits back up again. "What time is it?"

I look past her at the time on the cable box. "Seven-thirty."

She lays back down and groans. "I have to be at work in less than an hour."

"I don't need that much time."

"Owen," she starts and sits up again, running her fingers down my chest. Her touch sends tingles through me, and my dick starts to rise. "I didn't mean it like that."

"If you're taking back wanting to have sex, then you need to stop touching me. You have no idea how hard it is to resist you, Char."

She smirks. "I do know how hard it is."

"Ohhh, a dick joke. Nice."

"I learned from the best." She lies down next to me again and I take her in my arms.

"Then what did you mean?"

"I don't really know," she admits. "But I do know you make me happy and being with you feels...feels good."

"I can make it feel better."

"Can we just start with this?" She pats my chest.

"Snuggling and keeping it all above the waist?" I raise my eyebrows. "You're not going to make me wait three years to get into your pants again, are you?"

"Make it four." She sits up again and rubs her eyes. "I don't know what I'm doing."

"Maybe you're still a little drunk. Or sexually frustrated. I can help you with that."

Laughing, she grabs the water bottle from the nightstand and twists off the cap. "Do you work today?"

"I do."

"All night?"

"No, I'm opening this morning and I'll be home by five or six."

"That's a long day." She takes a big drink of water.

"It is. But I own the place. Co-own, sorry. Logan gets his panties in a bunch if I leave the *co* out of it."

"I'm going to take you out on a date tonight."

"Where are we going?" I push up on my elbows.

"It'll be a surprise."

I bring my hand to my chest in fake shock. "How will I know what to wear?"

She laughs. "I'll buy you a fancy suit and send it to you in an overly ostentatious gift box."

"If it doesn't have a big red bow, I'm going to be disappointed."

"And then my driver will pick you up at seven." Still smiling, she leans in and puts her lips to mine. It's a quick kiss, and she gets up and goes into the bathroom right after that. But hey...I'll take whatever I can get.

Because this is all I need. My second chance to prove to Charlie that I'm serious this time around. She's all I've ever wanted, and now she'll know it.

CHAPTER 28

"You're in a good mood today." Amy opens the box of donuts I brought into the office.

"I am," I agree. "Which is surprising since I didn't get much sleep last night. I get a little cranky when I'm tired."

"Were you getting a little something else?" She wiggles her eyebrows, and I laugh. Before I can tell her no, my dad comes into the office and we both stop talking about where I was last night. I don't know Amy well, and the fact that she's slept with Owen weirds me out, but she's nice and I get along with her just fine.

Though it seems like Owen has slept with most of the women in this town, so if his ex-lovers weird me out, I'm going to be limited to talking to only those he's related to. But the past is in the past, and I can't hold that against him.

He asked me what changed my mind about being together and I couldn't give him a clear answer. Because I don't really know, and when I think about it, it doesn't make sense.

I thought things would only work if he changed and wasn't the same Owen Dawson that he used to be. But after last night, I realized he was the same Owen Dawson that he used to be…and that's the man I loved back then.

Can't it be the man I love now?

Owen was thoughtful, kind, caring, and devoted back then. Well, until he wasn't and broke up with me. And this is as far as I get in my logic without being tripped up. But last night wasn't the first time he stopped me from taking things further in the bedroom. It would have been all too easy to sleep together last night, especially with the way I was throwing myself at him.

But he didn't want me to regret it in the morning, just like he did when we were teenagers. That's Owen, though. He might seem like he puts himself and his pleasure first, but he doesn't. At least not when it comes to me.

We broke up because he didn't want to get married and have kids. That was years ago, and I've seen the way he is with his nieces and nephews. He'll be a perfect father—someday. I need to be upfront with him this time.

I still want to get married

I still want to be a mom.

Not tomorrow. Not the next day. Or even within the year. But it is what I want, and if settling down isn't for him, then we'll forever be star-crossed lovers destined to want what we can't have.

But I have a good feeling about things this time around.

"Does the drive-in still play movies?" I ask Amy. "It's been years since I've gone."

"They do." She takes a bite of her donut. "Are you thinking about going?"

"Maybe. Since I'm staying in Eastwood, I figured I should know the ins and outs of this town again."

"There's not much to know. Though we do feel all sorts of modern now that there's a Starbucks in town."

"I do appreciate that. Though the diner coffee is still the best in the county."

"I totally agree." She smiles. "Whatever kept you up all night is good for you." She gives me a wink and Dad whirls around, looking at me in question.

"Ohhh, it's time to get up to my desk," I say, forcing a smile. "See you at lunch, Dad."

"Right," he mumbles, shaking his head. He doesn't want to know, I'm sure. Grabbing a donut, I leave the break room and go into my office. I'm sharing it for now, but Timothy won't be in until after lunch. I'm meeting with one of his clients today to see if they'd like to switch over to me or go elsewhere. Until then, there's not much for me to do. I pull out my phone, set on texting Marcus, when I see I have a text from Owen.

I smile right away and my heart swells in my chest. Baby steps. I need to take baby steps.

I open the text and it makes me want to take a flying leap. Owen sent a picture of himself, sitting on the screened-in porch drinking coffee. He's still in his boxers and looking incredibly hot, but the best part is he's holding Tulip on his lap.

Needing to put the phone down before I respond with eggplant and water-dripping emojis, I drop it onto my desk and spin the chair around, stupid smile on my face. My phone rings, and I grab it expecting to see Owen's name pop up. It's Marcus, and I answer on the second ring.

"Hello?"

"Hey, girl. Haven't heard from you in a while. What's going on with that sexy ex of yours?"

"I almost slept with him last night."

"What stopped you?"

"He did."

"What? Why?" Marcus gasps. "Have you not been shaving or something?"

"I don't think Owen would mind if I stopped shaving, actually, but no, that wasn't it. I was kinda drunk and he said he didn't want me to wake up and regret it in the morning."

"Wow. That's shockingly sweet and disappointing at the same time."

"I know, right? But it made me want to give things another go."

"That's even more shocking."

"Is it?" I spin around in the chair. "I like being with him. He's funny and makes me laugh, and his family is just the best."

"Are you dating him for his family?"

"No," I laugh. "And I don't know if I can even say I'm dating him. I mean, I am kind of living with him already, and I plan to tell him tonight that I want to get married and have babies."

"What the fuck is going on?"

I laugh. "It's not how it sounds. My sister's dogs attacked my cat, and we're all stuck at my parents' together until an apartment opens up for me to move into. I've already put down the deposit for it, and Owen offered to let my cat live at his place for a while."

"He's babysitting your pussy."

"No, not you too with the pussy jokes."

"Can't help myself. So the cat is at his house. Why are you?"

"I don't really have a good answer. The first night I stayed because I didn't want to drive in a storm. The second night I fell asleep reading and it was late when I woke up. And last night I passed out drunk in his bed."

"Stop sounding like such a lawyer," he quips. "Just admit you like him."

My heart skips a beat. "I do. I do like him, and I like being with him. Am I being stupid? Getting swept up with the thought of how it used to be? Maybe I should just sleep with him and get it out of my system."

"We both know that's not going to work. I've heard your one-night stand stories."

"I know," I sigh. "I don't want to get hurt again. I'm scared. Really scared. That's why I'm going to tell him tonight that I still want to get married and have a family. He broke up with me back in college because he didn't want any of that."

"Good idea to put it all out on the table before you get in too deep."

"Exactly. I don't expect a ring or anything, but if marriage isn't something he wants, then we're not meant to be. I'll save myself from another broken heart."

"Will you, though?"

I swallow hard, knowing he's right. If Owen tells me he doesn't want to settle down, it will be just as crushing as it was the first time. I let myself get close to him again, felt welcomed back into the Dawson family, and don't want to have that all ripped away again.

"Yeah. It'll be fine. So, how are things in the office?"

"Ohhhh, girl, I do have some juicy gossip. Monica James, from your old firm, was caught fucking a client."

"No! How'd you find that out?"

"There was a screaming match between Monica and the client's wife in the lobby. I felt like I was watching trashy made-for-TV dramas in real life."

"Damn. That would have been a sight to see. I never liked Monica or her stupid designer suits."

Marcus laughs. "Don't drag poor innocent designer fashion into this."

"The jackets alone to those things cost five grand. I don't care how fashionable that is, it's crazy to spend that kind of money on a colorful suit jacket."

"Hun, we both know if I could afford that, I'd have one in every color of the damn rainbow."

"I might have too, just so I'd feel like I fit in," I confess. "I miss you, Mar."

"And I miss you, Char. You'll have to come back this fall and go to a show with me."

"Oh, I will for sure. Are you decorating anyone famous's house this week?"

"A *Housewife*, and she's a total nightmare." He goes on to tell me about his client from Hell before we both have to and get to work. My morning drags, and I find myself wistfully thinking about the fast-paced days spent at my New York firm.

With nothing else to do, I go online and look for any job postings at the firms in the city. Some of the more prestigious ones don't post listings, and you have to have a client list you could take with you, a killer reputation, and more importantly, know someone at the firm to get you an in.

Blinking, I close the internet tab. What am I doing? I'm making a life here. In Eastwood. And hopefully with Owen.

~

"I SHOULD WARN YOU, I DON'T PUT OUT ON THE FIRST DATE."

I laugh and hold my phone to my ear with my shoulder. "That's not what I heard," I say to Owen.

"Oh, you, uh, heard about that?"

I can't tell if he's joking or not anymore and I regret my words. Way to make things weird. Owen has quite the reputation around here, as I further discovered at lunch when I overheard a group of women talking about how much they love going to Getaway because of the hot bartender who's given more than one of them "the best night of their lives".

"About that," I start. "Not *that*, I mean the date."

"Are you backing out already?"

"No, but my dad asked if you'd come over for dinner."

"Sure. I haven't seen your folks in a while."

"You don't mind?" I put papers in a folder and slip it into one of the desk drawers.

"Nope. I've dragged you to two family dinners already and you've only been in town a few weeks."

"Yeah, but I like your family."

"Yours isn't bad either," he laughs.

"Great. I'll let him know, and then I'll see you at home later. Home. Your home. I'll see you at your house later."

"You might get back before me. It's pretty busy here and Logan is gonna be late coming in. He had to take Danielle to the doctor and they're just now getting done over there."

"Is she okay?"

"Yeah, everything is fine. She was feeling some pains but I guess it was normal. Danielle's a little paranoid, not that I can blame her considering what she went through."

"Right. I'd be the same way. I really hope things stay good with her."

"Me too. You know I've never really been religious but even I'm saying prayers for them."

"That's sweet. I will too."

"Thanks. See you tonight, Charlie."

We end the call and I finish straightening up the desk before leaving. I tell Dad we'll be over for dinner, and then head to Owen's house, smiling the whole way.

CHAPTER 29

OWEN

"Shall we?" I hold out my arm for Charlie to take. She loops her arm through mine and looks up, smiling.

"We shall."

I parked on the street, and we're walking up the sidewalk to her parents' house. Chaos reigns around us as soon as we step foot inside. Two dogs come running, and one wags its tail so hard it knocks over a decorative vase on the coffee table in the living room. Charlie's niece, Libby, is upstairs in what I think is supposed to be a time out. She's screaming and crying and banging on a closed door.

Her youngest nephew cries from somewhere deeper inside the house, and the TV is blaring *Mickey Mouse Clubhouse*.

"I have no idea why you left," I say and take my shoes off. "It's so quiet and peaceful here."

She rolls her eyes and takes off her heels. "Right?" Taking her phone out of her purse, she turns just in time to see one of the dogs pick up her shoe and run off with it.

"Drop it, Chewy!" she calls, chasing after the dog. "Those are Gucci!"

The other dog, a pretty cream-colored golden retriever, jumps up at me, tail wagging.

"Hey, buddy," I say and kneel down so the dog stops jumping. Looking through the foyer and into the living room, I'm taken back to the last time we were here.

This is where we sat when I broke Charlie's heart. When I told her I wasn't ready for a serious relationship and wanted to have fun.

Fuck, I was an idiot.

If I hadn't done that, I wonder where we'd be. Would that be our kid upstairs throwing a huge temper tantrum? Would we have two unruly dogs? Or—gulp—a dozen or so cats?

"Libby, if I hear one more—oh, Owen!" Carly comes through the dining room, looking up at the stairs.

"Hey, Carly. Long time no see."

"Oh my God, yes!" She sets down the toddler in her arms and gives me a hug. "I feel like you got taller. Did you get taller?"

"Maybe you got shorter."

"Fatter, that's for sure, but I don't know about shorter," she laughs.

"I see they're about to break ground on your lot soon."

She picks up the little boy again. He's eyes are red and swollen from crying and he rests his head against her, obviously ready for a nap he doesn't want to take.

"I am so flipping excited. Not that I'm not grateful to be here, but it'll be nice to have room to have all our things spread out again." Her eyes go to the formal living room, which is doubling as a playroom for now.

"Got it," Charlie says, coming back into the foyer holding her shoe. The dog follows behind her, playfully jumping and trying to get the shoe back. "These are going in here for safe keeping." She grabs her other shoe and mine as well and puts them in the front closet.

"Do you want a drink?" Carly asks over Libby's screams. The kid's got an impressive set of lungs on her.

"Sure," I say and Charlie eagerly nods.

Carly leads the way into the kitchen and I put my arm around Charlie, pulling her close. "You still want to have sex, right? I'm making sure now in case you get shit-faced again."

She laughs and pushes me away. "I did not get shit-faced last night. And about the other thing." She purses her lips together and shrugs. "Let's see where the night takes us."

Carly goes around the island counter and crouches down, opening the wine fridge. I take her distraction to my advantage and grab Charlie around the waist and bring her to me. We're around the corner, but if Carly takes a step back she'll see us.

"What are you doing?" Charlie hisses. She goes to push me away again, but I can see the lust in her eyes.

"Trying to sway you." I put my lips to hers and she melts against me. Heat pours off her body, and she wraps her arms around my neck, standing on her toes and pushing her hips against mine. My tongue slips into her mouth and the same desperate passion we felt last night takes us over. I press her against the wall and she groans as I deepen the kiss.

"What about red Moscato?" Carly asks and sets a bottle on the counter. Charlie and I break apart, both breathless.

"Not fair," she whispers and wipes her mouth with the back of her hand. "Yeah. Carly, that sounds good."

"What about you, Owen? I can try to make you something. I know there's whiskey in the pantry."

"Wine is fine," I say and adjust my pants when she turns to grab two glasses. It was just one kiss and yet I'm getting turned on. Charlie plants her hands on the counter and lets out a breath. It's safe to say she is too.

"Where's Mom?"

"She took Matt for a bike ride," Carly tells her.

"How old is he?" I ask.

"Six."

"My nephew lives a few blocks away. They're around the same age."

"Jackson, right?"

I nod. "That's him."

"They played at the park together just yesterday. Jackson is a cute kid."

"He gets that from me," I say with a smile.

Carly grabs three glasses and pours the wine. "How's Tulip?" she asks Charlie as we sit at the island.

"She's doing much better."

"Good. I still feel so bad about that."

"You should," Charlie says seriously before laughing. "I don't blame you entirely."

"Just a little?"

"Oh, of course."

The screaming upstairs stops. Carly takes a big drink of wine. "Finally," she sighs.

"What's Libby in trouble for?"

"Jack took one of her Barbies and instead of letting me handle it, she yanked it from his hand and pushed him. He hit his head on the dresser, of course."

"Awww, poor baby." Charlie picks up Jack. "You just wanted to play dolls, huh, little guy?"

He mutters something and reaches for Charlie's hair. She and her sister look alike. Charlie is much prettier, but I'd never say that to anyone out loud. Jack has light brown hair and dark blue eyes. He looks like his mother, which in turn makes him resemble Charlie.

She'll make a good mom someday, and before I can even stop myself, I think of her pregnant with my child. Of us living together, happy, married and in love.

How it should have been.

How it will be.

This is my chance and I'm not going to blow it this time.

"I should go check on her." Carly drains her wine and goes upstairs. Jack nestles down into Charlie's arms, head resting on her breasts.

"Kid's got the right idea," I say and Charlie glares at me. "I'll have to steal his spot later."

"Owen," she scolds.

"What? Thinking about is getting you all hot and bothered, isn't it?"

I expect her to tell me no, to get my mind out of the gutter and grow up. Something like that. I don't expect her to sink her teeth into her bottom lip and agree with me.

"I want you to kiss me again." Her voice comes out all breathy.

"I want to kiss you again too." I scoot my stool closer to hers and run my fingers through her hair. Her eyes fall shut and she lets her head fall in my direction.

Then the back door opens, and her other nephew, Matt, comes running into the house. His face is red and his hair all sweaty from wearing a helmet out in the heat.

"Hey, Aunt Charlie!" he exclaims, startling Jack, who was starting to drift to sleep. "Who are you?" he asks me.

"Hi, I'm Owen. I'll be your neighbor when you move into your new house."

He looks at me and then at Charlie. "Are you two having sex?"

Charlie's mouth falls open. "Matt! Y-you—where did you—no, we're—how do you know what that is?"

He shrugs. "Jacob's brother told us about it."

I let out a snort of laughter. "How old is Jacob's brother?"

"Fourteen."

"Kids are starting younger and younger these days."

"That's so not the point." Charlie shakes her head. "You shouldn't talk like that," she tells him.

"What'd he say now?" Carly comes back into the kitchen.

"I asked if they're having sex," Matt says proudly, and I have to turn away so the kid doesn't see me laughing. It'll only encourage him to keep saying it if he know people find it funny.

"Matthew James Tully. We talked about this. That is not appropriate."

"Keith says everyone does it."

"Lord have mercy." Carly grits her teeth and shakes her head. "Your father is going to deal with this one. Go wash your hands, please." She waits until he's out of ear shot to talk again. "He doesn't know what sex is. Justin and I talked to him about it. I thought he'd forgotten about it. I am so sorry."

"I think it's hilarious," I laugh. "Jackson went through a phase where he talked about how babies get put inside a mommy by a daddy."

"I'm sure you had nothing to do with that." Charlie raises an eyebrow.

"That was all on Dean, actually. Even I know better than to open that can of worms."

"The last thing I need is him asking people at school this fall if they're having sex."

Charlie laughs. "It is kind of funny."

"It kind of is. Like when Libby said *penis* all the time when she was three. But it's embarrassing if it's said to the wrong people."

"We're not the wrong people," I assure her. "You have nothing to worry about."

"Thanks. And I do wonder…" She looks at her sister and raises her eyebrows. Charlie swats her away and Jack climbs out of her arms, wanting his mom to hold him. Mrs. Williams comes into the house a moment later.

"Owen!" I get up and hold out my hand, but she pulls me into a hug instead. "How have you been, dear?"

"Good. Busy with work, but life's been good."

"Hopefully it's only getting better," Carly mumbles and Charlie elbows her again.

"Dad is bringing home steaks to cook on the grill," Mrs. Williams tells us. "He should be here any minute."

"Need any help with dinner?" Charlie asks and her mother shakes her head.

"I got everything else prepared already. Libby was a good helper with the pasta salad."

"I'm going to try to get this one down for a quick nap before dinner," Carly tells us and takes Jack into the living room.

"Is Justin working late tonight?" Charlie asks. I think Justin is Carly's husband. Charlie and I had already broken up by the time her sister got married. I don't even remember her dating anyone named Justin.

"Yes, he's been working all the overtime he can get lately."

"I can't blame him," Charlie says and looks at me with a wink. The house is chaotic and crazy. I might work extra to avoid it too. I went from living at home, living on campus, to living with Logan. I wonder how it would be to live with my in-laws.

Mrs. Williams pours herself a glass of wine and we move into the sunroom at the back of the house. The dogs follow but have settled down by this time and lie down on the cool tile floor. Charlie sits next to me on the loveseat, and I put my arm around her out of habit. She doesn't move away or flinch this time. Does it feel like habit to her too?

It's weird, how it feels both new and old.

When Mr. Williams comes home, I go out on the back porch with him, talking as he grills the steaks. I always liked him, and he reminds me of my own father in some ways. We talk about work and business and he doesn't bring up how I broke Charlie's heart all those years ago.

We were kids then. I've changed. She's changed. *We've* changed.

∽

"THAT WAS NICE." CHARLIE PULLS THE SEATBELT OVER HER LAP AND clicks it in place.

"It was." I start the engine. "Did you drink enough wine to get all frisky again?"

She laughs. "You know I don't need wine to make me frisky."

"Mmm, that sounds promising."

Shaking her head, she rolls down the window. The sun is just now starting to set. We stayed at her parents' later than planned. After dinner, we all sat around talking. I can tell Charlie's missed being around her family after being away in New York for years. And I really have always liked the Williamses.

"It's such a nice night." She sticks her arm out the window. "That breeze feels so good. Would you think it was lame if I asked if we could go on a walk after we get back to your place?"

"Not lame at all."

"Great." She smiles and brings her other hand across the center counsel and rests it on my thigh. I flick my eyes down, watching her long fingers spread out. I imagine them wrapped around my cock. I need to stop before I get a hard-on right here in the car. "I'll change my shoes first. These were expensive as fuck but not comfortable at all."

"Quinn likes all that designer stuff too. I don't get it."

"I don't really either," she admits. "I do like some of it, like the bags and the belts, and think they really are of good quality, but some of the other stuff is just ridiculous. There was an unwritten dress code at my old firm, though, and I'm ashamed to say that I wanted to fit in."

"I don't think there's any shame in wanting to fit in."

"Really? You've always done your own thing and not cared about what others think."

"Well, I'm awesome and the exception to the rule."

She laughs and runs her hand up my thigh, fingers inching toward the inseam of my jeans. "I wouldn't really say I'm a follower or anything, but I really did want to be in with my coworkers. I tried hard for the first year and then realized it was stupid. I wore the same clothes, carried the same bags, and went to the same overpriced salon, and still felt like an outsider."

"Why was that?"

"Because I was an outsider. It took me a year and thousands of wasted dollars before I admitted it to myself. You said it yourself. I'm not a big city person. I like the excitement of the job, but not the lifestyle or the pressure to look a certain way. Don't get me wrong, I think it's important to show up looking put together, clean, and professional, but does wearing a five-thousand-dollar suit make me any better than the lawyer in the eight-hundred-dollar suit?"

"Even eight hundred bucks is way too much for a suit."

She laughs. "It is." Taking her hand off my thigh, she turns on the radio. It's synced to my phone, and she flips through my playlist until *Defying Gravity* comes on.

"Maybe I should take this secret to my grave," I start. "But I still know the words to this song."

"You do?"

"Remember that weekend trip we took to Tennessee? You listened to this on repeat the entire time."

"Oh yeah," she laughs. "Why did you let me?"

I shrug. "If I knew I was getting some, I was willing to do just about anything back then. We were, what, nineteen?"

"Yeah. It was so hard to get my parents to let me go down there with you. They didn't think it was appropriate for me to be with you overnight."

"How'd you convince them to let you come?"

"I pretty much admitted that we were already sleeping together at that point and it didn't matter if we were alone over the weekend or just an hour."

"Solid logic, actually."

"Right? I never got why they cared so much about me being

with you at night. And we'd gone through a whole year of college together."

"We did have a lot of sex then."

"We certainly did." Her hand lands on my thigh again.

"We can have lots of sex again."

"We can," she says in a level tone. She's not saying we're going to go home and get started on that right away, but is more stating it as a possibility. I grip the steering wheel and resist moving my legs so her fingers inch closer to my cock. Though if she actually does start jacking me off while I'm driving, there's a good chance I'll crash.

She keeps her hand on my thigh the rest of the ride home. We go in and she goes upstairs, carrying a bag of clothes she brought back with her from her parents' house. I almost told her to bring all her stuff over, but I didn't want to freak her out and make her think things were moving too soon.

She still intends to move into her own place next month. And she should, right? But she could also stay here with me. Starting a relationship over when there's already so much history between us is tricky.

We're not a new couple. We still get each other, even after all these years. Yet those years did happen, and rushing back to where we were before just isn't possible. Still, she's in a unique situation and needs a place to live.

And I have that place.

I'm overthinking, which isn't something I usually do. I'm a shoot first, aim later kind of person, and while some may say that's reckless, it's always steered me in the right direction.

And right now, I feel like having Charlie move in with me is admittedly a little impulsive, but will put us right where we're meant to be: together.

210

CHAPTER 30

CHARLIE

O wen isn't in the kitchen anymore when I come back down the stairs. The house is dark, with the exception of a soft glow coming from the screened-in porch. A single candle is lit and sitting on the table out there, and Owen's back is to me as he looks at the fountain in the pond behind his house. There's a light in it, making the simple fountain look much fancier at night than it actually is.

Silently, I slip into the room. The candle is one of those meant to repel mosquitos, and the smell reminds me of summer nights spent on the front porch, both with Owen and my other friends. Life was simpler then, and while I can't get rid of my adult responsibilities, things don't have to be complicated.

Owen turns right when I get up behind him, and firelight flickers in his eyes. He takes me in his arms, and my heart skips a beat. I hook my arms around his neck and step in close. Being in his embrace feels so right.

It's like I never left.

He tips his head down, lips brushing against mine. Heat floods through me, and my eyes fall shut. The rushing of the fountain sounds behind us, and though I know there are other houses nearby, it feels like Owen and I are the only two people left in the world.

And I'm okay with that.

I bring my head up and push my lips against his. That's all it takes for the spark to ignite into a wildfire, and suddenly, desperate desire takes over me. Owen's arms tighten around me, crushing me against his chest.

I need to be closer. I need to feel him, all of him.

He slides one hand up my back, grips the base of my neck, and then plunges his hand into my hair. Holding my head like this while he kisses me is intimate, and makes me want him even more. His other hand moves down to the small of my back, and he pushes my waist against his.

His cock is just starting to get hard, and feeling that monster-sized dick come to life turns me on more than anything else. Knowing that I'm the one getting him off, that I'm the one his cock is hard for...fuck. It drives me absolutely crazy.

Taking his lips from mine, he moves them to my neck and bites and sucks at my skin. I grip his shoulders, needing to hold onto him for support or else I fear I'll melt into a puddle at his feet.

"Charlie," he pants, breaking away so he can look at me. Cupping my face with his hands, he kisses me once more. "Are you sure you want—"

"Shut up and kiss me."

"That's enough of a yes for me." We tangle together again, kissing each other like our lives depend on it. I'm getting so hot and so wet, and when Owen pulls me to him, I feel that hard cock in all its glory.

Moaning, I arch my back, rubbing myself against him. My pussy contracts just thinking about having that thing enter me. Filling every inch. Fucking me into oblivion until I'm screaming and seeing stars.

Owen takes another fistful of my hair and pulls my head to

the side, exposing my neck. His puts his mouth to it and sucks at my flesh, teeth nipping my skin at the same time. I put one hand on his chest and slowly move it down, breath hitching when I get to the button on his jeans.

Owen stops kissing me and looks down, watching me undo his pants. I lick my lips, eyes wide and heart racing. I pop the button on his jeans, and pull down the zipper. Looking up at Owen's face, I watch his eyes fall closed as I run my hand over his cock.

Holy fuck, it's even thicker than I remember. The tip sticks out over the top of his boxers, beading with precum that gleams in the candlelight. My lips part and hunger for that big dick takes me over. I drop to my knees, mouth watering, and pull down his pants.

I haven't *wanted* to give a blow job since I don't know when. But right now, I want to taste him, to take him in my mouth, and bring him as much pleasure as I can. Letting out a small moan, Owen parts his legs and rests hand on my head as I pull his pants and boxers down.

Pushing my hair over my shoulder, I lick my lips and open my mouth. His cock slides in past my lips, and I flick my tongue over the tip. Owen groans and pulls my hair. I take him in as far as I can and then slowly pull my head back, sucking hard. Cupping his balls with one hand, I wrap my other around the base of his cock. Alternating between sucking him hard and fast and then slow as I lick and suck the tip of his cock, I rub my thighs together, so fucking hot right now.

"Fuck," Owen pants. His balls tighten in my hand, but he stops himself before he comes. He moves back and reaches down, picking me up. Breathing heavily, he steps out of his pants and boxers. Before I even know what's happening, he picks me up and lays me down on the ground. He moves on top of me, kissing my neck as he reaches down, plunging his hand under the waistband of my leggings.

"Are you wet, Charlie?" he growls. "When my fingers touch your pussy, will I find it wet for me?"

"Yes," I breathe. "I'm so wet for you, Owen."

"This is what you want."

He's talking dirty, still being demanding, but double-checking my consent too. He cares so fucking much, and my heart swells in my chest. "It is." I squirm underneath him, clit begging to be touched. "I want it, and I need it. Touch me, Owen. Please."

With his hand under my leggings but still over my panties, he sweeps his fingers over my core. I swear I could come right now if he does it again.

"You are wet. I can feel it already." He moves to his side, slipping his other arm underneath me. His cock is against my thigh, and my pussy quivers. It's not fair that he's able to hold me here in this state of desperation.

"Make me wetter," I groan. "Make me come."

"With pleasure." He gently rubs me though my panties and my eyes roll back and I moan. He brings his hand back only to slip his long fingers under my panties. "Goddamn," he mutters when he takes in just how wet I am. If it was anyone but Owen, I might be embarrassed. He circles my entrance, teasing. I close my eyes and bend one leg up. He finds my clit right away, and slowly strokes it, rubbing me with the perfect amount of pressure and speed.

I'm so revved up already, it's not going to take long for me to come. And Owen was always good with his fingers. He understands the *less is more* concept when it comes to sex, which is a rare find in a guy.

But Owen...Owen plays me like a fine-tuned instrument he was born to play.

"Ohhh my God," I moan, feeling the orgasm build up inside of me. It winds into a tight coil deep inside me, and the muscles in my thighs tense in preparation for what's going to come.

Me. It's me doing the coming.

I grab Owen's arm, nails biting into his skin. The orgasm releases, rolling through every single nerve in my body. I'm still coming, pussy still wildly contracting, when he slips a finger inside of me, going right for my G-spot. He presses his fingers against it while gently rubbing my clit with his thumb.

Another orgasm comes on hard and fast, and this time, I come so hard Owen's hand is drenched. Slowly, he pulls his hand out of my pants and moves over top of me. Instead of lowering himself to me, he pulls my pants down. I'm still panting, still seeing stars and riding high. I try to lift my butt up off the floor so Owen can get my pants off.

Still trying to catch my breath, I feebly pull him onto me and attempt to take his shirt off. I can't quite get my hands and arms to work like they should, and stars are still dotting my vision. Owen flashes his trademark cocky grin, knowing the reason I've been rendered useless is him and him alone.

He pulls his shirt off over his head and moves back down between my legs. He's on top of me, completely naked, and nothing has ever felt better. Inhaling deep, I regain a bit of control over my body. I bend one arm up and run my fingers through his hair. He nestles his face in my neck, and gives me another minute before rolling us over.

I'm on top of him now, and his cock rubs against my clit. Already sensitive from the two orgasms he just gave me, I pitch forward, mouth falling open in a moan.

"Take your shirt off," he orders.

I nod, wanting nothing more than to obey him right now. Grabbing the hem, I pull it up over my head. Owen bites his lip as he reaches up and undoes my bra with one hand. He's always been good at doing that, and I can't even take my own bra off one-handed.

I lean forward again, letting my bra straps fall down my arms.

"You are so fucking gorgeous, Charlie," he groans, taking my breasts in his hands. He flips us back over and I widen my legs, welcoming him in between. Owen kisses me, hard and deep, just like before, and then makes his way down, kissing my neck, my collarbone, and my stomach. He doesn't stop until his mouth is over my pussy, and there's no hesitation, no warning. His tongue lashes out against my clit and my mouth falls open. I plant my hands against the floor, bracing myself for the third orgasm. This one hits me faster, awakening every fiber of my being. Owen's hands are under my ass, and he lifts me off the floor, holding my pussy against his face. He keeps licking and sucking as I come, and the pleasure is almost too much.

I'm moaning, screaming, writhing against his face. My ears ring, and I'm certain I'm not even in my body anymore. It's like Owen and I have been transcended to a place where only sex and pleasure exist. He flicks his tongue against me one final time and sets me down.

The house could be on fire right now and I wouldn't know. Wouldn't care to get up, even, because all that matters in this moment is how incredibly fucking amazing Owen can make me feel.

"Charlie," he groans, moving between my legs. He's antsy, rubbing his cock against me before he even enters me. He's close to coming too, and I want him to enjoy it at least half as much as I did.

"Fuck me, Owen," I growl. Sucking in a breath, I reach down and wrap my fingers around that big cock. I guide it to me and angle my hips up, offering myself to him. Owen's lips go to mine as he pushes inside me. I cry out again, and my hand falls back to the floor.

He slowly pushes in balls deep, making sure the tight fit feels good for me. As soon as he sees that it feels fan-fucking-tastic, he lets loose, fucking me hard and fast. He kisses me as he comes, filling me with everything he has.

With his cock pulsing inside of me, he lowers himself against me. His weight is crushing, but I know he needs a moment just like I did. Taking a breath, he picks his head up and kisses me on the lips before pulling out and moving to my side. He spoons his body against mine and I put my hands over his. My eyes flutter shut.

"Are you tired?" he asks, and the fact that he has his wits about him is beyond me.

"You...you wore me out." I look up at him. "I came three times. And each was more intense than the last."

"We were always good at this."

"We were...and we still are."

CHAPTER 31

CHARLIE

"I feel like such a lush," I laugh, settling into Owen's arms. We moved into his bed and he just brought me a glass of wine. "Sex, wine, and staying up past my bedtime."

He brushes my hair back. "I'm turning you into a rebel."

I take a sip of wine and set the glass on the nightstand. "You really are."

"I should be punished."

"Oh, you definitely should be." I move on top of him, and tingles run down my spine. We're both still naked, and I'm still floating high on adrenaline and sex. I don't know why I resisted, why I waited until now to finally relent and do what I wanted to do since the moment I saw Owen again.

And admit that I'm still very much in love with him.

Owen's hands land on my hips and his cock starts to get hard again. I lean over, breasts in his face, and rub myself against him, getting off before I reach down and guide him into me. My breath comes out in huffs as I ride him hard and fast. Owen presses me down onto him, then brings one hand down and gently rubs my clit with his thumb. It's all I need to come, and the moment the orgasm rolls through me, Owen groans and comes as well, and we finish at the same time.

I fall down onto him, and Owen playfully slaps my ass and rolls us over so he can pull out. He gets me a towel from the bathroom to clean up with, and it hits me that he just came inside me twice and I'm not currently on birth control. I stopped taking my pills after Todd and I broke up.

Statistically, the odds are against us. And since I went off the pill, my cycle hasn't been normal. At all. I push the thoughts out of my head, not wanting to ruin this moment. Because this moment is really damn perfect.

We get ready for bed and then slip back under the covers, snuggling close together.

"This feels almost as good as sex," I mumble, feeling sleep start to pull me under.

"It does," Owen agrees softly and kisses the top of my head. "Almost."

~

DAD KNOCKS ON THE OFFICE DOOR. I LOOK UP FROM THE FILE I'VE been going over and smile. I'm in another good mood today, pointed out by Amy.

"Hey, kiddo. We're all heading out for lunch. Are you coming?"

By "we're all" he means him, Tim, and Amy. The farmer's market is set up today, and the entire firm—all three of them—is going to get something from there.

"I'm meeting Quinn in about half an hour. Do you mind if I shift my break back a bit?"

"Not at all." Dad smiles, and I know he's happy I'm making friends here again. He and Mom of course want me to stay, but they also want me to be happy. "Enjoy lunch."

"You too."

Dad leaves the door open, and silence falls over the office. A few minutes later, the elevator dings. I set the file down and look out into the hall, not creeped out at all. Maybe it's just going haywire? No one should be in here.

Then the floor creaks and I shoot up, grabbing the stapler off the desk. With my heart in my throat, I move around the desk and inch toward the door.

"Charlie?" Owen calls, appearing in the doorway.

"Owen!" I let out a breath. "You scared me! I thought some creeper got in here."

He laughs and looks at the stapler in my hand. "Your plan was to staple them to death?"

"Not to death. But I did think one staple in the ball sack would be enough to get away."

He winces. "It would be."

"What are you doing?" I set the stapler down and go to him. He's holding a bag of takeout that smells like cheeseburgers and fries.

"I came to see you." He puts the bag on my desk and wraps me in his arms. "You're alone in the office?"

"Yeah. I'm meeting your sisters for lunch."

"I only have one sister."

"Scarlet, Danielle, and Kara are your sister-in-laws."

"True. When are you meeting them?"

I look at my watch. "Twenty minutes."

Owen's hands slide up and down my back. "And we're alone."

My lips part and I start to get wet just thinking about it. "In the office?"

His lips pull up into a grin. "On the desk. Or in the window."

"The window? People will see us."

"Maybe. Maybe not."

"They'll hear us, for sure." The windows are open today, letting in the warm breeze. This building is old and the third floor gets a little stuffy. The air conditioning isn't very strong and having the window open is a must until it gets replaced.

"Sounds like a challenge." His lips go to my neck.

"A challenge to be heard or not be?"

"Whichever one you want."

"We shouldn't." I start to undo his pants.

He bunches up my skirt. "Right. We really shouldn't."

I use my foot to close the office door. "This is unprofessional."

"Very." He locks the door. "I should probably leave now."

"Yes. You should."

With that cocky grin still on his face, he spins me around, pulling my skirt up over my ass. My panties come down next, and he lowers his pants so his cock is exposed. Pressing it against me, he pushes me forward. My hands land on my desk, holding me upright as he slides his fingers between my legs and rubs my clit, not stopping until I'm just about to come.

Then he stops, spins me around, and drops to his knees. My eyes roll back as he pulls my panties the rest of the way down, tossing them on the floor. I perch on the edge of the desk, knocking over my coffee mug from this morning. It's empty, thankfully.

Owen throws one leg over his shoulder and dives in, mouth over my core. A loud moan escapes my lips, and I clasp one hand over my mouth to muffle the others. It doesn't take long before I come, body shuddering with pleasure. Panting, Owen stands and moves between my legs. My pussy is still spasming as he enters me. I hold onto him, and the desk rattles underneath us as he fucks me.

"Holy shit," I gasp as he pushes in balls deep, coming just as hard as I did.

He lets out a deep breath and rests his forehead against mine. "Yeah, I'm good."

My lips curve into a smile, and I cup his face with my hands. I want to tell him I love him, that I've loved him this whole time and no matter what I did—even getting engaged to another man —nothing made those feelings go away.

Reaching over me for a box of tissues on the desk, Owen grabs a few and hands them to me. I clean myself up enough to pull on my panties and then use the bathroom. Owen is in the lobby outside my office when I come out with the bag of takeout on the coffee table.

"When do you have to go in to work?" I ask him.

"Pretty much whenever I want. Benefit of being the boss. I'm not bartending until tonight."

"I wish you could call off."

"Don't tempt me, Charlie. Because I would. Though I do have an office we can use at the bar."

I laugh and take a burger out of the bag. "Maybe I'll come in for a drink then."

"I'll have a stiff one waiting for you."

Laughing again, I bite into my burger. We talk and laugh as we eat, and then I realize that I was supposed to meet Quinn five minutes ago. I wolf down the rest of my food, and Owen walks with me out of the office and into town. My hand is in his when we find Quinn and Scarlet. They're each pushing a stroller, and Scarlet is wearing a tight dress with her hair up in a messy bun. She looks so effortlessly gorgeous, and I'll forever be impressed with how thin and tight her body is after having a baby only a few months ago.

Quinn is just as gorgeous, and I can't get over how grown up she is.

"Hey!" She brings her hand up and waves, then notices that Owen and I are holding hands. The biggest smile takes over her face, and she elbows Scarlet, who makes just as big of a deal over Owen's fingers laced through mine.

"What are you, twelve?" Owen quips, rolling his eyes. "Are you going to tell me I need a cootie shot next?"

"More like penicillin," Quinn shoots back then looks at me

and laughs. "I'm joking. He's not diseased. Well, as far as I can tell."

"It's okay," I tell her, leaving a lot unsaid, but I think she understands what I mean. Owen was a man-whore before. He's not now.

Because we're back together.

Jackson, who's sitting on a little bench-like seat in the double stroller gets out and runs to Owen, giving him a big hug. Emma is excited to see her uncle too, but she's more interested in the melting popsicle in her hand than getting out to hug him.

"Can you stay with us?" Jackson asks Owen.

"I'm sorry, buddy, I have to get to work. I'll see you on Sunday, though."

He smiles. "Is that tomorrow?"

"Not quite, but it'll be here before you know it."

Owen gives Jackson a hug and sets him back down. Scarlet calls him to get back in the stroller and he protests, saying he's too big to ride in a baby stroller and he should be walking or pushing the stroller himself.

"I'll see you tonight then," Owen says to me, hooking his fingers with mine. He steps in and kisses me, melting my heart all over again.

"Ewww!" Jackson cries, and I laugh. Owen smiles, says bye to Quinn and Scarlet, and then heads to his truck to go to the bar. I watch him leave, knowing I'm going to get a million questions as soon as I turn around.

The smile is still on my face when I do.

"Oh my God," Quinn gasps. "Are you guys back together?"

I try to play it cool. I fail. My smile widens and a flush comes to my cheeks. Owen and I haven't really talked about what we are, but there's no doubt in my mind we want the same thing.

"Yes, we are."

Quinn squeals with excitement. "Sorry. I promise I'm not this involved all the time. But I've tried so hard over the years to find the perfect match for Owen and I never have. Because no one was you."

I push my hair back, wishing I had a band to put it up. The sun is hot, and having my long, thick hair down my back isn't much different than wearing a shawl in this heat.

"We're going to take things slow," I say only because it feels like the right thing to tell someone. "We didn't work the first time because we didn't want the same things in life. I don't want him to do anything he doesn't want to do, but I have a better feeling this time around."

Quinn beams again. "I do too."

Kara joins us a few minutes later, and then we go to the bakery to get Danielle. Even though I already ate, I order a spinach salad, needing the extra energy boost. Owen and I had sex three times in under twenty-four hours. I'm a little tired.

I had a really nice time hanging out with the women who could very possibly be my own sister-in-laws someday. I don't want to go back in to the office, but the thought of being with Owen again tonight will get me through the rest of the day.

"Hey, lady," Amy says when I go through the lobby. "Did I see you with Owen?"

Oh shit. I can't deny it, but I don't have to act guilty. "Yeah. I was with him."

"I thought so. I was across the street and the market was busy."

Good, she saw us together at the market. Not fucking on my desk upstairs. "It was really busy! Is it usually like that? I don't remember it being so crowded before."

"It's gotten popular. People from Newport come now. It's trendy or something." She waves her hand in the air. "And I have to say I'm impressed to see Owen with you more than once."

"You are?"

She laughs. "That man is the definition of love 'em and leave 'em. Not that I mind. I mean, we all know what we're getting into with Owen Dawson, right?"

"Right." He's not that man anymore. Being with a different woman every night isn't what he wants.

He was holding out for me…right? Suddenly, I feel insignificant, like I'm not enough to make Owen change his playboy ways. I blink rapidly and shake that thought from my head.

I'm a strong, smart, confident, and beautiful woman. Any man would be lucky to have me.

But then again, Todd cheated on me.

Motherfucker.

I hate how easily I can be shaken like this.

Owen is with me.

Things are different now…unless they're not.

CHAPTER 32

The day has never gone slower. And the night? The night is dragging by so slowly I'm starting to wonder if I died in a freak accident on the way to work and went right to hell. Charlie isn't here, so there's no way this is heaven.

A group of guys are out celebrating a twenty-first birthday. They've spent a ton on beer and shots, and we've been watching them closely to know when to cut them off. It's late and the crowd is starting to dwindle, but they're still going strong.

This happens every now and then, and usually it doesn't bother me. If we're making money, I'll stay open for another half hour or so. But tonight, tonight I want to go home, strip off my clothes, and feel Charlie's body against mine.

Everything feels right in the world. Charlie is back, and this time she's staying. I want to tell her I love her, but won't. It's too soon. She wants something serious this time around, and I do too. But freaking her out isn't the way to go.

I turn on the lights, giving the birthday group a hint it's time to leave. We start cleaning up the bar, and one of my employees pays attention to how the party goers are getting home. We take drinking and driving seriously around here and do our best not to ever over-serve.

Once the group is finally gone, we clean up as fast as we can. I'm half-tempted to leave shit and come in tomorrow morning to get things neat and tidy, but Logan is opening with me and usually comes in early to do bookkeeping shit. I don't feel like dealing with him getting all pissy over the state of the bar. Plus, you never know when an inspector will come in, and we have a perfect reputation to uphold.

Getaway profits enough for Logan and me to both step back into more of a manager role and be less hands on, but hiring two full-time employees is an expensive endeavor and I've gotten quite used to my comfy lifestyle.

Finally, everything is spotless and ready for another day of the same thing tomorrow. I'm the last to leave and double-check the alarm system and locks. It's after three-thirty and Charlie is no doubt fast asleep.

I take a quick shower to get the smell of the bar off me and then get into bed still naked with damp hair. Charlie rolls over, eyes fluttering open. She smiles when she sees me and she wiggles closer, resting her head on my chest. As much as I want to have sex again, I'm beat, and holding Charlie is the most comforting thing in the world. She might be in my arms, but it feels like she's the one holding me.

～

"OWEN?" CHARLIE'S LIPS PRESS AGAINST MINE.

"Are you waking me up for sex?" I blink my eyes open and pull her back into bed. She's dressed, with her hair and makeup done.

"I wish. I'm running late, actually. But I wanted to say bye before I left."

Wrapping her in my arms, I nuzzle my head into her neck. "Call in sick."

"I can't. I'm meeting another client today."

"Another boring client?" I squeeze her ass and my cock jumps.

"This one doesn't sound boring. It's a young nurse. She got hired, went through orientation and then got fired once the employer found out she's six months pregnant. They told her she was disabled. Can you believe that?"

"What an idiot. You can't do that."

"Exactly. I'm sure we'll come to a settlement outside of court, but this is the kind of case that reminds me why I became a lawyer. To get justice and try to make the world better in a legal way. Remind assholes they can't treat women that way."

"You're amazing, Charlie."

"Thanks. I'm just doing my job." She sits up and runs her hand through my hair. "Do you work again tomorrow?"

"Yeah, but during the day. I'll be done by six at the latest."

"Do you want to go out for dinner? I can make us a reservation at the one and only fancy place to eat downtown," she says.

"Yeah. I'd like that."

"Good, because I want to talk, which I know is something people say when things are bad, but it's not. I just want to make sure we're on the same page with everything."

"If that page means my cock in your pussy, we are."

"I'm serious," she giggles. "I like this. I like us. But I'm still a little scared," she admits. "I don't want to get hurt again."

"I will never hurt you, Charlie. Trust me."

She puts her lips to mine. "I do."

Then she leaves, needing to go to work. I fall back asleep until my alarm goes off. Then it's up, eat breakfast, get dressed and head into work myself. Maybe I will look into hiring someone else. Or at least trying to get on more of a daytime schedule. I'm the boss and can move my shifts around as I want. Well, as long as it's doable with everyone else.

I'm the boss—okay, one of the bosses—but I'm not an asshole. We have a good thing going here, and I like knowing that our employees generally enjoy working here.

Getaway is busy today, busy enough that even I wait on a few tables and run food out to the lunch crowd. Charlie called me while she was on her break but I missed it. I call her back and get her voicemail. She must be with her client, and I know she's going to win this case with ease.

There's a lull around four o'clock, and I go into the office to eat my lunch and get off my feet for a few minutes. Wes, Scarlet, and the kids are at a table when I come back out, and I start to head over there to say hi.

Weston meets my eye and then looks at a guy in a navy blue suit who is sitting at the bar. He looks back at me in question, and I shake my head, not sure what he's trying to ask.

"What's going on?" I ask, pulling a chair up to their table.

"That guy," Weston starts. "Do you know him?"

I lookback at the bar at the guy sitting there. The guy has an air about him that screams asshole. "Never seen him before in my life."

"I think that's Charlie's ex," Scarlet whispers. "Quinn and I kind of stalked her social media to get clues on how to push you two back together." She holds up her hand, silencing me before I can tell her that was borderline creepy. Though I did have Quinn do something similar. Call it a dirty move, but it made Charlie happy, didn't it? "Quinn was able to recover or unlock or something—whatever—and we found one photo of Charlie with her ex. I think that's him."

"What's he doing here?" I ask though I'm sure I know. He's here to try and win Charlie back. Too late, asshole. "And it'll be easy to figure out if it's him or not. Her ex's name is Todd."

"We had Logan ask for his name, and he told him it was Dan." Scarlet shakes her head. "Can't you go card him or something?"

"Not unless he orders alcohol."

She looks at Wes. "Pretend you're investigating him or some-thing them."

"I can't do that."

She bites her lip and hands Violet to Wes. "Don't arrest me, babe."

"What are you going to do?" Wes asks, cradling the sleeping baby.

"I'm going to find out that guy's name." She pulls her dress down, exposing enough cleavage to make me feel like I need to look away. Then she fluffs her hair and saunters over to the bar, sliding up next to the Mystery Man.

In under a minute, she has him buying her a drink. I watch, impressed, as she goes on to spill a bit down her breasts. Mystery Man reaches over to give her a stack of napkins and makes a move to wipe the alcohol off her chest. Wes starts to get up.

"She knows what she's doing," I assure him and he sits back down, eyes narrowed. Another minute passes and Scarlet catches my eye, and motions for me to join her in the back. Pretending to go to the bathroom, she slips into the office.

"I forgot how much fun that was." She smiles and takes a sip of her drink. "I mean wrong. How morally wrong that was."

"You just talked to him for less than five minutes. What's wrong with that?"

She cocks an eyebrow and holds up a wallet.

"You picked his pocket? Damn. I'm impressed, Scarlet."

She bats her eyes. "Thank you."

I take the wallet from her and look at the guy's ID. Yep. This asshole is Todd.

"What are you going to do?" She takes the wallet back. "Kick him out? Beat him up?"

"I want to, trust me." And I would have in the past. I've gotten into my fair share of fights over the years. But I want to prove to Charlie that I've changed. I'm not that guy anymore. "But instead,

I'm going to talk to him." I look at the wallet. "You're giving that back, right?"

She purses her lips. "Yes. Though if that is Charlie's ex, he's exactly the kind of guy who needs to be taught a lesson."

"Easy there, Lucifer. Leave the punishing to the law."

She lets out a sigh. "That's so boring."

"It is." She goes back to the bar, telling Todd she saw his wallet tumble out of his pocket. He checks it right away for any missing cash, and seeing that there isn't any, he offers to buy Scarlet another drink. She turns him down and goes back to the table with Weston and the kids, leaving Todd sitting there dumbfounded.

No wonder she liked hustling so much. It comes naturally for her.

I go back around the bar, fill a few drink orders, and put in an order for sweet potato fries.

"You passing through town?" I ask Todd.

"Do I look that out of place?" he chuckles.

"You do."

"I'm trying to locate a friend."

"Who are you trying to find? I know most people in this town since they tend to pass through here too."

He looks me up and down. "You wouldn't know her."

I arch my eyebrows. "You'd be surprised who I know. So this old friend…you two lost touch and you don't have their number anymore?"

"Something like that."

It's more like Charlie either blocked his number or won't take his calls.

"Ever think they don't want to be found?"

He laughs. "Trust me, she needs to be found."

"Needs to be?" I plant my hands on the bar and narrow my eyes a bit. "You make it sound like she's in some sort of trouble."

"If she's here, she is. She doesn't belong here."

It's getting harder and harder to keep my cool. "Have you asked her what she wants? Maybe she likes it here."

He shakes his head. "You know how women are. They might think they know what's good for them, but really, they need someone to show them."

What the fuck was Charlie thinking, getting engaged to a guy like this?

"I disagree. And I have a feeling this *friend* is much better off here than in New York with you."

"H-how do you—who are you?"

I smile pleasantly just to piss him off. I extend my hand to shake. "Hi, I'm Owen Dawson. And Charlie and I are back together."

Todd stands up so fast the barstool falls to the ground behind him. Then he balls his fist and tries to punch me right in the face.

CHAPTER 33

CHARLIE

"Hey," I say to Owen's voicemail. "I know you're still working, so I'll go ahead and meet you at the restaurant so we don't miss our reservation. If you're going to be late because of work, no big deal. Just let me know and I'll order an extra glass of wine and bring a book to keep myself entertained." I walk out of the office and head toward my car. "And I feel like saying I wanted to talk this morning was more dramatic than it needed to be. I do want to talk, but not in a bad way. It's in an 'I want to be with you and still want what I wanted before' way. Marriage and children—not right away," I add quickly. "But they have to be on the horizon, and this time…this time I don't think it'll be an issue. I'm looking forward to seeing—and doing you —later."

It's an awkward as fuck voicemail, but whatever. It's Owen. He never makes me feel awkward. Putting my phone in my purse, I pause at a crosswalk.

"Charlotte!"

I look up, not sure if someone is talking to me or someone else. Everyone here calls me Charlie, which I prefer. The only person who always called me by my full name was—

You have got to be fucking kidding me.

"Todd?"

He's across the street, separated by the passing cars. I could turn and run back into the office, lock the door behind me, and wait until he goes away. Or I could face him now and get this over with.

"What do you want?" I ask when he crosses the street. There's a bruise on his face and what looks like dried-up blood under his nose. Did he get into a fight?

"You," he pants. "I want you."

"Okay, good for you." I shake my head and start to walk forward. He grabs my shoulder.

"Wait, Char."

"We're over, Todd. What you did was unforgivable, and like I said, we had our issues before. We should have ended things long before then."

"Come back to New York."

"Didn't you hear anything I just said?"

"I did." He brings his hand to his forehead and winces. There's another bruise along his hairline. "And that's why I need to tell you something."

"What, Todd? What could you possibly have to tell me that's so important?"

"It's about Owen."

"What about Owen?" I roll my eyes. I've mentioned Owen before. Todd knows we dated in the past, but he had no idea that I still had feeling for him. Hell, I didn't even let myself acknowledge my feelings for him.

"I know you guys are together."

"Yes, we are. Are you going to scold me for moving on or something? Get over it, Todd. You slept with someone else while we were engaged."

"If you're together then he's cheating on you."

"That's ridiculous."

"Is it? I went to that bar, what's it called, Getaway? He was there. With another woman. Some pretty blonde with a tight ass—"

"Seriously?"

He shakes his head. "We got to talking and it came out who I was and who he was…and then when I was leaving, I saw him in the parking lot with some other girl. I'm so sorry, Charlie. I confronted him and he hit me."

I cross my arms, looking at Todd with disdain. "Whatever, Todd."

"He's no good for you, Charlie."

"And you are?"

"No," he says, which surprises me. "Neither of us are. If there's a type I know, it's assholes. Trust me, that guy is an asshole. You said it yourself about him breaking up with you in college."

"That was a long time ago, and I'm done with this conversation, Todd. Owen and I have a date tonight, and I need to go home and get ready for it." Without another look, I cross the street, running to avoid being hit by a car. My heart is in my throat, along with chunks of rising vomit.

I call Owen as soon as I get into my car. He doesn't answer. I call again, and get sent to voicemail after one ring. What the hell is going on?

Nothing. Nothing is going on.

Owen isn't a playboy anymore. I didn't freak him out by leaving a voicemail saying that I want to get married and have his babies. Because he wants it too. I know he does.

I start the car, roll down the windows, and drive to my parents' house to get another dress to wear tonight. I might as well take all my clothes over to Owen's at this point. Or enough to get me through the next month…when I move into my own apartment.

Which seems silly to do now.

Because Owen has enough room at his place. And we're

together again. Why would I move out only to move back in a few months later? I park along the street and go inside, heading up to my old room. Our dinner reservation is in half an hour, and it makes sense to change and get ready here and then hang out instead of driving across town to Owen's. He's most likely going to meet me there and not go home either.

Refusing to let Todd's words get to me, I change, brush out my hair and use Carly's curling iron to freshen up my waves. I call Owen again on my way to dinner and get his voicemail. He'll be here, though. He has to be.

I'm seated at the table, order one glass of red wine, and open the Kindle app on my phone, reading to pass the time. But then fifteen minutes pass and Owen still isn't here. I get another glass of wine, read three more chapters, and call him.

He doesn't answer, and suddenly I can't breathe. Did something bad happen? If it did, I'm sure one of his siblings would get a hold of me. Weston is the sheriff and Archer works at the local hospital. One way or another, we'd know if something terrible happened.

Needing a distraction, I log onto my social media accounts. Five minutes ago, Danielle posted a photo of her, Logan and Dexter. They're smiling and looking picture-perfect. I'm confident Logan would be able to sense something bad happening to his twin, and he wouldn't be smiling for a photo with his wife and dog if Owen were dead in a ditch.

Which means my worst fear is coming to life.

Owen doesn't want the same thing I do. We had sex and then what? He decided to ditch me?

Fool me once, shame on you. But fool me twice...

CHAPTER 34

OWEN

"Fuck." I rub my wrists where the cuffs had been.

"Sorry," Weston says, shaking his head.

"It's not your fault."

He shakes his head and runs his hand through his hair. "You're free to go now."

"Took long enough. That little shit got out of here hours ago, didn't he?"

Wes opens the holding room door for me. "His lawyer screams scumbag but had good connections."

"What good is the legal system when rich assholes can buy their way out of situations like this. He hit me first. Well, tried to hit me." I smirk. "That cocksucker can't throw a punch to save his life."

After Todd tried to hit me and I easily blocked it, he stepped back and fell right onto Marty Pickens, one of our resident drunks. Along with being a drunk, Marty is paranoid and thinks the world is out to get him. We serve him at Getaway because he's safer in the bar than out on the streets, and we're able to give him food and a cool place to wait out the sun in the summer.

But the second Todd touched Marty, he freaked out, saying the FBI sent Todd. He started beating the crap out of Todd, and it was a good thing Weston was there to break things up because I would have stood back and watched with pleasure.

Then Todd went after me again, and this time I did hit him back. Popped him right in the nose, and as soon as Todd saw the first drop of blood, he was dizzy and about to pass out. Instead of leaving things at that, the fucker called the police once he realized Weston was my brother.

Which is why I'm just now leaving the police station.

"Can I have my phone? I was supposed to meet Charlie for dinner." I rub my temples. "Shit. She's going to think I blew her off or something."

I walk with Wes through the station and get my phone and wallet. It's not my first time being booked for fighting, but this is the first time regret and anxiety forms in my stomach over it. I hate that I left Charlie hanging, but once she hears how Todd got his ass handed to him, she'll be laughing.

I have a bunch of missed called and texts from Charlie. Wes and I walk outside so he can give me a ride back to the bar so I can get my car. I call Charlie right away. She doesn't answer. Hoping she's not too mad, I text her telling her I'm sorry I missed dinner but have a good reason.

"Thanks," I tell Weston as he drops me off at Getaway. "For everything."

"You're lucky it was me."

"Oh, I know." I shut the door and race to my truck. I call Charlie three more times and don't get a hold of her at all. I race to my house, not sure what to find.

She's not there, but Tulip still is. That's a good sign, right?

Exhaling, I sit at the kitchen table and put my head in my hands, letting out a sigh. She'll come home. She has to. Her stuff and her cat are here.

I get up to plug my phone in to charge the battery. Pacing around the house, I pick up the black-and-white cat.

"Where would she go?" I ask the cat. "To her parents'? Yeah. That's the only other place I can think of too." Tulip follows me into the kitchen, meowing for food. I don't think Charlie came home to feed her yet, so I open a can of cat food, slop it into a bowl and hurry out of the house.

The old Mustang isn't parked along the street, but that doesn't mean much. There's a covered garage in the backyard, butting up to an alley. I'm starting to freak out a little, and am worried Charlie is hurting, thinking that I blew her off because I don't want the same thing she did, like she said in her voicemail.

I check my security system activity log and see that no one opened or closed any doors at the house, so she hasn't gone back there. Too upset to go home and sit in the house by myself, I go to Wes and Scarlet's place. They're only a few blocks away anyway. Jackson is outside with Scarlet, and Violet is in the stroller in the shade, fast asleep.

I put on a fake smile, not wanting to freak Jackson out. Scarlet took the kids into the office when the other cops arrived, letting Jackson play games on her phone while I was cuffed and arrested.

"Uncle Owen!" Jackson kicks a soccer ball over to me.

"What's going on?" Scarlet asks. "Are you okay?"

I slowly shake my head. "Yeah. Fine."

"Hey, Jackson," she calls. "Do you want your Kindle time now?"

He gets excited to be able to watch videos and play games on the tablet and runs inside.

"Owen," Scarlet starts. "What happened?"

"I think I fucked shit up with Charlie." I sit on the top porch step.

"Why? Because of the fight?"

"Not entirely."

Scarlet checks on Vi and then sits next to me. "They why?"

"I broke up with her back in college because she wanted to settle down and I didn't. I've regretted it every damn day, and then she finally gave me a second chance. I was supposed to meet with her for dinner tonight and obviously couldn't. Now I can't get a hold of her and I'm not doing a very good job showing her I changed. Getting arrested doesn't say *I've grown up and changed*, does it?"

"No, it doesn't. But you have grown up and changed. You have just in the short time I've known you. And getting arrested was bullshit. You didn't do anything wrong, and you have Wes to back you up on that."

"I know. It feels...it feels like I blew this second chance, though."

"I get it," she tells me. "And I know how weird a second chance can feel even when you don't blow it. I haven't always made the best choices, as you know."

"True."

"Go find her and kiss her and tell her you love her. We all know you do. Acting like you only get one shot is the best way to actually blow your second chance, you know."

I inhale and feel a little better. "Thanks, Scarlet."

"Anytime. And Owen?"

"Yeah?"

"You do deserve a second chance. Even if you don't think so." Violet starts to fuss, and Scarlet gets up to get the baby. Her words hit me deep, though, and only someone who's lived the kind of life Scarlet has would see the pain I've hidden from myself. I don't feel like I deserve Charlie, and I'm going back to fucking up just like I did the first time.

Thinking that she's better off without me because I love her more than I'll ever love myself.

Taking another breath, I walk down the sidewalk and run down the street. I don't stop until I'm at Charlie's parents' house. This time, the blue Mustang is parked out front. My heart swells in my chest when I see a flash of blonde hair in the fading sunlight. She's on the porch swing, and I'm going to race up the steps and kiss the breath right out of her.

But then I see that she's not alone. Todd is sitting on the swing next to her.

CHAPTER 35

CHARLIE

A slight breeze rustles my hair, and I look out at the street. My heart is sitting at the bottom of my chest, and all the cracks are starting to separate. It won't be long until it shatters into a million pieces again, and this time, there'll be no putting it back together.

My ex-fiancé is sitting on the porch next to me, waiting for his ride to come pick him up. He cheated on me. Embarrassed me. But it's not him who's hurting me.

It's Owen, and I don't understand how I could have been so wrong. Again. Things were so perfect between us. And then he didn't even have the decency to call me. I need to get Tulip from his place, and it's going to be so fucking awkward.

"I can put in a good word for you at another firm," Todd says. "It's the least I can do after…after…"

"After fucking your assistant while you were in a relationship with me?"

"Yeah. That. I'm sorry. Really, I am."

I hold up my hand, stopping him right there. "What do you want me to say? That it's okay and I forgive you? It's not okay and I don't. Live with that."

"I miss you."

"Too bad." I let out a breath. The only reason I'm sitting out here is because I don't want my niece and nephews asking about Todd. They've met him and don't need to see him again. Because it doesn't matter.

"If you're handing out second chances…"

"I'm not."

"Really? You're back in town less than a month and you're with your ex."

"That was different.

"What's so different about Owen?"

"Yeah," a deep voice comes from the sidewalk. I turn and see Owen's handsome face. His eyes are filled with hurt and his jaw is tense. "What is different about Owen?"

"What are you doing here?" I get off the swing, heart swelling in my chest when I see Owen. "You…you ditched me."

"I didn't, and I don't know what that asshole has been telling you, but it's his fault."

"You're supposed to be in jail." Todd gets up and rounds on Owen.

"What?" I go down the porch steps, putting myself between Owen and Todd, hoping to prevent a fight from breaking out. Because Owen looks like he wants to tear Todd apart limb from limb.

"I told you, Charlotte. He hit me and got himself arrested."

"Is that true?" I ask Owen.

"Yes," he says and takes a step closer to me.

"Because he caught you with another woman?"

Owen makes a face. "No. There is only one person for me, Charlie, and it's you. It's always been you. He threw the first punch and then fell onto Marty Pickens. It's all on camera. Irrefutable evidence right there."

I look back at Todd and squeeze my eyes closed. "You lied to me?"

243

"Char, look at him. Look at this town. You don't belong here. You belong in New York, at a real firm with real cases. Making real money."

I put my face in my hands, head spinning as I try to process everything. "You came all this way just to manipulate and lie to me?"

Todd lets out a nervous laugh. "When you say it like that, it sounds bad. If we rephrase—"

"Shut the fuck up, Todd. I'm not a client."

"He doesn't deserve you," Todd snaps.

"It's true," Owen says. "I don't deserve you, Charlie. I never thought I did, and that's why I broke up with you all those years ago. I was certain you'd be disappointed if you stayed with me. I felt selfish making you settle, so I ended things. I've regretted it every single day since then, but I thought it was the right thing to do. That I was holding you back and you'd someday resent me for it."

My lips part and tears fill my eyes. My emotions are all over the place.

"I missed dinner tonight because I was in a holding cell while this prick had some fancy lawyer putting in calls and pulling favors that held shit up and not even Weston could get things smoothed over right away."

I blink and a tear rolls down my face. "I wish you told me sooner."

"About the fight?"

I shake my head. "About why we broke up. All those years I thought it was something I did. That I wasn't enough."

"No, Charlie, that's not it at all."

I wipe away a tear and shake my head. A black Toyota pulls in front of the house to pick up Todd.

"Charlotte," he starts.

"Just go," I say, voice thin.

Hanging his head, he walks down the sidewalk and gets into

the car. A sense of relief washes over me when the car pulls away. Owen steps up next to me and takes me in his arms. It feels so good to be here again. It's where I belong.

But I can't. Not yet. Not right now.

"Owen," I start, pushing away. "I…I need some time."

"Okay," he says, voice shaking. "Like a minute? Fifteen?"

"I…I don't know."

He runs his fingers through my hair. "Okay," he says again. "Whatever you need."

Sniffling, I turn and walk into the house. Tears fall as soon as the door closes behind me. Mom, who I'm sure heard the whole thing, comes rushing to me from the kitchen. She takes me in her arms and guides me to the couch.

"I don't know why I'm crying," I say as she hands me a tissue. "He didn't really do anything wrong, did he?"

"What happened, honey?"

"I thought Owen blew me off on purpose but the situation was really out of his control. But then he told me the only reason he broke up with me was because he thought I could do better. That's not fair, though. Who is he to decide what's good enough for me?" I blow my nose. "I spent years, Mom, years wondering what I did wrong. Why I wasn't enough. Why he left me when we were so happy and in love. He was everything I wanted."

"I know. And I agree with you. It's not right to decide what someone else does or doesn't deserve. It sounds like he had your best intentions at heart, though."

"How can you say that? Because we broke up, I moved to New York and almost married Todd. Everything that happened after Owen broke up with me is all his fault."

"You won't agree with that after you calm down," Mom says gently. "But I see your train of thought. If Owen hadn't broken up with you, you wouldn't have left Eastwood."

"That's exactly what I just said!" I grab another tissue and lean against the back of the couch. "I wish he hadn't told me. Because now I'm mad and questioning everything."

"Do you think he cares about you now?"

I nod. "Yeah. I do."

"Can you forgive him for breaking up with you?"

Swallowing hard, I shake my head. "I don't know. I hurt so much for so long after."

"I remember." Mom lets out a deep breath. "I wish I had better advice, honey. You're happy when you're with him, and people make mistakes in the past. Especially when they're young."

I just nod and mop up more tears. Mom puts her hand on my shoulder and stays with me.

"Charlie?" Carly says softly, coming downstairs. "Are you okay?"

I glare at her with tear-filled eyes. "Peachy."

"I was listening to what Mom said, and I agree."

"Then we all can agree we don't know what to do. Great."

"Only you can decide what to do." Carly sits on the floor by me.

"That helps me even less. Maybe the only thing Owen and I are good at is hurting each other." I'm being dramatic right now and don't care. Not at all.

"You were blaming Owen for Todd, but right now, we can blame Todd for Owen. If Todd hadn't shown up, Owen wouldn't have missed dinner. And you wouldn't have assumed the worst, right?"

"Right."

"What if he told you about why he broke up with you during dinner? If he said the same exact words. What would you have done?"

I shake my head, trying to really think about it logically. "I don't know. I think I'd still be upset for having to go through years of my life feeling like I let the only person I ever loved down."

"But would you go home with or without him?"

I swallow the lump in my throat. "I don't know."

"Look, thinking he knows what's good for you is shitty. But breaking up with you hurt him too, especially if he did it because he loved you enough to let you go."

I take in a shaky breath. "I didn't think of it that way."

"Good thing I'm here." Carly smiles. "You should talk to him. Get everything out in the air. If you can't move past the past, then you can't go into the future."

Nodding, I wipe my eyes and smear the rest of my mascara down my cheeks. "Where's my phone?" I ask. "I'll call him."

"No need." Carly winks. "He's still on the porch."

CHAPTER 36

OWEN

The front door opens, and I spring up, half expecting it to be Carly telling me to fuck off. But it's Charlie. Her eyes are red and swollen from crying, and it kills me to see her like this.

"Can we talk?" she asks, voice thin.

"Of course."

She motions to the porch swing and we both take a seat.

"What do you want to talk about?" My heart is beating so fast I fear it might beat right out of my chest. I'd pick it up, dust it off, and offer it to Charlie. It's hers to keep. It's always been hers.

"First things first," she starts. "Do you still feel like you know what's best for me?"

"No. Though if I were to give you advice right now it would be to come home with me tonight."

Her lips curve into a half-smile. "Okay. Did it hurt when you broke up with me?"

"Yes. And I hurt every day since then. I've had a void in my heart, Charlie, and nothing could fill it. Nothing but you."

She nods and looks down at the boards on the porch. "Do you want to get married and have kids?"

"Yes. I do. Part of me was scared to start a family back then too. Being a dad...that sounded terrifying."

She smiles again. "We were young. I thought I'd want to pop out babies right away but changed my mind too. It would have been hard to finish law school with an infant."

"I like being an uncle," I assure her. "And I was happy with that, but only because there was no one in the world except for one person who I could even imagine settling down with."

"And who is this lucky girl?" She looks up, eyes locking with mine.

"It's you. It's always been you." I take her hands in mine. "I want to spend the rest of my life with you, Charlie. We lost so much time that I don't want to waste another day. I love you. I've always loved you."

Her eyes fill with tears again, but this time she's not sad. "I love you too, Owen. Even when I tried not to."

I pull her to me, kissing her hard. "Come home with me, Charlie. And spend forever with me."

"That does sound nice."

"Will you?"

"Are you proposing?"

"If I was, would you say yes?" I give her a smirk.

She smiles right back. "I would strongly consider it."

"Then I'm not quite proposing because I don't have a ring. Yet. But keep this in mind."

"Trust me, I will."

"I love you, Charlie. I've always loved you and I always will." She moves closer and I wrap her in my arms. The swing sways back as we kiss, and I have to remind myself that I'm on her parents' front porch and her mother is most likely watching.

"Say it again," she whispers, cupping my face with her hands.

"I love you."

Smiling, she closes her eyes again and kisses me. "So, can I get another cat?"

I laugh and kiss her again. "You can get whatever you want."

"You don't think we're moving too fast if I move in with you?"

I pull her to my chest and push off the porch, sending the swing back again. "It feels right to me, and I know there might be unwritten rules or timelines or whatever, but fuck 'em. Move in with me. I'd say we should get married at the courthouse tomorrow, but I know you want to plan a wedding. And I might have thought about how I'd propose to you a time or two if things had been different."

Her face lights up and we kiss again.

"Can we go home?" she whispers. "You're turning me on, Owen, and if this was our first fight or misunderstanding or whatever, then I think makeup sex is the next step."

I take her hand. "What are we waiting for?

She really is perfect for me.

～

I PUT MY HAND ON THE SMALL OF CHARLIE'S BACK AND BRING MY beer to my lips. "It looks good, babe," I tell her.

"Are you sure?"

"I am. This is the first time this dining room has ever been used like this, you know."

Charlie laughs and spins around. She takes the beer from my hands and puts it on the table. It's been three weeks since I told her I love her, and things have been perfect.

"That's a shame," she says, hooking her arms around my neck. "But it'll get used now."

"Right. With all the fancy dinner parties you're going to have."

She laughs. "I don't think having your family over counts as fancy."

"You spent like an hour decorating the table."

"Tablescapes are fun."

"If you say so." I bring my head down and kiss her on the lips. "I'll go check on dinner."

"I'll come with you."

"You just want wine, you lush."

She slaps my butt. "I'm saving that for later."

I laugh and whirl around, picking her up, I kiss her hard and set her on the counter in the kitchen. Her legs go around me and she runs her fingers through my hair. My eyes fall shut and I put my head against her breasts.

"I love you," I whisper.

"I love you too."

We kiss again, right as the front door opens. Breaking apart, I go through the kitchen to welcome my parents into the house. We invited everyone over for dinner tonight. It was Charlie's idea, as a bit of a celebration for her officially moving in. We held off for a while before deciding it just didn't make sense for her to pay for an apartment when she'd be here most of the time anyway. She was able to get her deposit back and everything. Another reason it was meant to be.

"Dinner smells amazing," Mom tells Charlie.

"Thanks," she says. "Though I can't take credit. Owen made it."

"Really?"

"Thanks, Mom." I laugh and open the fridge, pulling out a beer for Dad. Logan and Danielle are the next to arrive, and Danielle comes bearing gifts. Specifically, leftover sugar cookies from the bakery. She and Charlie hung out three times this week, making this whole thing even more perfect than I could ever imagine.

My twin's wife and my girlfriend—who will be my wife soon enough—are friends.

Quinn, Archer, and their kids walk through the door and Wes, Scarlet and company are next. Dean and Kara are always the last to arrive, and I don't understand why they're almost always late and the two couples with multiple children get here on time. Regardless, things go along just fine and everyone enjoys dinner.

Logan and Danielle stay a while after, and we have every intention of playing a few rounds of Mario Kart. But Danielle falls asleep on the couch and apologizes when Logan wakes her up.

"Don't worry about it," Charlie says. "You're growing a human. That takes a lot of energy."

"I used to think people exaggerated how tired they were during the first trimester but the exhaustion is real."

"Let's go home," Logan tells her and helps her to her feet. We walk them to the door, and then Charlie and I go back into the kitchen to finish putting dinner dishes away. Charlie freezes as she puts one of her million coffee mugs away.

"Owen," she exclaims.

"Yeah?"

"I just realized something."

"You want to go upstairs and have sex?"

She gives me a pointed glare. "I do, but also…I, uh, haven't had a period in a while."

"How long is a while?"

"Since before we got back together."

"Do you think you're pregnant?"

She slowly shakes her head back and forth. "I…I don't know. Maybe."

CHAPTER 37

CHARLIE

I pace back and forth on the front porch, swatting away bugs. Owen ran to Walmart to get a pregnancy test. I don't feel pregnant. Not at all. I have zero symptoms, and while many women can go through the whole nine months without "feeling pregnant," I know I wouldn't get that lucky.

Still, we want to be sure.

I chugged a big glass of water when he left, and now I really have to pee. Headlights illuminate the street and I hold my breath, hoping that truck belongs to Owen. It doesn't, and it goes right past our house. Getting close to needing to do the potty dance, I decide I'm going to give Owen five more minutes before going to the bathroom. Luckily, he pulls into the driveway only a minute later.

He stands outside the bathroom door, waiting for me. The test said to wait a few minutes until you check, but I look at that baby right away. The control line pops up first. I watch, waiting for the second line. I don't see one, so I set the test down and pull my pants back up. After washing my hands, I open the door and Owen picks the test up off the floor.

"You're not pregnant," he says after looking at the test for a good minute. "Is it weird I'm a little disappointed?"

"No." I move next to him and hook my arm through his. "Because I am too."

Owen sets the test down on the counter and wraps one arm around me. "This isn't the first time we've thought you might be pregnant. We had a few scares there in college."

I nod. "I remember those. And seeing the negative was such a relief. But now...now..." I trail off and shake my head. "I shouldn't want to be pregnant. We're not married yet."

"Yet?" He raises his eyebrows. "Are you proposing? Don't spoil my surprise. Though I do want a hint so I can get my nails done beforehand."

I laugh and look up at him. "You really would have been happy if I were pregnant?"

He brings his head down and kisses me. "Yes. I love you, Charlie. So fucking much. You know I meant it when I said I'd go to the courthouse and marry you right now if that's what you want." He takes my hand and leads me into the bedroom. He pulls me into his lap and sits on the bed. "Until then, though, we can practice for when we really do want to have a baby."

"Didn't we get enough practice in this morning?"

He laughs and kisses me. "You can never be too prepared, you know."

"You actually can, though. You need to save it up and not deplete your sperm count."

"So romantic."

"I know, right?"

We fall back on the bed, and it only takes a minute of Owen kissing my neck while rubbing my back to get me in the mood. After sex, we shower and then finally go downstairs to finish in the kitchen. We both have to work in the morning and go up to bed. I snuggle close to Owen, feeling like I'm where I'm meant to be.

With him.
Together.
In love.

∾

"I'm running a little late," Owen tells me. "Go ahead and start dinner without me."

"Okay. How late are you going to be?" I shut my office door and get into the elevator. I was at work late tonight too. It's seven-thirty and I'm just now leaving. Dad scheduled meetings with clients today, and our last one didn't start until seven. The entire client meeting was bizarre too, and after talking about nothing that had to do with what the client wanted to hire us for, he left.

"Maybe an hour or so. It's been really busy at the bar all day."

"Well, that's always a good thing."

"Yeah. It is. Are you heading home now?"

"I am. I'll see you in a bit then. Love you."

"Love you, too."

I end the call and walk down the block to my car. My new car, which I bought only a week ago. It's a Jeep Grand Cherokee, and I love it. The four-wheel drive will come in handy in the snow, that's for sure. Summer is just now coming to an end, and while I'm not looking forward to the cold, Midwest winter, I might be a little excited to try out just how well the Jeep handles.

Owen's truck is in the garage when I get home, which surprises me. Maybe he and Logan drove together to work? They've done that in the past, though it doesn't really make sense since we live on opposite ends of the town. The house is unlocked too, but when I step inside and go to turn on the lights, nothing happens.

"Owen?" I call, reaching into my purse for my phone to use for light. He doesn't answer, but something shuffles inside the house, and flickering light pours from the screened-in porch. "Owen?"

Breath hitching, I slowly walk through the house and peek into the screened-in porch. Owen is in there, looking out at the fountain. Several candles are lit, and there's a little table set up with dinner.

"What is this?" I ask, a smile coming to my face.

"Surprise." He strides over and pulls me into his arms.

"Owen! This is so sweet! Is that—"

"The fancy pasta you like? Yes, it is."

I lean up and kiss him. "I love you."

He gives me a wink. "I know. We should eat before the food gets cold." He breaks away only to come right back. "Fuck it."

"Fuck what?"

"I was going to wait until after dinner, but I want to ask you now."

"Ask me?"

He drops down to one knee and pulls out a ring. "I love you, Charlie. I've always loved you and I always will love you. Will you marry me?"

I bring my hands to my face, tears filling my eyes. "Yes!"

He takes the ring from the box and slips it on my finger. It's a perfect fit. It's dark in here, so I go closer to a candle to look at the ring. It's gorgeous.

"This whole thing was a set-up!" I whirl back around. "You saying you're working late and that bullshit meeting at work."

"Yeah." Owen smiles and takes me into his arms again.

"My dad was in on this!"

"He was. And he's probably waiting for you to call him so he can act like he had no idea."

"Oh, Owen!" More tears fill my eyes, and I hold onto Owen as tight as I can. This time, I know there is no letting go.

EPILOGUE

OWEN

"What about this one?" I point to a pink-and-purple sheet set. Charlie looks at it and then shakes her head.

"It's too girly."

"We're buying it for a girl."

"I know," she agrees. "But I don't want to set her up with gender stereotypes from infancy."

"Babies don't even see in color when they're born."

"Aww, you did read the books."

"Cover to cover." I motion to another sheet set that's white with colorful birds on it. "This one?"

"Ohhh, that is cute!"

"It's not too girly?" I give her a smirk and she playfully nudges my arm. "These birds look pretty girly."

"I like them."

"That's the whole point of this," I whisper-talk. "We get to pick out what we like."

Charlie rests her hand over her stomach. She's just now

starting to show, and we found out we're having a girl only this morning, continuing with what Quinn insists is karma for being raised in a house full of older brothers. Though she's expecting her third and they're not finding out what they're having. My money is on a boy.

And who knows, maybe our next one will be a boy as well.

Things can change, but right now our plan is to start trying again when our sweet little girl is around nine months old. As Charlie puts it, we're not getting any younger, and we want nothing more than to keep growing our family.

She found out she was pregnant two weeks before our wedding, and it was really hard hiding it from everyone. I caved and ended up telling Logan, but I held out longer than Charlie, who told her own sister the same day she found out she was expecting.

We shared the news the day after the wedding, making it obvious she got pregnant before we were actually married. That wasn't why we kept things a secret, though. Planning the wedding was stressful enough. We didn't want to add anything else to the mix.

"You're probably going to nix this one right away." I grab a pale yellow blanket with tiny flowers stitched along the hem. "But I like this."

Charlie smiles as she takes it from me, running her fingers over the flowers. "I like it. And yellow is neutral enough."

"If picking a changeable sheet set is this hard, how the hell are we going to decide on paint colors for the nursery?" I laugh.

"I actually like it the way it is," she insists. "It's all about accent colors, and pale pink and yellow would look really pretty."

I grab the corresponding sheets that go with the soft blanket. We came to the store with the intention of just looking at baby stuff and making a preliminary list of things to register for, but caved and decided to buy just one thing.

"We're still meeting Logan and Danielle for lunch, right?" Charlie asks.

"Yeah, what are you craving today?" We walk up to the register.

"Greasy diner food. Still. I'm going to be a million pounds when this baby is born."

"Your tits have gotten bigger but that's really all that's changed."

"My ass too."

I grab it just to check. "I don't feel any difference, and trust me, I know this ass well."

She laughs and pushes me away. "Not in public, Owen!"

"Want to sneak into a bathroom?"

"Now that the second-trimester hormones are hitting me, I'm very tempted to say yes."

I take her hand and kiss the top of her head. We pay for the baby blankets and then head into town, going to the only place other than Getaway to order cheeseburgers and fries. I call Logan to let him know where to meet us.

Charlie and I get there first, and she puts in an order of French fries right away. Logan, Danielle, and their baby, Paige, get here right as the fries are served.

"How'd it go at the doctor today?" Danielle asks Charlie.

She smiles and looks at me, and I give her a nod.

"Great. We found out the sex."

"And?" Danielle's eyes widen.

"It's a girl!"

Logan claps me on the back. "Congrats, man."

"Thanks." Charlie reaches across the table and takes my hand. I give her fingers a squeeze and look into her eyes and feel like the luckiest man in the whole fucking world.

And really, I suppose I am.

We got lost along the way but found our way back to each

other. The journey was full of pain, tears, and heartbreak, but I wouldn't have it any other way. Every little thing shaped us, made us who we are today.

And if you ask me, we're pretty fucking perfect.

THANK YOU

Thank you so much for taking time out of your busy life to read an early copy of Fight Dirty! I hope you enjoyed Owen and Charlie's story. I LOVED writing it so much! The cocky asshole who just needs a hug is my favorite to write ;-)

I appreciate so much the time you took to read this book and and would love if you would consider leaving a review. I LOVE connecting with readers and the best place to do so is my fan page and Instagram! I'd love to have you!

www.facebook.com/groups/emilygoodwinbooks
www.instagram.com/authoremilygoodwin

ABOUT THE AUTHOR

Emily Goodwin is the New York Times and USA Today Best-selling author of over a dozen of romantic titles. Emily writes the kind of books she likes to read, and is a sucker for a swoon-worthy bad boy and happily ever afters.

She lives in the midwest with her husband and two daughters. When she's not writing, you can find her riding her horses, hiking, reading, or drinking wine with friends.

Emily is represented by Julie Gwinn of the Seymour Agency.

Stalk me:
www.emilygoodwinbooks.com
emily@emilygoodwinbooks.com

ALSO BY EMILY GOODWIN

First Comes Love

Then Come Marriage

Outside the Lines

Never Say Never

One Call Away

Free Fall

Stay

All I Need

Hot Mess (Luke & Lexi Book 1)

Twice Burned (Luke & Lexi Book 2)

Bad Things (Cole & Ana Book 1)

Battle Scars (Cole & Ana Book 2)

Cheat Codes (The Dawson Family Series Book 1)

End Game (The Dawson Family Series Book 2)

Side Hustle (The Dawson Family Series Book 3)

Cheap Trick (The Dawson Family Series Book 4)

Dead of Night (Thorne Hill Series Book 1)

Dark of Night (Thorne Hill Series Book 2)

Made in United States
Orlando, FL
15 February 2023

30057697R00148